A CARDBOARD COTTAGE MYSTERY

DICE
on a DEADLY SEA

JANE ELZEY

Scorpius Carta Press
Arkansas

Scorpius Carta Press
P.O. Box 11, Beaver, AR 72613

First Scorpius Carta Press Hardcover edition: May 2021
ISBN 978-1-7346428-3-4

First Scorpius Carta Press Paperback edition: May 2021
ISBN 978-1-7346428-4-1

First Scorpius Carta Press Digital edition: May 2021
ISBN 978-1-7346428-5-8

The interior of this book is typeset in Adobe Caslon Pro.
Cover design by Bailey McGinn.

For Arielle

"Live with no excuses and travel with no regrets."
—Oscar Wilde

CHAPTER ONE

"You're not going to believe this," Amy squealed into the phone. "The governor wants me to speak at the tourism conference!"

"What? At the Governor's Conference?" Genna's voice echoed from the hands-free speaker then boomed as she pressed the phone to her ear. "You? Why?"

Amy hugged the phone to her chin, tugged at her purse strap, and shifted the heavy package on her hip. "The speaker panel is for women-owned businesses throughout the state. He wants me to represent our cooperative at the Cardboard Cottage!"

She didn't try to disguise her excitement, but only silence came from the other end. Amy set the package on the counter when the paper bag ripped at the seams and produce spilled out. She and Victor both chased a lemon across the kitchen floor. He sniffed the rind and blinked before she snatched it from his paws.

"Silly cat."

Genna exhaled into the receiver. "Jim Henry called you? The governor himself called?"

"Well, no. It was someone from the agency who organizes

the conference. A Mary Weather or something. I was so excited, I didn't quite catch her name."

"Merriweather Hopkins," Genna said sourly. "I should have guessed."

"I knew you were behind it," Amy gushed. "She even mentioned you in the phone call. She said to make sure to tell Genna Gregory hello."

"Hello, *darrling*," Genna said in her Lower Arkansas accent as if speaking to the agency woman herself. "So nice to hear from my dear old friend. Even if it is a knife in the back."

Frowning at Genna's tone, she pictured the tall, svelte woman at the other end of the conversation. Her long silver hair would be pulled tight behind her, a barrette holding it severely in place. Her periwinkle blue eyes would be squinting against the cigarette smoke curling around her head. Her mouth would have a slight squint of disapproval, too. The joy Amy felt moments earlier rushed from her chest like a deflating balloon. Her pride shrank with it.

"Isn't this good news?"

"Yes, well, it pays to have friends in high places. Even if they are scoundrels and swindlers who double-cross their friends."

"I would never double-cross you! Never!"

"Oh for crying out loud, Amy. I'm not talking about you. I'm talking about Merriweather Hopkins. The only reason she called you was to get a dig in at me. She is aware I'm affiliated with the Cardboard Cottage. She knows I would be a better candidate for the panel. She knows I would decline the invitation."

"Ouch. That feels more like a dig at me."

Genna puffed her cigarette, and the slow exhale hissed into the phone. "That's not at all what I meant."

Amy waited for an explanation, the groceries now unpacked

and Victor's bowl topped with treats that promised to clean his teeth and satisfy his wild feline hunger. The silence stretched on.

"The least I can do is write the talking points for you to follow," Genna said finally. "And I will pick out an outfit for you to wear. No T-shirts with bling, my friend." Amy's heart sank a little further into her chest.

"Believe it or not, Genna, I can dress myself!" She regretted her words. There was nowhere to go from here. She couldn't back down. Well, she didn't want to back down. She would not let Genna's old war wounds—or whatever they were—stand in front of the success of the Cardboard Cottage & Company. She held too big of a mortgage risk. The four businesses that occupied the historic building would gain by having a prestigious place at the Governor's Conference on Tourism. That, and the recent photo spread in *Belles and Bloom* magazine made a winning combination. Genna took credit for that. Her connections scored the four-page spread in the magazine, and her story read like catching up with old friends.

No, she would not let Genna or *old Merriweather Hopkins* steal her enthusiasm.

She steadied herself against the kitchen counter. "I do want your input. You could counsel me on how a panel works and how to prepare for it. I've never done anything like this, and I want to sound smart."

"Of course you do. And it really is good exposure, Amy. I should have thought of it myself. Which is exactly what she was thinking. If Merriweather wants to resurrect that stale dalliance, I will douse it with a fair measure of salt. She'll have nothing to do but lick her wounds." Another hiss of exhaled smoke whispered through the phone. "Bless her heart."

They hung up, and Amy let herself revel in the victory. The

annual Governor's Conference brought in hundreds of journalists and tourism leaders from all over the state. Genna claimed everybody who was anybody of stature in Arkansas attended—and of course, she represented Bluff Springs. A semi-retired public relations operative, Genna worked with all the big names in the heyday of her career, at least those with enough budget or prestige.

Genna would shove talking points at her whether she wanted them or not. She did want them. Genna knew how to make anyone sound smart on paper. She had a talent. And she had a flaw. She could write speeches that lifted spirits and inspired the gods themselves, but she couldn't deliver them. Not in front of anything but a mirror, and never, ever at a podium. It was hard to believe Genna was fearful of anything. Or anyone. But everybody had something they were afraid of. Genna was afraid of public speaking. *Glossophobia.* What a cruel twist for someone who loved words and the soapbox that went with it. No wonder some old spat had provoked Genna's temper, and maybe a dose of envy, too.

The cat clock kept time with its long black tail sweeping the kitchen wall. It would soon be time to open the shop. She had awakened early, coming face to face with the green-eyed creature staring at her from above, his paws kneading into her nightgown, his ragged purr reaching a familiar crescendo. Victor, her Maine coon nearly as big as a bear cub with dark tabby stripes, was better than an alarm clock. When he flicked his tail across her face and bounced from the bed, that was her cue for his breakfast. He even came with a snooze button, reminding her of her duty if she tried to ignore him.

Instead of lounging over her standard three cups of espresso, she decided to run out for groceries rather than leave it to the end of the day. She had been on her way back from the market when Merriweather Hopkins called to talk about the tourism conference and a place on the panel if she wanted it. Of course she wanted to be part of the panel. What a great opportunity. Not only would she be promoting the Cardboard Cottage and Bluff Springs to tourism leaders from all over Arkansas, but the success of women-owned businesses, too. Who wouldn't want to speak to a room full of people about all that? Genna wouldn't. Genna couldn't.

Was this invite a dig at Genna? Was Merriweather Hopkins taunting her? Rubbing salt in an old wound? That wasn't the impression at first, but now, it seemed that whatever Merriweather Hopkins did to make Genna resentful, it was neither forgiven nor forgotten.

Bless her heart.

Now, quickly filling the crockpot, she set it for a slow cook and dreamed of dipping into hot chili for dinner. She put away the last of the groceries, and Zelda, her best friend and confidant, waved from the picture on the front of the fridge.

Bold red marker declared *T-Minus 10 and counting* at the top of the brochure with four exclamation points. Zelda's punctuation overkill. There was no need for the reminder that in less than a week, she and her friends would be in the Galápagos Islands.

That was a surprise. The eco-adventure wasn't the cruise she thought Zelda would choose. She pictured Zelda on a mammoth cruise ship with shopping malls and umpteen decks of pools, restaurants, and bars. She imagined the four of them celebrating Zelda's birthday on a city-size ship floating through a windswept sea. Zelda chose the *Darwinian* instead, a small ship sailing with only one hundred passengers and its crew.

It was Rian's idea. *Archipiélago de Colón, Las Islas Galápagos.* Nineteen islands about six hundred miles off the coast of Ecuador and a bucket list destination for many. The Galapagos! Paid for by Zelda. Every. Last. Penny. Just as she had promised.

In the bathroom mirror, she checked her copper-red curls, smoothing them from her rush of errands before bundling them into a bun on top of her head. She made sure her freckles were still hidden by makeup then added a smudge of color to her cheeks. She brushed on mascara to brighten her hazel eyes, and now, satisfied with her appearance, she kissed the air with a neutral lip. Good enough. She didn't have Zelda's green eyes and cute little nose. She didn't stand as tall and elegant as Genna. Nor could she pitch a ball and run the bases like Rian. No, she was just Amy Sparks, thank you very much. Owner of the Tiddlywinks Players Club at the Cardboard Cottage & Company.

Victor waited on the hall tree bench near the door, his tail slapping the wall before he bounded down the stairs ahead of her. Twenty-nine steps from her apartment above the shop. She loved that these stairs were her commute to work, and she counted them every day. Twenty-nine. And that included the last two skips in the hopscotch grid under the Cardboard Cottage & Company sign, with its painted daisies and curlicue font.

As she passed the bakery window, she caught Sammie's eye and waved. In a flour-stained apron, dark hair piled in a messy bun, Sammie waved back as she bustled happily behind the counter. Her bakery was already clogged with customers. Crumpets and Cones proved to be one of the best promotional tools possible, because anyone in town with a sense of smell and a taste for sweets found their way here. In the morning, regulars bought freshly baked cinnamon buns, crumpets, brewed coffee, or tea. In the afternoon customers lined up for waffle cones piled with fruit and fresh whipped cream. Ice cream cones were commonplace in town, but Sammie's treat in a cone was one of a kind.

She unlocked the stained-glass entry, and Victor blasted through the door and leaped onto the wingback armchair in the front window. He settled on his throne across the top. The front door jangled again, letting in a familiar whiff of perfume and Zelda Carlisle.

"*Yoo-hoo!*" Zelda called as she stuck her head through the door of Tiddlywinks. "What are you doing, Sparks? Standing there all dreamy queen? Those games aren't going to sell themselves."

"Mind your own shop," she teased. "You have less than a week to find someone to mind your business while we're away. That's not much time to get them hired and trained."

"Tell me about it," Zelda agreed. "I am so excited about the trip, I can't stay focused on anything. If I can't find the right person to take on Zsa Zsa Galore, I'll just lock the door and count my losses."

Amy frowned. Been there done that. They all had. She had missed the playful chatter of tourists at the game tables when the building closed for repairs then stayed closed a little longer because it seemed like the right thing to do. It was the right thing because Zelda was mourning, if she could call it that, and they were all recuperating after a misadventure in the backwoods of Arkansas.

An innocent game of dominoes and a birthday wish set those gears in motion. And a snippet, too. One of those odd dreams that made her question whether it was an accidental murder or a premeditated one. She had been compelled to find the truth. She had been determined to hunt down a killer she hoped wasn't one of her friends. What a ride! At least it was one Hummer and one hundred miles in the past now. She wanted to keep it there—in the past—where it belonged, and Zelda seemed to agree.

Zelda's designer heels clicked on the wood floor, echoing down the hallway to her cubbyhole shop. Aptly named, Zsa Zsa Galore Décor catered to shoppers who were not on a budget. Although tiny, the shop showcased a hodgepodge of collectibles for home and garden. Zelda's customers loved it.

"Hey," Rian said, zipping past her, pulling her shop key from the pocket of her blue jeans. Directly across the hall from Zelda's shop, the Pot Shed housed the fourth business in the cooperative.

The building, which stood the test of time for more than a hundred years, sparked Amy's imagination the moment she stepped over the wide threshold with the real estate agent. With cash from her divorce and a hefty mortgage later, she felt honored to own such a stately and historic piece of Bluff Springs. Well, the bank owned it, but she enjoyed working with her friends close by, especially since she jumped into debt all but dragging them with her. No regrets. The mortgage got paid on time, and she stayed ahead of the bills. It wasn't Boardwalk, but it was at least Marvin Gardens with a house and a lucky cat.

"Good day, O'Deis," Amy called, enjoying the pun. "You are opening early."

"I'm interviewing today," Rian called over her shoulder as she unlocked the door. "We only have a few days left to get staff hired. I ran an ad in the newspaper, but I should have followed your lead earlier. You already have your temps on the payroll and stocking shelves, don't you?"

Amy didn't bother to answer. She did have them on the payroll already.

"Well if you don't want them, send them my way," Zelda shouted from across the hall. "I need help, too, and haven't done a thing about it. Not even an ad in the paper."

"I doubt if you would want my castoffs. They'll all be long-haired *nuevo* hippies in Birkenstocks and baggy tie-dye. Not the kind of style your housewives are accustomed to."

"Don't be so smug. I have plenty of baggy tie-dye."

"In your rag bag maybe," Rian muttered.

"I heard that. Send them my way, anyway. You never know who you might dress up in heels. Besides, hippies are honest to a fault."

Amy followed Rian into the Pot Shed, and the heady perfume of herbs and ornamentals filled the crisp morning air. "Genna could help you both find help. She's skilled at scrutinizing the innocent."

"I already asked her. She's filming a television commercial over in Buck Ridge. Some patriot's running for office and wants the famous Genna Gregory spin. The fool doesn't have any idea what he's stepping into."

Amy laughed as she fingered the petals in a pot of chamomile. "Genna can't keep her nose out of other people's business, can she? She may say she's retired, but she'll never pass up an opportunity to put words in other people's mouths. Not as long as there's a politician who needs words strung together."

"And willing to pay for it," Rian added.

"Speaking of politics," Amy said as Zelda joined the other two, a cup of tea in one hand and a crumpet dripping lemon curd in the other. "I've been invited to participate as a panelist at the Governor's Conference. I'll be representing our cooperative."

"Bravo!" Zelda said, licking the dregs from her fingers. "That's amazing!"

"Better you than me," Rian said, stuffing her fingers in her jeans pocket. "I can't imagine being in a room with all those people."

"Genna's going to write my talking points."

Rian rolled her eyes. "Of course she is."

"Do you know a Merriweather Hopkins?"

Zelda stuffed the last bite into her mouth. "Should I?" she mumbled, shaking her head. "Your big gig better not interfere with my cruise. When is it anyway?"

"The conference is not until spring. And nothing could interfere with your birthday cruise."

Zelda smiled, crinkling her nose the way a child greeted a candy cane. "Girls just want to have fun," she chirped and disappeared into her shop.

Back at Tiddlywinks, Amy set out a puzzle on one of the library tables. The collage of old-time candy wrappers reminded her of hot childhood summers spent in a cool theater. Hayley Mills and Julie Andrews were her favorite actors on the screen then. Her favorite candies, which cost less than a dollar, were Junior Mints and Sugar Babies that stuck in her teeth. Memories like these fueled her passion for old games and the nostalgia that went with them. She funneled that energy into Tiddlywinks with the same craving for camaraderie that drew her and her friends to the game table every week. Games just made life more fun.

She looked up as the jangle of the front door announced customers.

"Welcome to Tiddlywinks Players Club," she said in greeting. "We're an old-fashioned game parlor. We have games from every era." She smiled when their eyes widened with the possibilities.

"Play any game you want from here." She pointed to the section of games on the library shelves. "Or work the puzzle. The rest of these games are available for purchase. If you join the Players Club, you play for free. Five bucks for adults, and kids are always free with their parents."

Glancing from one to the next, she studied their family genetics. She always enjoyed that game. Here were Mom and Dad, two siblings—that seemed obvious. Mom's sister—they shared the same eyes and smile. And a cousin.

She ran her hand lovingly over the spines of the cardboard game boxes. Her very own Vanna White. "We have all the old standbys and new games, too."

"Whoa," the cousin said.

"Totally," said one of the siblings.

"Pandemic! I love that game!" the dad said. His family groaned behind him, and he raised his hands in defeat. "Okay, okay. What game do you want to play?"

Mother and sister eyed Amy with a grin. "We want to shop," the mother said.

"We want to play games," the father said.

"Yeah," said one of the boys. "We want to stay here."

Amy cocked her head. "That's usually how it works. We keep them entertained while you shop." She nodded toward the women, who beamed at the idea.

While the children searched through the games, the women

disappeared down the hall toward Zsa Zsa Galore Décor.

The bell jangled constantly as customers came and went. She loved the sound. She moved smoothly through the throng, her spiel welcoming. The other shopkeepers in town recommended Tiddlywinks, which was often full of husbands and cranky kids tired of being dragged behind die-hard shoppers. Tiddlywinks offered a win-win option and benefited the stores that needed to keep their shoppers engaged.

"I'm looking for a chess set," said a dark-haired woman motioning to the chess board set up between two wingback chairs. "I noticed this one in the window."

Victor tapped his tail rhythmically on the back of the chair. His eyes were closed.

"Beautiful cat."

"He's aware of it, too. His head gets fluffier with every compliment."

As they passed the locked cabinet where she kept collector's games, the woman gasped and stopped. "Ruth Haring actually played *this* set?" She motioned to the comment card inside the case.

Amy unlocked the cabinet door. "It belonged to someone who had a long friendship with Miss Haring. Which means they played many a game on this board."

The woman sighed. "She was my hero growing up." Her eyes brightened. "Do you play?"

"Not very well. Dominoes is my game." She pulled the set from the shelf, setting it on a table nearby, and the two of them stood over it as if they were admiring a precious diamond. She didn't need to love the game to appreciate the look of awe on the woman's face. She lived for that sense of discovery, the way a treasure hunter must feel when she dug up a chest of gold.

The woman nodded and picked up the queen, rubbing the ebony surface with her thumb. "I went to the University of Arkansas, too. Ruth's alma mater. Where did you find this?"

"Kansas City. I bought it at an estate auction. This set should be in the chess museum in St. Louis, but it isn't." Amy winked. "Not yet anyway. I think it needs a home."

"Is it expensive?"

"Not if you have to have it," she said with a conspiratorial giggle. "But then, who am I to say. I bought a two hundred dollar set of dominoes because the pips are real Swarovski crystals. I had to have them."

The woman smiled, her eyes sparkling. "How much?"

"Do you love it?"

"Yes," the woman breathed.

"Then how does two hundred sound?"

"Yes!" she breathed again. "And I still need one for my granddaughter. I want to teach her to play, too."

She left the woman to review her options and helped another customer discover a shelf of games from the 1930s. Back at the sales counter, transaction complete, Amy smiled at the woman who beamed back.

"Farewell and fond memories," she called as the woman left the shop, bag in hand, floating out on a cloud of joy. She knew that feeling. That's what Tiddlywinks was about—connecting players to their best childhood memories.

Tiddlywinks emptied and refilled with players and shoppers in a cycle that made the day go by quickly. The door jangled again, and Bruce the delivery hunk juggled a large box through the door and hoisted it to the counter.

"Our costumes!" She recognized the sender's name. "For the cruise," she added, but the hunk in shorts was already out the door.

CHAPTER TWO

The scream dragged her from a deep sleep. The blast of a ship's horn brought her fully awake.

Not again. Amy squeezed her eyes closed as if that would push it away.

Breathing in slowly, she hoped to slow the racing of her heart. Lavender linen spray. Lavender walls. *Boudoir Lavande*, a color Zelda chose for her. While color and scent merged, they didn't calm her fears.

The scream was not real. Not. Real. Or at least real only in her head. If the scream did not exist in reality, neither did the pirate with the cliché black patch and the pistol pointed at someone she couldn't see.

A sob choked in her throat. Not again. Couldn't this be a flash from a movie? Another silly dream? Not a premonition of something to come. Not a snippet. Not anything, not really. Impossible to understand.

She wasn't psychic. Neither was she clairvoyant or telepathic. She considered herself more tele*pathetic* than anything. She didn't channel wisdom or speak to spirits. She didn't believe in ghosts. She couldn't locate lost things unless finding misplaced car keys counted. She couldn't move anything without touch or foretell the future. And yet, here it was, another little snippet flashing through her dreams. Familiar and unwelcome, snippets haunted her sleep and never, ever made sense.

Tele*pathetic*.

Dreams. Visions. Hocus pocus. Genna would call it that.

She didn't believe in any of it. Not really. And yet, the last snippet had come true. Sort of.

Pulling the covers over her head, she sucked at the lavender scent with deep calming breaths. The picture of Zelda on the refrigerator popped into her mind.

T-Minus 10 and counting!!!!

CHAPTER THREE

"I'm not going to pay one red dime for that cab following us," Genna announced, bumping shoulders with Amy as she turned to glare at the cab behind them. The car appeared to be empty except for the driver, although the cab carried all the luggage that would not fit in one compact car. "If a woman has to bring four suitcases for a ten-day cruise, she can pay for her encumbrance."

"Relax," Zelda said. "I'm paying the cab fares. I'm paying for everything, remember?"

"Dimes are silver," Rian said. "Not red. Not even in Ecuador."

"Besides, one of the suitcases is empty."

"What for?" Genna demanded. "Are you going to smuggle contraband back to Arkansas? Peruvian diamonds? Cute little cabana boys with thick . . ."

"Shush!" Zelda glanced at the driver.

"I was going to say *accents*. Thick *accents*. Pervert."

"That would make an interesting souvenir," Amy mused. "What language do they speak in the Galápagos anyway?"

"Spanish, silly. Everybody knows that."

"I don't know Spanish. But Rian speaks Spanglish."

"I can ask for a beer and a bathroom. In that order."

"If you must know, I brought an empty suitcase to hold all the birthday presents I'm going to buy myself." Zelda adjusted her hat and shades with a brief look in the visor mirror. "Husband number five is not going to be one of them."

"Contraband is Rian's wheelhouse, anyway."

Rian poked Amy in the ribs with her elbow. "Thanks for the broadcast, Sparks."

"He can't understand us. We don't speak his language."

"I hope they speak English on board," Genna said. "I'm rusty with all my foreign languages."

Rian laughed. "You're just rusty."

Amy turned to Zelda, eyebrow raised in concern. "And you booked them both in the same cabin? One of them may not make it home alive."

The two cabs sped through the busy streets of Guayaquil, weaving in and out of the dense traffic. They rode in a constant blare of horns and shouts from the drivers with open windows, arms wigwagging out the window at each other. Amy felt like they were in a toy car, zipping through an imaginary track. There were no traffic lanes marked on the road. Cars zoomed by everywhere.

The four friends flew from Miami to Ecuador, spent a quiet night at a hotel, and now were headed to yet another airport to fly to San Cristobal, one of only four human-inhabited islands of the Archipelagos. Their ship docked there.

Amy sniffed the salt air and car exhaust coming through the cab window. "We are going to have so much fun! The Galápagos Islands! Isn't that on everyone's bucket list?"

"Bucket lists are for when you are old. Like Genna," Rian suggested.

"Old is a frame of mind," Genna snapped back. "And a lack of quality cosmetics."

Genna leaned her head out the window and burped. "I shouldn't have had that second sausage."

"You were not *hostage*. That was Amy."

"Seriously, Rian. I said, *sausage* not *hostage*. We're getting you a hearing aid for your birthday if we have to hold you down and tie you up."

"You'll have to catch me first. There's nothing wrong with my hearing. It's your mumble-jumble that's the problem."

"I don't even want to hear the word *hostage*," Amy replied. "That's one misadventure I hope never happens again."

"Touché," Rian said. "Easter clown and all."

She elbowed Rian for the painful reminder, but Rian had been a determined friend during her mishap with some good old boys down near Hot Springs. She solved the mystery with a little help from her friends but had found some trouble doing it. "How come you didn't bring Officer Handsome? He deserves some downtime, too."

Rian nodded. "Ben and I are going to go . . ."

Zelda turned from the front seat. "Hey, this is our trip! No men allowed! Girls want to have fun, and men just get in the way."

"Ben and I are meeting in Ecuador after the cruise and traveling on to Peru. We're going to climb the Machu Picchu."

"How fun!"

"I can't imagine how fun a thousand steps straight up to heaven could be," Genna mumbled.

"There are sixteen hundred steps," Rian said.

"I'd be wheezing at sixteen."

Zelda turned back to face the road ahead and the cars

zooming in and out of traffic. "And you didn't share this travel tidbit with us prior because . . . why?"

"Because you would want to come with us. We want to go alone."

"Well, that's just fine by me," Zelda said with an air of attitude. "The only men I want around are the men who drive the boat, make our beds, and serve us drinks when we snap our fingers."

Genna peered over her shades and down her nose. "You have a warped sense of entitlement, now that you're a rich widow."

"We're peas in a pod."

"I'd prefer pearls in an oyster."

"Time to pay up, little pod," Amy said as the cabs jerked to the curb at the airport hub, and the four friends scrambled out into the heat.

The flight from Guayaquil to San Cristobal took nearly two hours on a loud ride in a small plane, but every minute moved them closer to their destination. Stealing a glance at Zelda, who rested behind her oversized Fendi shades, she wondered if Zelda enjoyed her newfound freedoms. Zelda, now free of a bad marriage, would also be free of her forties. Amy wasn't sure if Zelda considered this as good a freedom as the other, but the half-century marker loomed ahead. This cruise with her best friends was the birthday gift Zelda wanted and made clear she would get. The only person who opposed the idea was now out of the picture altogether.

The plane bumped over the cracked tarmac as it landed, taxied toward a small concrete building, and stopped. As they disembarked into the heat of the blacktop, they were herded through another baggage check before meeting the ship's shuttle driver, who cheerfully ushered them on board the van and its cool interior.

Within minutes they were off the shuttle and aboard the *Darwinian*.

"Look at this!" Zelda stepped through the door of their cabin. Amy followed her inside, her eyes as wide with awe as Zelda's. Jeez Louise. So this was what a little money bought. Maybe this was what *a lot* of money bought. Zelda acted hush-hush about the cost of the trip, and frankly, she was glad. This was swanky.

The view of their mooring at the marina sparkled through the wide windows framed by exotic wood. Whether teak or mahogany or something equally as luxurious, the grain was polished to an amber shine. Turning in a tight circle, she gathered it in. Although small, the cabin felt plush from top to bottom. Two twin beds with navy duvets and a mound of blue and gold pillows were separated by a wooden nightstand. Across from the foot of the beds, a couch with wide-striped cushions matched the navy-and-white motif. A built-in table in the corner held a nautical lamp fixed in place. Smart décor. Ships tended to roll. She touched the patch behind her ear to make sure it was still on.

Near the windows stood a small table with two heavy chairs that swiveled. On the opposite side, a pocket door opened to a large dressing area with banquet seating in front of a wall-mounted mirror. Another door opened into the bath. The space felt cozy but roomy enough.

"My goodness."

"No joke," Zelda agreed, her eyes as green as the sea beyond the windows. "I'm glad I booked two cabins. We would be too crowded having all four of us in one."

Amy nodded. Too crowded and too loud. Between Genna's

and Zelda's chattering, there would never be a silent moment. What did she care? She would be happy to stow away in a suitcase of monkeys if she had to. The Galápagos! She might burst open with bliss like overripe passion fruit.

"I don't think you spared much expense. This is a boutique boat."

"Oh, let's don't talk about money."

Going from twirling to pacing, Amy wandered the space, touching surfaces and opening drawers. The wood felt smooth. The beds were comfy. The glass gleamed and sparkled.

"I'll take these two drawers," she said, motioning to the nightstand. "I didn't bring a lot. Not compared to you."

"I'm going to need every hanger and every drawer," Zelda said, opening the drawers and closing them before eyeing the ice bucket on the table by the couch. "Let's drink champagne while we unpack!"

The cork exploded across the room.

"To me!" Zelda said, raising a bubbling glass.

"To you! Fifty is going to look great on you."

"It is, isn't it?" Zelda turned to face the mirror. A well-filled flowered jumpsuit fit her ample curves. She twirled in the mirror, turning her heels in the reflection. Her mules were topped with a floppy bow in pink flowers and stripes. "Aren't these to die for? Tabitha Simmons. They're so girly."

Amy dropped her eyes to the gaudy shoes. They were hardly boat attire, but Zelda would argue the point. While Amy didn't understand the appeal of high-dollar shoes, shoes were Zelda's addiction, and one shared with oodles of women who loved a shoe-forward approach to life and ample closet space.

Amy inspected the well-worn sneakers on her feet, not feeling a bit envious. She preferred cheap and comfortable, although she did love a T-shirt with a little bling.

Still admiring her reflection, Zelda patted her hair. As dark as bitter chocolate, it landed just below her chin, curving seductively behind her ears. Bangs framed her brows in a slight, precise arc. The cut looked as if it were right off the page of a roaring twenties magazine when women were beginning to show their sass.

Amy grinned at her friend. Confidence came so easily to Zelda. Not vanity with airs of self-importance, but rather a simple appreciation for what she had. Most women who had curly hair wanted straight hair. Brown eyes wanted to be blue, and short wanted to be tall. Zelda was content with what she had. All of it. All of the curves, dings, and wrinkles. Her confidence, now days away from fifty, was enviable. Glancing at her reflection, Amy didn't see herself that way. She straightened her spine, sucked in her stomach, and heaved a sigh.

The steward knocked gently against the open door, motioning to the suitcases, now empty and lined up like dominoes waiting to be played.

"Take care of my babies," Zelda told him, one hand patting her designer luggage and the other tucking a twenty-dollar bill into his hand.

Amy drained the last of her champagne and grabbed Zelda in the crook of her arm. "Let's explore! Which deck first?"

Zelda wobbled on her mules. "Let's follow the champagne!"

"You're a bit tipsy already."

"I'm just getting my sea legs, that's all."

"We haven't left the dock, yet!"

She jumped sideways as a rattling groan came up from somewhere below her feet. "What the . . ." The ship shifted slightly, a gentle rocking as soothing as a feather floating down from the sky. The rattling ceased, and the scenery from the window began to slide by.

"Anchor's away!" Zelda pitched right into Amy. Righting themselves, arms linked, they stepped into the hallway and stumbled headlong into Rian and Genna.

"Sounds like they let Jacob Marley loose," Rian said, pulling herself free of Zelda's clutch. "The anchor and chains must be somewhere below our cabins. You all right there, Zelda? You're a little wobbly in those fancy shoes."

Zelda dismissed the comment with a flip of her hand. "We're going exploring! Come on. Let's go!"

"Exactly what we had in mind," Genna said, taking the lead down the corridor.

Following Rian, Amy zigzagged through the narrow hall as if she were a sailboat tacking in the wind. Tracking softly from one wall to the other, her feet felt awkward beneath her. "This is going to take some getting used to. I feel a little dizzy."

"I'm glad I have on my patch," Zelda agreed. "I could get seasick riding in a bathtub."

As they gathered at a diagram of the ship hanging on the wall, Amy pointed to the "You are Here" arrow. She felt comforted about being in a strange place and knowing right where she was. At least on the map. "What a maze," Amy said. "I hope we don't get lost."

"Oh, we'll do our fair share of backtracking before we get the knack of navigating our way around," Rian said. "That's part of the fun."

Three hundred feet bow to stern, the *Darwinian* was less than a quarter of the length of the cruise ships that sailed the Caribbean with thousands of passengers on board. This seemed to be the tipping point for Rian, who said she simply could not abide that many people all in one place. The idea, though, settled well with all of them. One hundred passengers and five decks of luxury, six isolated islands, and ten days.

When they reached the Sun Deck, an open sky covered them—a vast umbrella of blue. A brisk wind ruffled Amy's hair, and tiny whitecaps peaked like frothy egg whites in the giant blue bowl of a sea that carried them farther into the cold waters of the Pacific.

The naturalist guide on deck gathered a crowd around her, including Genna, Rian, and Zelda, all of them admiring the sky.

"These are frigate birds," the guide explained, speaking perfect English with a rhythmic Spanish accent. "We will see many of these birds during our voyage. They enjoy following us."

The giant birds did seem to be following the ship, soaring the wind currents with ease. Squinting into the sun, Amy watched the birds overhead.

"They have the largest wing-to-body ratio of any bird," the guide continued. "Even of the mighty eagle, for our US friends on board. Her wingspan is over two meters, about seven and a half feet. She is often compared to the pterodactyl, and perhaps she is their evolutionary sister. Her silhouette resembles this, with her forked tail, hooked bill, and long, pointed wings."

The silhouette did share a resemblance as if evolution held on to the past while moving toward the future. Frigate birds had been around much longer than humans, and their evolution from any connection to the dinosaur occurred eons ago. If that's where they came from. Still, it was thrilling to witness a possible link in the chain of time, however long the span might be.

"You can spot the females by her white underbelly. The

male, he has a distinctive red gular pouch, which he inflates to make him sexy. To female frigate birds, anyway."

Everybody laughed. Zelda sounded tipsy.

The guide talked about the bird's funny mating dance, his red-balloon throat, and noisy clattering bill. "We will see plenty of their antics!"

A single bird soared overhead, and all eyes followed its flight, riding the wind as a surfer rode a wave. The massive dark wings were the only color in the sky beyond blue. The bird caught a downdraft and swooped low over the deck. Amy ducked instinctively.

The crowd around the guide grew tighter as the wind gusts strengthened. A pair of tall, sandy-haired men stood rapt in the guide's story, the wind pulling at the strings of their hats. Time to play her game. She couldn't help it.

These two men didn't look like brothers—their jawlines and smiles seemed to share no family genes. Maybe they were friends. Maybe they were a couple. Too soon to tell that, but they were definitely here to drink in the wildlife. Cameras and binoculars hung from their necks the way rappers wore gold chains, but their rap leaned toward feathers and species found here in these islands. Bird nerds. Ornithologists! Both men were dressed in expensive-looking clothes for the posh traveler. They were all posh travelers on this boat. Even if *her* posh belonged to someone else and she came along for the ride.

She watched another couple as they leaned into each other. She hoped they were tipsy from the champagne, or bracing against the wind, not seasick. He stood tall and rotund, his belly big enough to reach the bar before his elbows did. He was an odd color, too, like a big gray can of putty, or a bucket of cement. She saw no genetic resemblance. Husband and wife, probably, although she looked much younger. Tall. Big-boned, buxom, not at all delicate. With beautiful red hair. The kind of red she wished her curls would be—smooth, dark, and sultry, like a spiced rum drink—not the copper wire at the end of a plug.

Why did she do that? Why did she always put herself at the bottom end of the scale? She was a Moscow Mule. That's the kind of drink she was by comparison. A bright copper mug with tangy lime, sweet mint, and just enough kick. Much better. She would work on that. She would work on her confidence as Zelda suggested. It was okay to believe in yourself. Having confidence didn't take confidence away from anyone else.

The rum redhead grabbed the man's elbow and ushered him to a chair. He pulled a handkerchief from his pocket and mopped his brow. Amy averted her eyes. If he was seasick, she didn't want to look.

Her attention returned to the guide, still talking about the birds and her chicks. She should be listening, but her attention drifted to the passengers. It was then that he caught her eye. Leaning against the rail, a fair distance from others, stood a tall man with broad shoulders, dark hair, and an eye patch slung over one eye. Her hands tightened on the arms of the chaise.

A pirate! Just like in her dream.

A shadow covered her as though a cloud passed over the sun, only the sky was cloudless. Zelda loomed over her and the man disappeared from her view.

Zelda wobbled on her high heels. "What are you looking at?"

"Just taking it all in."

Zelda teetered again. "We have a little time before dinner. I think I'll take a teeny nap."

"Me, too," Genna said, joining them. "A siesta sounds good."

"We don't have to dress for dinner, do we?" Rian dropped into the chair beside Amy. "I didn't bring fancy."

Genna tugged the sleeve of Rian's T-shirt. "Of course you didn't."

"Well I *do* have a dress code," Zelda said a little too loudly. "And I spent a small fortune acquiring it. Tonight is the costume party. We'll have cocktails and dress up. It will be fun!"

Amy skimmed the deck again, but the man with the eye patch was gone.

CHAPTER FOUR

"So what do you do?" Poseidon asked. Or, he was dressed like him. The man and the woman sitting beside him were the same couple from the deck. He still had a ghastly pallor about him. Amy still envied the woman's gorgeous red hair. He introduced himself as Simon Monforte, a yacht dealer. From Maine.

Sleaze Ball from Anywhere, USA, was how Amy would put it. The minute he opened his mouth, Amy took a disliking to him. That was not her norm. She preferred to give everyone the benefit of the doubt and had lots of practice. People of all ilk wandered into Tiddlywinks, and she had learned how to trust her intuition without being unkind.

But here they were, stuck at the dinner table for the duration with a man who made her skin crawl.

What do you do? Could she ignore his question? She wanted to ignore him altogether, but then he leaned toward her, fork waving at her food as if to stab a bite on her plate. Too hard to ignore that. Nor could she ignore that he was dressed as Poseidon, or at least his version of the King of the Sea on a ship in the Galápagos in October. What a fantasy spoiler. She thought of Poseidon as a tall, muscular guy with broad shoulders and a trident full of magic. This Poseidon had an over-indulgent gut and a crown made of plastic starfish and glitter. Somebody's five-year-old could do better. Simon was bald, except for a few strands of white behind his ears, which had more hair than his head. The real Poseidon had hair like Fabio.

Simon Monforte scanned the guests seated at the table as if they were pawns on a chessboard. What did it matter what she did? He turned his gaze back to her expectantly, though he still didn't introduce the redhead sitting next to him.

Ignoring Simon, she caught the woman's eye instead. Her gown was beautiful silk in deep lavender. The deep-vee of the neckline dropped to a necklace so large it couldn't possibly be real amethyst. With her hair piled in a classic New York beehive, she appeared ready for breakfast at Tiffany's. The whole effect said she had taken *costume* with a grain of salt. Her outfit was not a catalog kitsch selection.

Glancing down at her white shift, Amy felt dowdy, even under the weight of the fake gold tiara and matching sandals borrowed from Zelda that laced to her knees.

"What do you do?" he repeated. "Miss Cleopatra. Queen of the Nile."

She was stuck.

"Queen of *De*-Nile," Genna remarked. Amy shot her a glance.

"I own and operate a game shop. In Bluff Springs, Arkansas."

"Video games!" Simon bellowed. "I used to own a video shop. A Blockbuster. Back in the day when people bought videos. No money in that now."

She forced a smile. "People collect board games, especially vintage games."

"Vintage!" he bellowed. "I have an entire basement full of vintage. You name it, I got it. Go ahead, name it. I got it."

The redhead spoke. "A game store. How fun! I love to play games, too. My name is Sheila by the way. I am also from Maine. And another mermaid costume tonight, but certainly not as beautiful as you," she said to Zelda.

Zelda's glee shone in her bright eyes. "I love a costume party!" She shook her shoulders, sending the sequins chattering like a wind chime made of shells. A shade matching Zelda's eyes, the skirt fit tight over her plump hips before spreading out into a flared hem resembling a mermaid tail. The merfolk scales shimmered to the floor. Zelda flicked her foot out from under the table, showing high heel pumps that matched the skirt.

"They are not designer, but they sure are cute."

"*Seeexy*," Genna said. Dressed in a flirty blue sailor suit with brass buttons and a white rope trim, Genna looked svelte and commanding all in one capri-length jumpsuit. The jaunty sailor cap made her even taller in the chair, her long silver ponytail tossed over one shoulder. She grinned with a coquettish smile.

"I agree," Sheila said. "Don't you, Simon?"

"Games," Simon slurred, draining his tumbler on the rocks. "No money or power in that."

Genna coughed into her napkin and narrowed her eyes at the target. Oh, boy. Ammo loaded. She knew that expression and the emotion behind it.

"Oh, for pity's sake. Amy is being humble," Genna said, hard *H*, her southern accent dripping from behind a two-martini start. Stirred by Simon's arrogance, no doubt, and a lack of nicotine, Genna was about to shake up the Gregory poison and serve it over ice. Simon wouldn't know what slugged him.

"My dearest friend, Amy"—Amy winced at the exaggerated

tone—"is the CEO and founder of an enterprise in a restored historic landmark, a national treasure, no less, which is the headquarters for the four prestigious *women-owned* companies that serve a lucrative tourism clientele." Genna's gaze remained steady and holding. "We were all featured not long ago in one of the nation's most popular magazines. There's power in that. And . . . Amy's up for the Woman Entrepreneur of the Year Award. If I'm not mistaken."

Genna had that mischievous twinkle in her eye. Amy couldn't tell if the joke was on Simon or herself.

No one else spoke, and Genna still had Simon's attention. "I should also add that Amy is the *president* of our chamber and sits on the Governor's Board of Tourism. She will be the featured speaker at the Governor's Conference in the spring. He's a dear friend of mine."

Amy hid her smile. What a whopper. She *belonged* to the chamber and she *subscribed* to the state's tourism newsletter sent out every month. Her participation in the conference was minor, albeit important to her and the Cardboard Cottage. As far as she knew, there was no woman entrepreneur of the year competition in Arkansas, and she sure wasn't up for it if there were.

"Well," Simon responded, his eyes on Genna. "That is quite an impressive resume. For a woman."

"*Indeed*," Genna drawled. "Impressive. *For a woman*. And I . . ." she continued, letting the vowel linger there, too, "am a PR counselor for people of interest, as with our dear governor. Not that that might interest you, I don't expect. My clients are men of stature and style."

Wham! Why couldn't she sling dirt like that? Zelda and Rian hid their amusement behind napkins.

Rian begrudgingly agreed to a costume after a playful-but-serious quarrel with Zelda. Amy liked Rian's idea of the Amelia Earhart costume better, and she couldn't keep the disappointment from her voice when Rian changed her mind. Rian's reasoning was sound enough. Amelia's plane went down over the Pacific.

"I wouldn't want to jinx the boat," Rian had said.

"Ship," Zelda corrected.

"Boat," Rian said stubbornly.

"Spoilsport."

"Don't wear that eye patch," Amy had begged.

Rian had crossed her arms stubbornly. "That may be all I wear."

And now, Rian sat directly across the table from her in a white ruffled shirt, a wine-red vest, and the eye patch flipped up so that it rode inverted above her eyebrow. Her linen drawstring pants reminded Amy of MC Hammer days. They were probably authentic fashion from the back of Rian's closet at home.

Sheila grinned, and her eyes sparkled. She was on to Genna's bunk.

"Your enterprise sounds fun. And ambitious," Sheila said.

"Well, actually . . ." Amy started.

"Well, actually," Genna interjected before Amy could rework the spin, "we are all engaged in this business. Rian is an herbal practitioner, and Zelda, who will be celebrating her birthday on this cruise, is one of the most popular interior design consultants in the entire region."

"That is true," Zelda said. "My birthday is Thursday."

Sheila chuckled softly. "Wonderful to meet you, ladies. We are delighted to have such accomplished women at the table. Don't you agree, Simon?"

Simon sucked the ice cubes from his scotch on the rocks.

"Right, delighted," he parroted, turning to catch the waiter's eye.

The man sitting beside Genna leaned forward. "My name is Broderick," he said, browsing each face. "Andrew Broderick. No, no relation to Matthew. None at all," he added as if anticipating the question. "I teach science and history at a private school in southern Louisiana."

His gaze landed on Sheila, then on Simon, then finally the man sitting to her right. "This trip has been a dream of mine," he continued, his eyes still on the man beside her. "Ever since I first read Charles Darwin's *On the Origin of Species*."

"And it changed your life, right?" Simon's tone was jarring.

"It has eased my struggle," Andrew admitted. "I have always wondered about our true origin. I was raised in a strict Catholic home with a father who was not present." His cheeks colored. Straightening the ruby-colored ascot at his throat, he brushed at a dark bang that had fallen forward. "Darwin was a devoted scientist. A keen and impartial observer, even though his work fell prey to the unfortunate criticisms of his time."

"I get it now," Zelda said. "You're dressed as Charles Darwin without his hat."

Andrew nodded. "It wouldn't be proper to wear a hat to dinner. Or a beard." He smiled warmly at Zelda.

Now Zelda's cheeks colored. "Are you traveling alone?"

Andrew seemed startled. "Alone? Uh, no. I am traveling with—uh, with a friend," he said, frowning after the last word. "Sharing a cabin made this trip affordable."

"Tell me about it," Simon thundered. "This trip is costing me a fortune. Not that I'm complaining. There's plenty where that came from. But the food and booze better be top-notch and plentiful." He scowled at the one person at the table yet to be introduced. Amy sat sandwiched between them.

"My accountant and attorney," Simon said. "Two for the price of one. Meet William B. Forthright the *Third*. Now isn't that a name to live up to?"

"Simon," Sheila said sternly. "Behave."

William smiled at Amy by way of introduction, then glared at Simon with veiled contempt. The exchange said a lot about their history. And something else. Was he afraid of Simon? Or was it the other way around? Their eyes locked briefly, then Simon turned his gaze away.

"My apologies," he said thickly. "We're on a business trip, with business to do, so why wouldn't you need your accountant and attorney along with you?"

The man smiled and nodded to the guests at the table. "A pleasure to meet you. Call me Bill if you will. I prefer that. Much less formal than William."

Bill forked chocolate cake into his mouth and chewed with vigor. He looked younger than Simon, but not by much. His dark hair was smoothed flat, a stark white part on the side.

"What are you dressed as?" Amy asked. "What's your costume?"

"Me?" Bill chuckled. "I'm dressed as myself. I don't go in much for costumes or disguises."

"I hear that," Rian said. "I got bribed into this costume myself."

"Don't let him fool you," Simon muttered. "He's about as transparent as a brick wall."

"Simon," Sheila said sternly.

Music blared from the speakers near the stage, quieted, then the emcee announced the evening entertainment, including the costume contest, for which he needed volunteers and entries. The emcee barely spoke the words before Zelda sprang from her chair and bobbled to the stage.

"Come on now," the emcee begged. "Don't be shy. Let's see your costumes. Come strut your stuff. You all look *mahvelous*. Absolutely *mahvelous*."

"Zelda's got this in the bag," Amy said. There were several costumed contestants on stage now, but Zelda stood out as the most beautiful. Circling the stage to audience applause, Zelda sashayed her hips to make her fins swim. The contestants made three rounds, each time getting a little bolder, and the crowd a little louder with their applause.

"Our winner!" The emcee said, standing next to Zelda, presenting her with a gift certificate and a bottle of wine. "Wonderful costumes! Thank you all for playing along. And now, as dinner has concluded," he said, motioning to the doors, "join us for live music and dancing on the Moon Deck under the stars."

Zelda joined Amy and Genna at the table, still beaming from her win. "Did you see me? Did you see how sparkly my fins were? Hey, where's Rian? Where did she go?"

"Disappeared about the time you hit the stage. Slipped out the door like a thief on the run."

"Stealing some time alone," Amy suggested.

"We have to change tables," Genna declared. "I can't suffer through another meal with that man. I overheard him when I eavesdropped earlier. He said he didn't know his wife was coming on the cruise, and the mistress said that was the most ridiculous thing she ever heard."

"Who said Sheila is his mistress?" Amy asked.

"You don't have to be Magnum PI to see it. She has much

bigger bling."

"Sheila had some pretty impressive bling. Didn't you see the size of those amethysts?"

"That's my point," Genna said. "Sheila didn't introduce herself as Simon's wife. She said she was '*also from Maine.*'"

"So *Sheila* is the mistress and not the wife," Zelda said.

"Exactly."

Amy frowned. "So where is the wife? Wouldn't she be at dinner with the rest of his brood?"

"Not if the mistress is sitting there, too!" Zelda exclaimed. "That would be unbearable!"

Genna surveyed the room with a discriminating eye. "*Simon's* unbearable. Disgusting chauvinist pig. I won't spend another dinner hour with the likes of that!"

"His poor wife," Zelda said.

"Poor wife," Amy agreed. "They never know about the mistress. Trust me, the wife never knows."

Zelda nodded and looked around the room. "Say . . . he's cute. Oh, they're twins! What if we ditch this table for that one over there? Oh, and the pirate. I like him, too."

"Of course you would," Genna said in jest. "If there's a bad boy on the boat, you're bound to fall hook, line, and sinker."

"That's not fair."

There were several pirates in the dining room, not counting Rian, but she recognized the man Zelda meant. Leaning against the wall, the pirate observed the guests as they left their tables and exited through the open door. He was the same man she observed on the deck earlier. Out of the bright sun and dark shadows, she saw his features more clearly. Tall and dark-haired. Ruggedly handsome, with a chiseled jaw and a two-day shadow popular with men these days. What caught her attention yet again was the black patch strung over one eye. A small gold hoop hung from his left earlobe.

"I don't think you should go anywhere near that pirate."

"I agree. He's mine! I saw him first." Genna smiled. "He was on the Sun Deck watching me. You know, *watching* me. I don't think the patch is his costume."

"I'm not hunting a man, anyway," Zelda said, flipping the ends of her hair. "You just go right ahead. You just take that bait. Hook, line, and sinker!"

The pirate nodded in greeting and smiled as they passed him on their way out the door. Genna turned and peered over her shoulder, the cute little sailor cap still perched on her head, an extra swing in her hips.

Amy shivered as she stepped onto the deck. The chill at her neck had nothing to do with the brisk trade wind blowing across the polished deck of the *Darwinian*.

CHAPTER FIVE

"Where have you been?" Zelda asked after Rian knocked then entered the cabin. The three of them sat at the small table, a game of dominoes displayed helter-skelter over the tiny surface. "You missed my debut! I won the contest!"

"Good for you," Rian said earnestly, popping the cap from a bottle of beer in the ice bucket. "I went to explore the bottom of the boat. I thought I could find where they keep Jacob Marley."

Amy grinned. She could smell *Jacob Marley* on Rian's clothes. "So is that your new code word for pot?"

Rian grinned. "No, that's what I call the anchor, but I did run into someone down there who speaks just the right amount of English."

"Unbelievable," Zelda spat.

"We were wondering if we had to honor the Loser Rule while on board." Genna shifted so Rian could sit beside her. "Since Amy is such a stickler for the rules."

"Who made that rule anyway?" Zelda pondered. "Winner supplies the food, and the losers buy the booze. Did you make that up?"

"It was Genna," Rian said. "That was the year of Genna's winning streak. Remember? We ate hummus and celery sticks for every game."

Genna frowned. "I have no idea what you're talking about."

Rian nodded, one eyebrow raised. "Oh yeah, that was the year of the garbanzo gruel. I still can't face a bowl of hummus."

"Uh-huh." Zelda tapped the dominoes with a manicured fingertip. "I remember. It took us forever to figure out how Genna was winning. She told us she put that feng shui mirror up to redirect the energies, but she was eyeing our bones and pips in it the whole time."

Genna grinned. "I put up that Bagwa to ward off bad juju." She pointed a long finger at Amy. "You of all people should understand superstitious whatnot."

Amy played a double five spinner.

"*Whoo-hoo!*" Zelda slammed her tile with a loud *clack*. "You of all people should understand not to play that when I have every other five from the boneyard."

"And now we know," Genna said. "You'll never play another five as long as I live. Or this game ends. Whichever comes first."

"Why are you even in the cabin? There's a boat to discover and stars to see."

"We were waiting for you," Zelda said, looking over her red readers and down her nose. "We thought you had been kidnapped by Genna's pirate."

"Genna's pirate?"

"He's very sexy," Genna added.

"At least he's not Jacob Marley. Or Bob Marley, or whoever you found below deck."

"Freedom," Rian said softly.

"You're just dazed and confused," Zelda said.

"No, that's Led Zeppelin."

"I knew that." Zelda played a bone without scoring points.

Genna was keeping her word about the fives.

"Ten!" Genna slammed the domino on the table. "And Robert Plant is pretty sexy, if you ask me."

"No one asked you," Zelda said.

Genna ignored the gibe. "If you could have any rock star you wanted, who would it be?"

"Do I have to marry him?"

"No! No more husbands," Amy and Genna chanted in unison.

"What's there to eat?" Rian asked. "I'm hungry."

Zelda grinned at Rian. "If we were back home, we would be eating hummus and your brownies."

Rian frowned. "No hummus for me, thanks."

"I grabbed a piece of cake left on the table at dinner," Amy said, "and a fork."

Rian accepted the plate and dug in. "I'm going to say Bono. From the band U2," she interjected between bites. "He has a passion for what's right. A fighter for the underdog. And all the right sexy in all the right places. If I could have any rock star, he would be it."

"His real name is Paul."

"Don't ruin my fantasy, Genna. Ben bears a resemblance, doesn't he?" Rian noisily scraped the plate with the fork.

Amy nodded. "Must be the dimpled chin." Rian's semi-secret boyfriend, Ben Albright, served as a cop in the next county over. He came to her aid with a drill and a hammer when Tiddlywinks was broken into. He came to her aid again when she hunted a killer down near Hot Springs. Amy didn't know a lot about Ben the Boyfriend. Rian kept it that way. But she liked him. They all liked him. She thought of him as Dudley

Do-Right, and he was a good match for Rian, even if they didn't get romantic details.

"I wanted to marry David Cassidy. He was so dreamy," she added.

"David Cassidy!" Zelda swept the room with her hands. "I had him hung all over my bedroom walls! Who didn't want to marry him?"

"I didn't," Genna said. "Too young for me."

Zelda eyed Genna over her glasses, making the rhinestones glitter in the light. "Don't tell me you were an Elvis fan."

"What's wrong with Elvis?"

"There was a lot wrong with Elvis, but we don't need to go there."

Genna pulled bones from the boneyard. "I had the hots for Engelbert Humperdinck."

The three of them howled.

"Humperdinck!" Amy squeaked between breaths. "You just wanted to say his name!"

Genna grinned. "I did. I thought I was saying a dirty word and getting away with it. But really, it was the sideburns."

"He doesn't count," Zelda said, finally recovering her breath. "Humperdinck didn't sing rock and roll."

"He did."

"He did not."

"He was more of a crooner," Amy said. "Like on the Firestone Christmas records. But who spins vinyl anymore?"

Rian ditched her plate and grabbed her beer. "Vinyl is making a comeback. Along with magic mushrooms and tie-dye."

"Tie-dye," Zelda echoed. "I wonder how our hired help is doing back in Bluff Springs."

Genna snickered. "I can't believe the two of you hired the same person."

"She was the only candidate who showed up for the job," Zelda said simply. "Share and share-alike. Tie-dye and Birkenstocks. Just what Rian ordered."

"She's going to get run ragged. I hired three people to handle my shop."

"How hard can it be? You smile, you take money. Besides, no one ever goes into the Pot Shed unless they're picking up a tin of cookies. They won't be doing that while we're gone."

"I have a lot more customers than my weed eaters."

"Name one thing you sell out of the Pot Shed that's not illegal."

Rian clicked her tongue. "It shouldn't be illegal. Besides, I'm legit. No more green goodies. No more sweaters for Granny. And for your information, Ms. Nose-in-My-Business, right before I left, I sold three kitchen herbs and a salad garden setup, including two pairs of rubber boots. Tie-dye wellies. Fifty bucks a pair!"

Zelda snickered. "Tie-dye wellies."

"Spoilsport," Rian returned. "You sell pots with holes in the bottom."

"They're called shabby chic."

"Whatever."

Amy smiled at her friends. You had to be quick to catch all the nuance and innuendo of their banter. Like a wild tennis match of doubles, they served and volleyed in all directions, out of turn, out of bounds. Balls and rackets slamming quips and one-liners all over the court. Somehow they kept track and kept score. Tie-dye, shabby chic, vintage games, and Irish pastries. The Cardboard Cottage & Company was all that *and* an anchor in her life. It played an important part for them, too. Even when they were halfway around the world. "You don't always get what you want, but you always get what you need." They were proof of that.

CHAPTER SIX

"Look who's drunk and passed out under the stars," Genna said loudly enough for Simon to hear. "That bore of a boat dealer from Maine."

They came up to the Sun Deck from the port-side stairs to see the stars as Rian suggested earlier. Genna hoped to sneak a cigarette, although Amy reminded her smoking was still not allowed on board. It wouldn't be the first time Genna disobeyed the rules, and Amy knew it wouldn't be the last.

The Sun Deck was located one deck above their cabins. Simon Monforte lounged on one of the wooden deck chairs, his mouth open to the night air and his arms dangling at either side. The butt of a cigar smoldered between his fingers.

"If he can smoke, I can smoke." Genna pulled a cigarette from her shoulder-slung bag. "Simon," she said, moving toward him with her cigarette in hand, "can't you offer a lady a light?"

Simon didn't respond.

"I said, a light," Genna announced dramatically as she marched the few steps to his chair. "Look at that . . . drunk and sleeping it off. He would look better in a coffin like Nosferatu!"

Zelda stumbled on her sequined heels as she reached the top step. "Genna! That's a little over the top. Who's Nosferatu?" she whispered to Amy.

"Vampire," Amy answered.

"Eww."

"Nobody burns my friends and gets away with it," Genna declared. "Let's dump him in the towel bin and let him sleep it off there. He'll wake up tomorrow and wonder what happened! Let sleeping dogs lie."

"Let lying dogs sleep," Zelda said.

"He's not sleeping," Rian said. "He's dead."

Amy's head peeked out from behind Rian's shoulder. "How can you tell?"

"This bullet hole was my first clue."

"What bullet hole?"

Rian turned her penlight toward the face staring up from the chaise.

Amy gasped. "He's dead!"

"I believe I mentioned that."

"Oh, dear God!" Zelda cried, nudging her way forward. "He's dead! How could he do that on my birthday cruise!"

His face looked gray beneath Rian's light, the eyes wide with terror, the mouth open as if caught in a scream, the bullet hole neatly between his brows.

"He was murdered." Amy's voice trembled, her body shivering against the night wind. The creep of doom and dread rose from somewhere within her. It was happening again.

"Murdered?" Zelda threw her hands over her eyes. "I can't look!" She tottered on her sequined high heels and then grabbed Amy for support. "We have to call somebody—do something!"

"He looked about that same color at dinner," Rian posed, the beam still trained on his face. She passed the penlight over the body, revealing a terrycloth bathrobe similar to the ones hanging in their cabin closets.

"Turn that thing off." Genna stood behind Zelda, a bird's-eye view over the top of Zelda's head. "That blowhard. First, he brings his wife *and* his mistress on the same cruise, and now he goes and gets himself killed."

"What are you saying?" Rian asked.

The moon made a halo around Genna's head. "That woman at dinner, Sheila, the one with all the bling 'also from Maine.' I saw the two of them together earlier. I overheard him talking about his wife. We don't know where the wife is hiding, but you can be sure—"

"Are you quite sure he's dead?" Zelda interrupted. "Couldn't you be mistaken?"

Rian's penlight clicked on again and focused on Simon's brow. "He hasn't taken a breath since we got here."

Amy stared into the circle of light at the dark hole in his head. She clenched her teeth. She might hurl her dinner.

The cigar butt fell from his fingers and rolled under the chaise. Zelda jumped and stumbled. "Do something!" she fussed. "You have to do something!"

"Like what?" Amy yelled back.

Rian focused the light on his bathrobe pocket. With a gesture so quick Amy barely noticed, Rian slipped her hand in and out. She looked at her hand. "Another cigar and a lighter. No gun." Rian clicked the light toward the other pocket. "Check that one."

"No, you do it!"

"Amy," Rian said. "Go ahead. Do it."

Her hand shook as she reached toward the pocket then jerked it away.

"Amy. Do it."

She squeezed her eyes shut and reached into the folds. "Just his cabin key," she said, holding her hand out to the flashlight beam. "And a note." The page was from a notepad similar to the one in their cabin, with *Darwinian* printed across the top in an expansive scrawl.

We must to meet en S Deck 23:00, it read. *You must pay, you get.*

"You must pay, you get? What does that mean? Was he being blackmailed?"

"It means we have a killer on board," Genna said. "Whatever he bought killed him. Well, whoever he bought it from. A smarmy old-fashioned 'double-cross, take the money, and run.'"

"How could this happen?" Zelda wailed. "He's going to ruin everything! Why are men always getting in the way of our fun?"

"We could leave him here and pretend we never bumped into him," Rian said. "Someone will find him sooner or later."

"But if they find him, they'll send us back to port, and we will have to go home. All my birthday wishes doused! All that money wasted!"

"We could dump him overboard," Genna suggested.

"No!" Amy shouted. "We can't do that!"

"Why not?"

"Because we can't. We just can't!"

Rian clicked the penlight switch on and off, on and off. The sound the switch made seemed eerily loud in the darkness. The light was a slow-motion strobe.

"We have to do something," Zelda whined. "You can't let him ruin my birthday. Can't we hide him somewhere until the cruise is over?"

Genna let out a laugh that sounded like the blast of a horn. "And I always thought I had questionable morals."

Rian swept her hair back from her face, and the eye patch flipped back over her eye. "Aye, matey," she said, holding the light under a grim smile. Despite the gallows humor, the shadow effect was chilling. Amy stepped back quickly, tripping over the chair behind her and landing with a thud into the chaise seat. She was now too close to the body beside her. The snippet, like a flash from the past, filled her memory as if she were back in the dream. A scream, a blast from a horn, a pirate patch. And a bullet hole in Simon Monforte's head. The scene was so familiar, she could have been in the snippet itself.

"If there is *no* body, there is *no* crime," Genna said. "Maybe we *could* hide him until the cruise is over."

"No! We have to tell the ship authorities!"

"And say what?" Genna snapped. "That we found him dead and picked his pockets?"

Amy studied the key and note still clutched in her hand. In a rush, she pushed them back into his pocket.

Zelda planted her hands firmly on her hips. "No body, no crime. And no sudden end to our fun."

Amy rose from the chair and they moved into a semicircle around the foot of the chaise. "I can't believe we're doing this." Simon was unaware of their consternation about his final resting whereabouts. But still . . .

The boat rocked gently as Rian put the penlight back in her pocket. "We'll have to pick him up."

Zelda clasped a manicured hand over her mouth. "Eww, disgusting. Is there going to be blood? Will his brains be hanging out?"

"I didn't see brains. It's a small hole. The bullet is probably still in there."

"Double ew disgusting."

Genna tapped Amy on the shoulder with a nod toward the side of the ship. "Grab that thing."

"What thing?"

"That towel bin. Roll it over here. We can hide him in that."

She and Zelda rolled the towel cart to the chaise where Simon sprawled, and they stood in position at all four limbs.

"I don't think I can do this," Amy said.

"He's going to ruin everything if we don't," Zelda replied. "We can't let that happen. You're my best friend, Amy. I can count on you, right?"

"One, two, three, lift," Genna charged, and they each hefted a limb.

Amy squeezed her eyes shut.

"Ewf," Zelda breathed. "He's heavy. Too heavy." She teetered on her heels, and the foot she held dropped from her grasp, landing with a dull *thud* to the deck. Zelda gagged.

"In for a penny, in for a pound," Rian said. "One, two, three."

The body landed with a *thump* in the towel cart. Rian pushed lightly at the hand caught on the cart rail. They covered him with the towels and rolled the bin back into place.

"What is it with us and dead husbands?"

"*Wasbunds*," Genna said. "A husband that *was*."

"That's not funny," Zelda said.

"It is, too."

"I had a husband that was."

Amy glanced at Rian. "Déjà vu. Another murder, right under our nose."

"Yep," Genna said, "and there's no shortage of suspects in this dicey, pricey game of sneaking around."

"Who's sneaking around?"

"We are, Zelda!" Amy exclaimed. "We may need that get-out-of-jail-free lawyer after all."

CHAPTER SEVEN

Amy tossed in her sheets. Two o'clock and her eyes were open. She turned and groaned. Zelda was sound asleep, little nipping snores proof that she wasn't tossing and turning in her bed. What had they done? Had they thought it through, they never would have dumped a dead body in a towel bin! Who would do such a thing?

They would. They had.

She flipped again, dragging the sheet with her. Two fifteen.

It sounded so logical at the moment. A perfect cover-up to a horrible crime.

But not *their* crime. They just happened upon it.

Bad timing. Or good timing. Who could say? If there was *no* body, there was *no* crime. She didn't want to admit it, but Genna might be right about that. Sooner or later the body would be found. Towels had to be washed and folded. Towels were no permanent resting place for dead husbands. Or wasbunds. Or dead bodies of any kind.

If the four of them had not bumped into the body, someone else would have. Someone would have screamed loud enough to wake the captain, and the boat would have taken them all back to port. And maybe to the pokey, too. Or whatever they called a jail cell in Ecuador. It would have rats. A jail cell in Ecuador would have rats. Or maybe hamsters. They ate guinea pigs in Ecuador. Nope. Not going there. She turned in the sheets. Three o'clock was ten minutes away.

The hard metal chair at the police department in Bluff Springs popped into her head. She remembered how the sweat dripped down her bra as the detective grilled her about the crime. She didn't know anything, but that did not stop her from making up lies to protect her friends. What were they going to say now? *Honestly, officer, we didn't notice the body in the towel bin. We didn't notice the bullet hole in his head.* She kicked the sheets free at the bottom and hung her toes off the bed.

Another dream had become her reality.

~ ~ ~

The knock on the door resounded loud enough to wake her and Zelda from a deep sleep. She had not been asleep long. Dawn came before slumber. The morning sun shone well above the deck, streams of light flickering in through the curtains at the cabin window. The knock came again.

"You must open the door," a deep voice resounded in a heavy Spanish accent. "*Abierta. ¡Instante!*"

Amy lurched from her bunk.

"Who is it?" she called, dragging the sheets from Zelda's also tangled bed.

"What is it? Amy, what's going on?"

"*Abierta. ¡Instante!*"

She flung the door open. The man, poised to rap his knuckles against her forehead anticipating the door, dropped his hand to a crisp uniform pocket and snapped his heels.

"The captain must meet with you this moment of time." He looked past Amy to Zelda. "*¿Comprende?*"

Amy nodded, her hand already closing the cabin door. He pushed her hand aside and shook his head. "No! *¡Ahora!*" he said.

"Now?" they chimed in unison.

"*¡Si!* Now!"

They shared glances, Zelda's eyes wide as she tumbled from her bed and grabbed her Mimi Havana silk robe. The pair followed the uniform through the door. Rian and Genna were already a few steps ahead of them in the narrow corridor.

They followed in a single file, disheveled, still groggy with sleep. Their rumpled nightclothes were a stark contrast from the crisp white uniforms of the two crewmen. One crewman led the way, the other one trailing close behind them. Amy's skin prickled at the back of her neck. Her heart beat against the thin cotton T-shirt she wore to bed. Tugging at the corners of her now too-short PJ boxers, she could only hope nothing too dimply hung out.

Zelda managed to wrap herself in the robe and cinch the sash, giving her a best-dressed air even in this circumstance, but her eyes were wide with terror and her hair was a dark tangle.

As they approached a stairway crossed with a length of rope, the crewman stopped, unhooked the clasp, and gestured for them to climb. Amy tugged at the hem of her shorts. The stairwell was cool as it curved upward. A man in a bright white uniform stood at the top of the stairs, like a spotlight shining down on them, his dark, heavy brows drawn into an expression of impatience.

"What is the meaning of this?" he insisted, his ire unmasked. "What is the meaning of such a joke? What is the punch, as you say, to this line?"

No one spoke.

"You must answer!" he shouted. "I am Captain Chavez. She is *my* ship. You must answer the questions I impose!"

"What joke?" Genna asked. "What are you talking about?"

"I am talking about this!" The captain spun to face a video monitor. The grainy black-and-white footage showed a pirate, a mermaid, a sailor, and the Queen of *De*-Nile standing on the deck, their arms animated in conversation as they moved across the screen. In the next frame, they were lifting Simon's body to the towel cart, rolling the bin back into place against the deck rail.

"Oh, *Humperdink*," Genna drawled. "Not the best light for our cameo."

The captain huffed.

Rian winced. The technician paused the feed just as Rian pushed Simon's hand from the rim of the cart.

"I must understand what cruel joke was this? Why was this man put in the conveyance? If he was too intoxicated to return to his cabin, you should have alerted one of the crew. What is your relationship with this passenger? What business do you have with him?"

Amy studied the captain and then the screen.

"If he presses charges for this misconduct, I will have charges brought against you!"

The captain lowered his hands to his side as if pushing his anger down with his fists. The room seemed to lighten. Just barely.

"May I ask where he is now?" Amy tried.

His dark eyes landed on her, and heat rose in her cheeks.

"You may ask," he said gruffly. "I do not have the answer.

He has yet to leave his cabin this morning. Too many dog of the hair. His wife breakfasted early, the steward reports, but there is 'Do Not Disturb' instruction on his cabin door."

The friends exchanged glances.

"So, he's not still in the towel bin?" Rian asked.

The captain's dark eyes narrowed at Rian. "He most certainly is not!"

"But he is still ali—"

"Alone," Genna interrupted before Zelda could finish her thought. "Is he still alone?"

"I have no confidence to answer! I don't have his status in the cabin." He brushed dark hair from his brow where a curl had fallen away from the rest. "I understand American women conduct themselves with peculiar social norms. Tell me at once why you landed el señor Monforte in the cart in such a manner?"

Only a breath of time passed. "He was drunk," Genna said with venom. "He was drunk and lecherous, and we had enough of his smarmy advances. He passed out, so we dropped him in the towel cart to teach him a lesson. If he makes a complaint against us, we will retaliate with a complaint of our own!"

Captain Chavez eyed Genna closely, his lips pulled into a thin line. "To teach him a lesson? An American custom also?"

Genna seethed with indignation. "Women no longer have to tolerate the lewd, unwanted advances of men. Of any culture. Of any status." She glared at the captain. "We will not tolerate this intimidation and innuendo any longer. We will fight to gain our equality in every sense of the word!"

Jeez Louise. Not only was Genna lying about what happened, but she was up to her soapbox in rhetoric. Was she really taking a stand against the captain and his culture? Or was she fanning a smokescreen to confuse him?

"Furthermore . . ." Genna started, but the captain raised his hand for silence, and she pressed her lips closed.

"I understand now the situation," he said. "I will take this under consideration should el señor Monforte file a complaint. However . . ." His voice deepened with authority. "You will not conduct yourselves in this manner going forward. You will approach a crewman for assistance if you have any further concerns about el señor Monforte—or any other passenger—or I will remove you from this vessel. Furthermore," he said directly to Genna with a squint to his eyes, "this ship is equipped with many security cameras. I will observe your behavior."

He turned his back to them, and without further comment, they were ushered to the stairwell by the same two men who had escorted them in. Was that a hint of a smile from the crewman at Genna's elbow? Amy was sure it was.

~ ~ ~

"You told us he was dead," Zelda said when they were back in her cabin. One shaking hand grasped a tall Bloody Mary with two vodka shots and three olives. "The captain believed Simon was drunk."

"He was dead and he still is," Rian insisted. "Simon Monforte had a bullet hole in his head. We're lucky the captain thought otherwise, but how did he get out of that towel cart? He sure didn't climb out on his own."

"Where is he now?"

"Someone had to be there watching us," Genna said. "Whoever shot him must have watched us. They were hiding near when we loaded him into the bin."

"We must have arrived right after he was shot then," Rian said. "Although I don't remember the smell of gunpowder in the air."

"You know how gunpowder smells?" Amy asked.

"Doesn't everybody?"

She didn't bother to answer.

Genna shook her head. "The killer must have pulled him out of the cart after we left."

"Then, why wasn't that caught on the security cam?"

Rian grabbed a dark curl and tugged. "We don't know that it wasn't. The captain didn't realize Monforte was dead when we put him in the towel cart. He thought he was drunk as Genna said. So why think otherwise when the camera records whoever pulled him out?"

"And who would that be?"

"I'm going to say his wife." Genna's eyes glistened with intrigue. "She shoots him, hears us coming, and hides in the shadows. We put him in the towel cart; she pulls him out. She carries him to their cabin and hangs the 'Do Not Disturb' tag on the door."

"And then goes to breakfast," Zelda said with sarcasm.

"It took all four of us to get him in the cart," Rian mentioned. "Even that was a struggle."

"Then the murderer had an accomplice," Amy said. "Maybe it took two—a man *and* a woman."

"That's a bit sexist," Genna said. "Women are strong, too."

"It doesn't matter if they are from *Texas*," Rian said, a frown on her brow. "You can be strong and not be a longhorn."

"Texas?" Zelda burst into laughter, sputtering as she sucked at the ice cubes with her straw. "A sexist from Texas! I swear, Rian, your hearing is like a gnat's."

"I think gnat refers to brains," Genna said. "My guess is that even gnats are not hard of hearing. That would sure cut short their time in the evolution pool."

"You see? Just more mumble-jumble," Rian said.

Genna ignored her. "We should ask what's-his-name. That guy from dinner."

"Matthew Broderick!" Zelda said. "No, wait. *Andrew* Broderick. Charles Darwin incarnate."

"The one who flirted with you at dinner," Amy teased.

"Stop, he did not."

"What about that other guy? Boatright or Tightright. Remember?"

"Tightright," Amy repeated. "That's a suitable name for an accountant-slash-attorney. Bill Forthright. The *third*. He must be involved somehow. I knew I felt the animosity between the two at the table, couldn't you?"

Zelda nodded. "And why is he on this trip?"

"Something about being on a business trip. But what do you buy in the middle of the Galápagos? And why do you bring your accountant with you?"

"Why indeed," Genna said, pondering the question. "I'd say because they needed his presence."

"As a witness," Zelda said.

"As a witness to a crime," Rian added.

"As a witness to *a murder*," Amy said. "No, as an *accomplice* to murder. That's why you bring him with you. The wife and the accountant are in cahoots." Amy bit her lip. "But what about Sheila? Is Sheila the wife or the mistress?"

"I still say she's the mistress. We haven't met the wife." Genna grinned and sipped her Bloody Mary. "Maybe she's the big-boned Texan."

Zelda laughed. "She's a big-boned girl from southern Alberta."

"No, she's from Amarillo!"

Rian was the only one who didn't laugh.

"So why was the wife not at dinner? And why was Sheila seated at our table?" Amy asked.

"Because she could," Zelda said. "She knew she could. There's something odd about this little group from Maine."

"We're going to have to keep an eye on them," she agreed.

The day's itinerary arrived, slipped under the cabin door. Fernandina would be their first island excursion. The ship would be underway the rest of the morning, arriving after lunch for a mid-afternoon landing.

They decided to find the Monforte clan and eavesdrop for clues. "The lounge is the most likely place to find anyone this time of day if they are not still in bed or sunning on the deck," Amy suggested.

The Beagle Lounge was located on the Sun Deck, where only a few hours passed since they climbed these stairs to discover Simon's dead body. If she counted the rungs, she might keep her mind off that dead body on the deck chair, and off of how it felt when she lifted his heavy, hairy leg. Last rung. Nine steps. Not enough to keep her mind occupied for long. Something glinted in the sun, and bending down, she picked up a shirt button and slid it into her pocket. Not a lucky penny heads up, but you never knew when you might need another button.

She grabbed the pull handle of the lounge door when the blast started. The ship's horn with its loud and brassy blare filled her head like a migraine on steroids. Once, twice. Again and again.

"What's going on?" Zelda screamed. "Are we sinking?"

The short blast sounded three more times and then blew steadily. Throwing her hands to her ears, she waited for silence.

"This is a safety drill," a deep voice intoned, which seemed to come from everywhere. "Make your way rapidly and safely to your assigned muster station. Procure a life vest from your muster crew attendant, and await further emergency instructions. This is a mandatory muster drill. I repeat. All passengers are required to make their way now to your assigned muster stations."

"What despicable timing," Genna said. "I was only ten feet away from another Bloody Mary."

"What muster are we?" Zelda asked, her voice still pitched with worry.

"Two A," Amy answered, remembering the notice on the back of the cabin door. "Located on the starboard side. We've got to go around to the other side."

The four of them kept close as they scrambled single file around the deck at the bow and around to the starboard side of the ship, passing others doing the same. Although one hundred passengers didn't sound like a lot, it felt crowded enough. Amy couldn't imagine the bustle of three thousand passengers scrambling up and down the companionways deck to deck on their way to an assigned muster station. There were only two decks open to the air, the Sun Deck and the Moon Deck above. The muster stations were marked, and as they passed the little groups gathering in place, they found 2A.

"Hello," she said to Bill and Andrew, who were already in the line, life vests zipped to the neck. "Fancy meeting you here."

She accepted the vest from the crew attendant, who nodded as she pulled it on, zipped it, belted it, and snugged the strap between her legs.

"Gross," Zelda said, doing the same. "This is not the fashion vibe I was going for today."

"This is a thirty-minute routine that could save your life," Rian said sharply. "Be quiet and do what they say."

Amy was surprised by Rian's tone, but Rian did have experience with emergencies on open water, and while it had been a long time ago, it was a memory that had not faded.

"Yeah," Genna said. "Shut up and do what they say."

"Where's Sheila?" Amy asked. "And Simon?"

"In another group," Bill said shortly. "Not here. Obviously."

She tugged the edge of the vest away from her chin, glancing at Bill out of the corner of her eye. He appeared composed, although a bit pale. Simon Monforte would not be reporting to his muster station, and Bill would know that, too, if he was the accomplice or the witness or whatever role he played. Bill tugged violently at his vest. What would the crew do when Simon didn't answer the roll call? What would happen when they discovered the "Do Not Disturb" tag on the cabin door meant something else? Had Simon been pulled from the towel bin and laid to rest on his bunk? Gawd. What a thought.

There were two lines, five passengers in each, all stuffed into their life vests like pimento cheese sandwiches. Amy made herself listen as the crew attendant stumbled over the language, butchered their names in the roll call, then demonstrated the use of the safety equipment. His spiel was the equivalent of a flight attendant pointing out exits, seat belts, and oxygen masks. Except there were no exits, seat belts, or oxygen masks. There were no lifeboats, either—only the three rubber pangas. Not enough to save them all. If they went down in the sea, they would float to the next island for rescue. A shiver ran up her spine.

CHAPTER EIGHT

By the time they were freed of their vests and obligation, took a pitstop at their cabins, and returned to the Beagle Lounge, the room was crowded.

"Look what the tide dragged in." Genna nodded to the door. Sheila and another woman they didn't recognize entered the lounge and moved to the farthest end of the bar. They sat close together, their heads bowed in conversation, their faces turned more to the shadows than the light coming through the portholes.

"We have to hear what they're talking about," Genna whispered. "Let's move closer."

"That won't be too obvious," Zelda said. "Why don't we go to the bar and eavesdrop from there?"

"Why don't I just go ask them what they're talking about?" Genna returned with sarcasm.

"You don't have to be so snarky. My idea is as good as yours."

"Hold on," Amy whispered.

The two women were laughing, their mimosa glasses clinking in a toast. They moved their barstools closer, and Sheila touched the woman's shoulder lightly.

"Do you think they're a couple?"

Genna straightened in the club chair. "Ah-ha! What if Sheila is the mistress, just not *Simon's* mistress. Is that his wife?"

"She doesn't seem upset about her dead *was*band," Amy said.

Zelda's eyes widened. "Maybe she doesn't realize he's dead."

"Of course, they do," Genna replied. "Look at them! They're already celebrating." Genna set her glass on the table with a heavy hand. "They put the body in the cabin, just as we thought. But the wife doesn't stay in Simon's cabin. The wife stays in Sheila's cabin. That's why Simon didn't think his wife was on the trip. He wasn't aware of their relationship!"

"We need to get a gander at that video feed after we stuffed Simon in the towels," Rian decided.

"We need to find out who is sleeping where and with whom," Genna said.

"Now you're just being nosey," Zelda said. "Even so, how would we do that?"

All eyes turned to Amy.

"Oh, no. I'm not doing any more of that hunting-down-killers stuff. I learned my lesson the last time." Amy rubbed her wrist tenderly as if it still hurt, although the cast had long since been removed.

"Hey, there's your man," Zelda said snidely. "Your tall, dark, handsome pirate."

Genna smiled as he entered the lounge. He caught her gaze and smiled back. "He does give me the gillies."

"What's a gilly?"

"Those butterflies you get when you see something you want."

Rian grinned. "I don't think that's what a gilly is."

"You're right, Genna. The patch is not part of his costume," Amy said. "That's real."

"All the more daring." Genna picked up her empty glass and wandered toward the bar.

Amy frowned. "Genna's spinning her web, and I have a bad feeling about it."

"Oh let her be," Zelda scolded. "What harm is there in a little flirtatious camaraderie while on the high seas?"

"He's at least twenty years younger for one."

"Even better," Zelda said. "Even better."

Sipping her drink, Amy surveyed the lounge with its round game tables and club chairs. Her gaze caught a group of men engrossed in a game she didn't recognize. They were playing dice. Except this wasn't Yahtzee or Bunco. The players each held a rolling cup and a set of colored dice. They rattled their dice, slammed the cup down on the table surface, and in Spanish, she assumed, they went around the table bidding the way players do in the game of Spades or Bridge. Only there was no money showing. And, neither were their dice.

What was this game? She didn't want to stare, but she did. One of the players raised his eyes to hers. Caught. He smiled. She smiled back and he waved her over.

"Come," he called. "Come play Perudo."

She couldn't ignore her curiosity.

"Come." He motioned with a curl of his hand.

She slid off the barstool, glass in hand, and approached the table.

"I don't know how to play. I don't even recognize this game you're playing."

"No?" His accent was thick. He jumped from his chair. "Sit.

Please."

She sat. He pulled another chair from a nearby table and placed it beside her, sitting down with a soft *whoosh*. He smelled of fresh air and Spanish laundry.

"I will teach you. I will teach you the ancient game of Perudo." He grinned wide, a bright smile on his tan, handsome face.

"Perudo?"

"¡Si! Perudo! A game that traveled to Spain from Peru and is now back in favor once again. A long journey!" He laughed loudly. "It is the game for liars!"

Amy laughed. That fit. A game of dice for liars. Genna would be pleased.

"You speak Spanish? *¿Hablas?*"

She shook her head. Time to get serious about putting that one on the bucket list, too.

"It's okay." It sounded more like *ezzokay*, but she knew what he meant.

"This is Paco, as in taco, *mi hermano*. My brother. His brother, Juan." He tilted his head at her with a coy smile. "Si, he is my brother, too. They are *gamelos*. Twins, yes?" Paco and Juan smiled. "And this is Alejandro, Sandro, and I"—he turned to face her—"I am Piero. I am the excellent Perudo teacher. You will learn." He grinned. "You are . . ."

She felt overwhelmed. "I am what?"

"You are called by what name?"

She laughed and her cheeks burned. "Amy. Just Amy." It sounded so plain among all those exquisite names that rattled off his tongue in a flourish of rolling Rs and breathy vowels that made her want to stare at his mouth more than anything.

"Now"—he popped the table with his open hands—"we begin."

The game reminded her of liar's poker played with the serial numbers on dollar bills. The players spoke English for her benefit, and while their English was far from perfect, they spoke far better English than any Spanish she could manage. She followed their bids, which began with each player's guess about how many of any one number dice—from one to six—were showing on all the dice hidden under the cups among the players. Perudo was a game of liar's poker, Yahtzee, and Farkle all rolled into one.

"I have four fives," Piero said.

"I have five fives," another said.

And so it went around the table, and the round ended with one winner, four losers, cheers, and deep male laughter. She realized how much she missed the sound of male laughter.

"So you begin." Piero turned again to face her. "You must lie to win."

Amy laughed. "Liar's dice. I like it." Genna would, too. She could lie without cheating. Zelda wouldn't have to count pips on her toes, and Rian could tell the truth or a lie, and it wouldn't matter at all.

"Perudo! You say you have six fives, I say, '¡Dudo! I doubt it!'" He laughed heartily and the other players joined in. "Are you ready to play?"

"¡Si!"

They all laughed, and Piero offered her his cup and dice so she could play the round. Tumbling the dice in their cups with a noisy rattle, they slammed them to the table one by one. She followed their lead. Glancing under her cup, she took note of the near straight of her dice. Great hand for poker. "I bid five sixes."

She hedged her bet that each of the other players held at least one six in play, she had two under her cup, and her bid was the last of the round.

"¡Dudo! I doubt it!" Paco yelled cheerfully, raising his cup to reveal a solid run of threes. The others revealed their dice.

"¡Ay, mi amiga!" Piero counted the sixes in play. She had not even come close to winning.

"¡Dudo!" Amy laughed, and Piero gestured to the bartender.

"The famous pisco sour," he said as the drink landed in front of her moments later. "If you enjoy Perudo, you will appreciate this tradition as well!"

"Delicious." She licked the tart foam from her lips. "What's in it?"

Piero laughed. It was a loud chortle, and compelling, and it made her want to laugh, too.

"This is not a Peruvian secret. It is *pisco*, which is a liquor we invented early in our history, and the juice of lime . . ." He waved his hands. "And other things. A charming taste. You agree?"

Amy nodded.

"Another round of Perudo?"

Amy nodded again.

Plates of food showed up several minutes later with another round of pisco sours, and Amy realized she had forgotten all about Simon and Sheila and even her friends. She had been playing Perudo for more than an hour. She scanned the room but didn't see Zelda, Rian, or Genna. "Oh, no! I'm missing my friends!"

"You are among new friends now! Please. Stay. Your company is much enjoyed. Your friends will be with you again. We are all at sea together!" He laughed again and she felt tempted.

"I shouldn't. The island excursion begins soon. My friends will never forgive me if I miss it."

He rose and pulled her chair from the table, taking her hand in his. "It is my loss that you go, but I will be with you again, yes?" He chortled once more. "We are at sea together!"

Amy left the lounge with her head in the clouds about a brand new game and a player named Piero.

CHAPTER NINE

Zelda peered over the neck of her orange life vest at the Zodiac rocking not-so-gently in the waves. "I'm not sure about this."

"You can do it." Amy nudged her in the back.

"You're holding up traffic," Genna snapped as the line formed at the rubber panga, one of the large gray inflatable boats used to ferry the passengers by the dozen from ship to island. To protect the fragile ecosystems, the *Darwinian* stayed in deep water, bringing in a curated number of explorers at a time. The passengers were under strict orders to take nothing but water to the islands and bring nothing but the empty containers back.

Before they could go anywhere, Zelda needed to step from the safety of the ship gangplank to the raft. Both were rocking. Her canvas wedges didn't help. Amy smiled at the guide apologetically. He shrugged and reached for Zelda's hand. Before she could protest, Zelda was pulled gently from ship to raft as smoothly as a dolphin slipping through the water. Smooth move. Zelda was in the boat and seated before she knew what happened. Amy gave him her hand, and as smoothly, she was sitting beside Zelda at the stern. The raft filled with other passengers, and they motored over the waves toward the island.

As she trailed her fingers in the swells beside the boat, she tried to describe to herself the colors of the water below. She wanted to name the hues, name them all to lodge this moment in her memory. Shimmers and shades swirled to the horizon. There were shades of blue everywhere. Lighter blues on top, deep-sea blues underneath it, strung as gemstone beads. All in a haiku of color.

Amy turned her face to the sky. The air felt cool, and the sun flashed hot. The waves rocked gently beneath the boat. Licking the salt from her lips, she smiled. Paradise was worth a thousand freckles if that was its price.

Genovesa, the craggy tower of an island they passed yesterday, was a breeding ground for blue-footed boobies and giant frigate birds nesting on the sun-bleached, windswept rock. Today, the *Zodiac* motored for several minutes and then drifted into a narrow mangrove inlet. While the passengers climbed out onto a ledge of rock at the bank, bright orange crabs scrambled in a dance for shelter. "Sally Lightfoot crabs," he explained as he held the boat to the shore.

As they emerged from the dense thicket of mangroves, the island opened to an expanse of flat, dark rock. The ground seemed to flow beneath her feet as if it were in motion, an ebony black river of hardened lava, absorbing the light from above.

"Fernandina is the newest island in the Galápagos as it is still forming. We are standing on lava flows that came from the volcano at the very center of this island. The island formed as lava cooled and hardened with the cold ocean beneath it."

She imagined the noise it had made, hissing and spitting like a giant cat as the huge fissures of steam spewed skyward and the red molten lava flowed into the water.

"This occurred more than seven hundred thousand years ago."

Seven hundred thousand. Amy let that sink in.

"On the other side of the island, the volcano is still active."

He beckoned the group forward, and they followed in single file until they reached a dark mountain of miniature dragons, white smoke streaming from their nostrils. Amy stopped mid-step.

"The famous Fernandina marine iguana." He spoke in a near whisper.

Licorice-black, spike-horned creatures sprawled in confused heaps on the rocks, long placid tails dragging as they moved in a slow boil.

"These are the world's only sea lizards. They dive into the cold waters after algae, their food. The steam from their nostrils may remind you of dragon fire, but this is only the saltwater."

One of the sandy-haired men spoke behind his camera lens. "Are they mating?"

"Because they pile upon each other? Great question. But, no, the marine iguana is not social, although he would appear otherwise. His interaction is simply evolution at work. He is cold from his swim and seeks the warmest place against the rock and other iguanas.

"Stay only to the trail. The lizard lays eggs in the sand, and we must not disturb their nests. If you see something that resembles a sausage, or bangers for our British friends, you have discovered an iguana egg."

He wagged his finger. "No touching. We have no idea how the most innocent interaction can change the course of life. With one brief touch, we could alter the evolution of a species forever."

The sightseeing group followed single file, leaving the dark lava flows behind, and climbed slowly down to the beach. As if on cue, a pair of sea lion cubs rolled in the surf like two puppies in a pond. Tumbling in the waves, flopping in the sand, one rolling over the other, the pups reminded her of Paco and Juan, the twins who played Perudo. They would have played in the surf as kids, too, with a mother watching nearby. While she didn't see the mother lion, the mother probably saw them. She watched from somewhere close enough. The pups were oblivious to everything, and they were still tumbling in the waves when the group hiked away from the shore.

Now threading through the rocky path, Amy dodged the wide cracks filled with bright red lava cacti dotting the dark canvas. They hiked the curve of the beach in silence until the guide pointed to a nesting ground full of gangly birds. "She is the Galápagos cormorant, a species endemic to the Galápagos Islands. She is the bird who has lost her ability to fly. You may wonder why.

"Evolution, we presume. Perhaps she does not need to fly. She lives in isolation in the middle of the sea. She doesn't have a predator she needs to take flight from, and all she could need for survival is right here." He swept his hands to the island, with its black twisted rock and stubby mangrove feet, and the ever-present sea surrounding them.

No predators. No struggle. No dead bodies you moved from a crime scene when you weren't thinking clearly.

A wave stretched toward her feet, and the heavy scent of the sea reached her nostrils. Sudden sadness washed over her. She felt disconnected from everything she knew. Everything familiar. Tipping a rock with her toe, she kicked the feeling away. Was this the bittersweet part of travel? The homesick feeling of being so far away from home? Or was this guilt creeping in again?

Evolution. Going forward meant you could never go back.

An unexpected rustle behind her made her nearly jump off the rock.

"I got to pee," Zelda whispered from behind. "You think the lizards would mind if I shared their rock?"

Amy laughed, her mood shifting abruptly back to the present. "Yep, that's not going to happen."

"How about that bush?"

"Zelda! Can't you wait until we get back to the boat? I think we're leaving soon."

Zelda sighed and eyed a mangrove a few feet away. "That guy just slipped behind the bush."

"Which one?"

"That one." Zelda pointed to the tallest of the two sandy-haired men Amy pegged as ornithologists—cameras, binoculars, and all.

"Did you see that?"

"What?" Rian and Genna joined the two of them near the shore.

Amy pointed. "He just picked up something and put it in his backpack."

Rian snugged the bill of her ball cap over her eyes and grinned. "Maybe he's smuggling those big birds."

"Maybe he's stealing iguana eggs."

"Maybe you have an active imagination," Rian said. "All I see is a place I could stay forever. I've never felt such peace."

"Here? It doesn't make you feel sad? Doesn't it make you feel lonely?"

"Not in the least. I could camp out right here."

"We could leave you here and pick you up in a week. There's plenty of bangers and eggs to eat. They're everywhere. And you can bunk with those seals for warmth."

"What? And miss out on your snoring?"

Genna put her hands akimbo, snapping her head at Rian. "I don't snore."

"How would you know? You're sound asleep. You only stop that racket when you wake up."

"For your information, women don't snore. We purr." Genna pulled her water bottle from her daypack and chugged, then cracked the nicotine gum with a loud *pop*.

"Well, your purring is keeping me awake. I might have to test the nine lives theory. You sound more like a John Deere tractor than a cat."

Genna grinned at Rian and hiccupped. "A Deere? A John Deere?" The corners of her mouth lifted and she hiccupped again. Then she burst into laughter.

The four of them howled.

"Oh, please!" Amy begged, picturing the bright green tractor as it chewed up the roadway in hot pursuit. A memory not that long in the past.

"Stop! I have to pee! Don't make me laugh!" Zelda cried.

Genna shook her head. "Can't smoke. Can't snore. Can't pee. Can't laugh. Who's life are we living, anyway?"

Amy grabbed Zelda's elbow and helped her climb onto the rock. "Darwin's?"

"Charles Darwin," Rian agreed. "The brave don't live forever, but the cautious don't live at all."

CHAPTER TEN

As she reached the top rung of the ladder and her feet were finally headed toward solid ground, Amy's view of the hub and bub of activity aboard the *Darwinian* stretched into focus. Passengers were scrambling around the deck in the same madness as during the emergency drill. A guide with a clipboard checked off names as they boarded the boat, and behind the guide, the two crewmen in white uniforms—both too familiar from their morning escort to the captain—stood watching.

"Amy Sparks," she said when prompted.

"Report to your muster station as soon as possible," the guide said. "Thank you."

"What's going on? Why are we having another drill?" Amy struggled to get out of her life vest, but the steward shook his head.

"Leave it on, please."

Zelda grabbed the guide's arm. "What's going on? Are we sinking?"

"We have a missing passenger."

"Who?" Her voice shook. She knew very well who was missing.

"I cannot say. An American who cannot be found."

Amy looked up as Captain Chavez strode toward them. His eyes locked on Genna's, and Genna's eyes were locked on his. He spoke rapidly in Spanish to the guide at her elbow, who immediately referred to the clipboard in his hands and nodded.

"You." He motioned to the four of them. "You will follow me."

They followed.

He waited until they were in private quarters, the door closed behind them, then said, "The wife of our—as you say—indisposed passenger claims she never saw her husband on board. Mrs. Monforte said she boarded late yesterday due to a transportation mix-up and then remained in her cabin ill with motion sickness the evening of our departure."

"Uh-huh," Genna hummed. "A likely excuse."

The captain turned dark eyes to the tall woman standing beside Amy. He and Genna stood eye to eye.

"He dined with the other members of his party, I am told, but they did not see him afterward. You, as I've learned, also dined with his party. However, you *did* see him afterward. We have proof of that."

"Uh-oh," Zelda said.

"And now he cannot be found." He trained his eyes on Genna, as if expecting her to respond.

Rian spoke up. "Whoever helped get him out of the towel bin knows where he is. Isn't that on your video feed?"

The captain didn't answer. He touched the bill of his hat and ran two fingers along the patent leather edge. "He is not in his cabin. Nor did he attend the emergency drill. He did not go to breakfast or call for cabin service. He did not keep his massage appointment this morning, nor did he partake in the Fernandina island excursion."

Captain Chavez stated these observations as fact, with the slightest edge of disbelief to his voice and a deep frown between his thick black brows. He turned to Rian before speaking. "We do not have a video feed of him leaving the cart. The event must have been out of range of the security camera. We can assume he climbed from the conveyance on his own once he regained his . . . equilibrium." He paused. "But we have no evidence of the precise time this may have occurred."

Amy's thoughts were racing. Now would be the time to tell the captain that Simon Monforte was dead when they put him in the towels, and they knew it. It would be the perfect time to describe the bullet hole and the cigar butt and the items in his pocket. But she couldn't find the words. Now would be the time to review the logic that got them to where they were. That once they had decided to hide the body so it wouldn't ruin Zelda's birthday cruise, things had fallen into place so quickly it seemed more like a blur than a reality. Those words didn't surface, either.

Where was Simon if not in his cabin? Had his killers thrown him overboard?

I have a suitcase I never use, and it's on wheels, she heard Genna say in her head, a comment made back in Bluff Springs while playfully planning what to do with husband number four.

"Where do you think he is?"

"That is why you are here. I am asking you."

Four pairs of eyes blinked at the captain.

"We have no idea," Genna said.

"No idea," Zelda agreed.

"But if *I* wanted to find señor Monforte," Genna started with emphasis, "*I'd* ask the wife, his mistress, and his accountant some pointed questions."

"His mistress?"

"We're not sure who is who," Genna said, letting him in on their secret, "but one of them is the wife, and the other is the mistress."

Captain Chavez shook his head slowly. Maybe he didn't want to open that can of worms. What people did in their private lives remained their business, especially on an expensive voyage. "Your unfortunate joke has become a delicate matter for me and my ship. You will notify me at once if you have any information that would help locate this passenger." He turned abruptly on his heels. He retreated, back straight, powerful shoulders swinging long, muscular arms by his side as he left the room. He did not say it, but Amy knew he considered it.

Simon Monforte was probably a man overboard.

CHAPTER ELEVEN

Amy and Genna were the first to arrive at their table for
dinner. The two of them had already agreed they would keep
their seats with the Monforte clan. They had a reason now that
Simon would be absent. More to the point, questions needed to
be raised, albeit carefully, and both she and Genna were eager to
get answers. The questions were burning a hole in her curiosity.
The captain may have considered this business about a mistress
an indelicate line of questioning, but Genna rose above
reproach. Amy trusted Genna to find a way to unravel this cloak
of secrecy the Monfortes were hiding behind.

With Simon's absence and the captain asking questions, it
would not be long before everyone knew he was dead, not just
missing in action. When that happened, the four of them needed
a few hard facts. She and her friends didn't come all this way to
face another murder rap for being in the wrong place at the right
time. They were still hanging tight to the "no body, no crime"
theory, but they could not hold on to that for the duration of the
cruise. It had been wishful thinking, anyway.

Amy was glad to have Genna as an ally at the table. Smart
and ruthless, Genna could turn any conversation to her own
benefit. Always a helpful approach when asking probing

questions—like what happened to the husband, who killed him, and where is he now?

Rian and Zelda were running late. Zelda's tardiness stemmed from her endless primping. She still fussed about which outfit to wear to dinner even when Amy left the cabin more than a half hour ago. No telling where Rian went exploring, but she wouldn't miss dinner.

They intended to position themselves at the table so they could corner the Monforte crew and pepper them with questions. They wouldn't succeed in their prearranged seating order if Rian and Zelda didn't arrive before everyone else. She felt anxious about who would arrive first when Andrew stepped into the dining room.

"Sit by me." Genna patted the chair beside her. "I'd love to chat with you."

Andrew obliged.

Zelda sauntered in with Rian behind her, looking a little lost. Behind her and among the rest of the passengers arriving for dinner were Sheila and the woman from the bar.

"I don't think we've met." Genna flashed a smile of *rose contretemps* that matched her manicured nails. Zelda slipped into the seat between them, and Amy caught a brief look of concern in Sheila's eyes.

"Elaine," the woman said by way of introduction as she settled at the table. Amy saw nothing inviting in her eyes, nothing to encourage further conversation. This hunt for details might be harder than they thought.

Genna paused, expectantly, then pushed ahead. "I'm Genna *Gregory*," she said, fishing for the last name. "And this is Rian O'Deis, and Amy Sparks, and Zelda Carlisle."

Elaine nodded in their direction, viewing each of them

without interest.

Andrew Broderick introduced himself to Elaine, his eyes following Bill, who joined the table and took the only remaining seat. He appeared wet from a shower and out of breath.

"And where is Simon?" Genna asked innocently.

"He's not feeling well," Bill said.

"Seasick?"

"Probably. He's not comfortable on the water."

Genna paused, glass in mid-air. "But he's a yachtsman!"

Bill chuckled and glanced at Elaine. "He buys and sells yachts. That doesn't make him a sailor."

"He's sick all the time," Elaine complained, a bite of bitterness on her tongue.

"Well, I don't mean to be rude, but why would he come on this cruise then?" Genna maneuvered the conversation like a tennis match. Serve and volley. She knew she was rude. That was the point. The three members of the Monforte clan spoke at the same time.

"Business," Bill stated.

"Bucket list," Elaine said.

"Pleasure." Sheila laughed lightly.

Bill laced his fingers over his plate. Was he praying? She studied his face. His lips didn't move and his eyes were open. He unfolded his hands and laid one alongside his plate. She noticed a wedding band on one hand and a large black stone ring on the other. "Our trip is not a secret matter," he said after a brief pause and a nod to Elaine. "The company had business in Ecuador. It made perfect sense to have all the vested parties benefit from the trip. This is a legitimate expense. Business, pleasure, and bucket list all rolled into one."

"What kind of business?" Amy asked.

"The Monforte Company purchased a fleet of boats that were being auctioned."

"Drug boats? Are you buying boats seized in drug operations?" Rian asked.

Bill fingered his wine glass. "In our business, we refer to them as narco-assets."

Rian leaned forward and put her elbows on the table. "Narco-assets! How does that work?"

"Governments sell narco-assets to recoup the expenses of their ongoing war against drugs. We have found this to be lucrative because the assets sell for pennies on the dollar. This benefits us, of course. They sell low. We sell high. These are one hundred percent legal transactions."

Drug boats, narco-assets. Yes, there was more to the Monfortes than met the eye.

"Why do they sell low?"

"Drug cartels are powerful and far-reaching in these regions. For a native local to buy narco-assets at auction is pretty foolhardy. They won't touch them."

"Because the new owners would become targets," Rian suggested.

"Precisely. There is widespread fear of retribution. The cartels go out of their way to spread that fear. If you lived in Ecuador and you were wealthy enough to buy such an asset, your family would become an enemy of the drug kingpins. Your family would be open to attack and in not-so-subtle ways. The people in South American cultures are very protective of their families."

Is that what happened to Simon? Had he gotten sideways with a kingpin? Wait. That meant the kingpin was on board! "Aren't you worried they'll attack you?"

"By the time we get these boats back to Maine and documented on US soil, no one will be the wiser. We've developed a . . . system, I guess you could say, for how to avoid this kind of danger."

"I've read about the pirates and the *enganchadores*."

The word rolled off her tongue as if Rian knew what she was saying.

"Pirates!" Zelda cried. "Not real pirates?"

Bill chuckled and tapped the table with his hand, and the bottom of his ring made a muffled sound against the tablecloth. "We are safe on this ship, but you can be sure it is going on all around us here in the Galápagos."

"What do you mean?" Zelda looked at Bill. "*What* is going on all around us?"

"Drug smuggling. Billions of dollars in drugs are shipped through the Galápagos Islands. Drugs come from Mexico, Peru, and Columbia. All on their way to the United States and Europe. But mostly on their way to the US. Americans have an insatiable illegal drug habit."

"That's because it *is* illegal," Rian said. "People are drawn to what's outside the law."

"*You're* drawn to what's outside the law," Genna scolded. "Don't lump us in that cesspool."

Rian rolled her eyes at Genna then turned back to Bill. "I've heard these drug traffickers lure local fishermen into transporting drugs on their boats. *Enganchadores* means *hooker* in Spanish. Am I saying that right?" Rian's stab at Spanish was a gamble at best.

Bill grinned. "Almost. My Spanish isn't much better. *Hooker* means something else down here. The fishermen are offered more cash for one drug run than they can make in an entire year fishing. The offer is one even the most virtuous find hard to refuse. They're hooked by the appeal of easy money. That's where the word comes from. How do you know so much about this?"

Rian sat back and steepled her fingers. "I have an inquiring mind."

The first course arrived, and the silence that settled over the table gave Amy time to think. They plowed into ceviche served with popcorn. This Ecuadorian staple she would need to mimic for their gatherings on Genna's deck back in Bluff Springs. Each bite was fresh and salty, tart with lime, and spicy with *aji* pepper. Popcorn gave it crunch, and every mouthful made her taste buds zing.

Eyeing Sheila and Elaine out of the corner of her eye so they wouldn't notice, she pondered. What *was* their relationship? Was Sheila Simon's mistress or Elaine's? Or maybe Bill's?

Genna dipped into her cup of corn and potato chowder that arrived swiftly after the ceviche. "Simon has missed a delicious dinner. I guess room service will take dinner to his cabin."

"Oh, yes," Sheila said. "A bland diet for the next few days is best. But he will resurface when he feels better. He's not one to miss out on gourmet food and drink."

"But he's missing!" Zelda blurted. "The captain said Simon isn't in his cabin."

"Oh?" Sheila's eyebrows rose. "You talked to the captain about Simon? Whatever for?"

Amy's cheeks clenched the seat.

"Just following protocol, I believe," Genna said quickly. "I understand Simon didn't attend the required muster drill."

"That doesn't surprise me," Bill said. "He's never followed rules and regulations. That's my job."

"And you do it very well." Elaine turned to Bill, a thin smile on her lips. "We couldn't do without you. We would be lost without your counsel."

Amy glanced at Genna. Elaine's smile of admiration, thinly veiled, wasn't lost on Genna either. Bill the witness? An accomplice? She and Sheila could not lift Simon without help.

Their roasted sea bass arrived sizzling with capers and pearl onions on a bed of rice, and baby carrots served with plump raisins and cinnamon. She launched a polite attack with her fork.

Genna broke the silence. "You mentioned a bucket list earlier, Elaine. Did you mean Simon's bucket list or yours?"

Elaine paused, a fish-laden fork midway to her mouth. Her dark eyes flashed, heavy and hooded, like the cold-blooded iguanas on Fernandina. The heavy lids made her appear tired, almost as if she could nod off on her plate at any time.

Sheila answered instead. "Isn't the Galápagos on everyone's bucket list? A must-do, whether you have one foot in the grave or not."

Amy almost choked on a carrot.

"I will agree with that!" These were Andrew's first words since dinner started. He shoved food into his mouth as though he had not eaten in days. "I always hoped I would visit the Galápagos before I grew too old to stumble out of a panga. I don't suppose it will be easy on old Simon, what with his condition and all."

"Condition?"

"Oh, you know," Andrew said.

You mean *dead*? She couldn't say that. "No, I don't know."

"I didn't speak out of turn, I hope. He didn't look all that great last night when I saw someone helping him back to his cabin. I think he had too much to drink. I offered assistance, but I don't think they heard me."

Was that before or after they had found him on the chaise lounge with a bullet hole in his head? Was that before or after they had dumped him in the bin?

"Where was that?" she asked.

"Near the Beagle Lounge. I played poker with some fellows from Brazil."

"You talked to Simon?"

Andrew regarded Bill and then shifted slightly in his chair. "No, sir. I did not have a chance to talk to Simon. Nor did I talk to the other person, who I could not see clearly enough to recognize."

"They were on the deck above you?"

Andrew nodded. "At the stairs to the deck."

"I saw you, too, Elaine."

Her eyes widened. "You did?"

"You were walking the track. You walked toward the stern."

"Oh. Yes. I remember. I like to walk."

"Elaine has trouble sleeping," Sheila said quickly. "You don't mind if I share that, do you?"

Elaine shook her head. "At home when I can't sleep, I often walk in our gardens above the water. I love the way the lights shine, and the boats are so peaceful in their slips, and the water is soothing and . . ." Her voice trailed away as if she had lost interest in her comment.

"We've all been under a lot of strain lately. You see, Simon has pancreatic cancer," Sheila confided, barely above a whisper. "We don't talk about it because *he* doesn't want to talk about it. So we don't. He's been very brave."

"He's been a boastful brat," Elaine spat. "He acts as if we are the ones responsible for his bad health and not the vices he's abused all of his life. Cigars. Whiskey. Too much food . . ."

"So, you are his wife?" Genna asked. "Do I have that correct?" Genna turned to Sheila. "Or are you?"

Sheila laughed. "I'm the company secretary. Although I admit I am a well-paid secretary with great perks." She lifted her glass and smiled. The bracelet on her wrist sparkled in the fake candlelight at the center of the table.

Zelda gasped. "Are those real?"

"These are. Narco-jewelry. They auction that, too."

"Wow." Amy mentally counted the carats. No wonder they all had so much bling, although the pearls at Elaine's neck seemed understated compared to Sheila's diamond bracelet.

Dessert came, and while she thought she could not force another bite, she did. The *canelazo* served in espresso cups tasted like manna from heaven. The warm rum-like *aguardiente* steeped with cinnamon, clove, and anise washed over her tongue. "This is delicious. I'll have another."

"Be careful, *aguardiente* will sneak up on you," Bill said. "I am the voice of experience."

"I'll keep that in mind," she agreed. "What did you think of Fernandina today?"

"I missed the boat," Bill said with a chuckle, humored by his pun. "I had some work to do and lost track of time."

Elaine and Sheila shook their heads. "I booked a massage down in the spa," Sheila said. "I didn't realize the two events would conflict."

"I went!" Andrew beamed. "What an amazing island! Amazing creatures! And tomorrow," he added, his enthusiasm mounting, "tomorrow we're snorkeling at the island called

Sombrero Chino, or Chinese Hat. It is named because of its shape."

He sounded as though he were reading the itinerary slipped under their cabin door.

"It is considered one of the most colorful dive sites within the Galápagos territory," he continued. "We're going to discover colorful fish and sea stars, which is what they call starfish in this part of the world. Hopefully, we will have an up-close and personal encounter with the Galápagos penguins!"

"I can't wait," Zelda said with a bit of sarcasm.

Genna turned to Elaine. "What did you find to do today?"

Elaine looked at Sheila before answering. "Nothing much."

"Really? Nothing caught your interest on this beautiful boat?"

Elaine frowned. "I slept late. I walked the track. I went to the library. Then I went to check on Simon, but he didn't answer the door. It was locked, of course, and the 'Do Not Disturb' sign hung from the knob. He probably took one of his pills and conked out. Then I went up on deck to read and then . . ."

"Elaine and I went over some documents Simon wanted her to sign. I hesitate to bother her with business, but it couldn't be helped."

Elaine nodded at Bill, but she didn't say anything more.

So Elaine didn't share a cabin with Simon. Did that mean anybody did? Probably not. If money was no object, the Monforte clan would each have their own cabin for privacy. And for sanity's sake, too. Rian's comment about Genna's snoring popped into her head. She could imagine Simon cut logs like a chainsaw when he slept. Only this was no option for Simon Monforte now. He was in the big sleep. The final bow. The bucket list finale.

She felt creeped out just thinking it.

It creeped her out, too, how cavalier they were that Simon was missing. But here she sat, with three killers calmly dining on Ecuadorian fare as if nothing were amiss. How could they be so calm while Simon was sleeping with the fishes, so to speak? Pretty cold-blooded. But then, what murder wasn't? Maybe they thought Simon would rest in his peace in the privacy of his cabin for the duration of the cruise. Maybe that was their plan. Maybe they planned to pretend he was ill right up until the end.

Do not disturb. Get out of jail free. ¡Dudo! *I doubt it!*

But the captain claimed Simon wasn't in his cabin. That messed up Genna's theory that they moved the body from the towels to his bunk. That also put a hole in Andrew's comment about a mysterious person helping him to his cabin after having too much to drink. Where did they take him if not to his cabin? The longer the Monforte clan postponed his discovery, the better off they would be. And she didn't want to change that. They were on the same page. Where was he? Overboard? In another cabin? Or maybe stashed in the killer's stateroom. She nearly gagged on her pudding. That would not make for pleasant sailing—bunking with a dead man—no matter how ruthless you might be.

Getting the body overboard would have been difficult. The rails on the ship were too high to heft someone that heavy. The four of them had to struggle to lift him the few feet to the cart. She made a mental note to check the height of the rail. Could three people heft a body that high off the ground? Where would it land if they did? Probably on the next balcony below. Or in the water. Who would take the risk?

"You don't have a key to Simon's cabin?" she asked abruptly.

Elaine's eyes widened in surprise.

"No," Sheila answered. "Privacy is important to Simon. Privacy is important to *all of us.*"

Amy got the message loud and clear.

CHAPTER TWELVE

Zelda held the purple wetsuit to her chest. "You've got to be kidding me. There's no way I'm going to get all this into that." She motioned over the girth of her hips, shook the wetsuit again, and unzipped the front panel.

"Same as pulling on some Spanx," replied Genna, already wriggling into hers.

Zelda narrowed her eyes. "You have never worn Spanx in your life. You're a twig with bark. Well, here goes nothing." She pulled one leg on and then the other, nearly toppling to the deck before planting her legs firmly. She hiked the sagging crotch into place. "I look like a baby whale in this thing."

"At least we're a pod of baby whales," Amy said, tugging at the heavy material. With more effort than seemed possible, she fit the wetsuit over her bathing suit and zipped it closed.

The divemaster issued instructions about the excursion and the wonders they would see below. She could barely focus on his words. As she peered over the rail into the pristine water, a pair of sharks circled the boat. "Uh, no way," she said. "There are hammerhead sharks in the water."

The divemaster laughed.

She narrowed her eyes. Did he think he consoled a child

from a bad dream?

"They are not interested in you. Trust me," he said. "They will smell only the neoprene of these wetsuits, and that does not resemble the food they eat." He spread a reassuring smile to the colorfully clad pod about to jump into the shark-infested abyss.

Genna pulled her ponytail so it fell below the band of the mask, and she tucked the loose strands into the neck of her wetsuit. "Hammerheads are vegetarians anyway. They only eat plankton. Same as whales. And marine iguanas."

Zelda turned to the divemaster. "Hammerhead sharks are vegetarians?"

He shrugged and handed her a pair of fins. "You will discover many things below. And yes, perhaps even a white-tipped reef shark. But do not be nervous. They are merely as curious about you as you are about them. You are not dinner."

"Hammerheads are vegetarians? Really?" Amy asked.

"Really," Genna said. "Get a grip."

After fitting their masks and snorkels in place, they padded to the platform a few feet from the water and jumped in. The cold sea nearly took her breath away as frigid water filtered into the wetsuit. From her expression, Zelda was as surprised by the cold as she. Dropping her face into the water, she swam away from the boat, her body shuddering with the cold that slowly warmed between the neoprene and her skin. A crystal-clear panorama of tourmaline blue spread in every direction, with nothing more than the clear window of her mask separating her from the sea and its creatures. From her periphery, she caught the bright colors of the other swimmers, but returned to the blue below, mesmerized by the world that lay before her.

Under the surface, the sea reminded her of how a blanket of snow quieted a landscape. The water felt nearly as cold. She heard her breathing through the snorkel and the muted squeaks of her surprise when a fish swam close. Mostly what filled her ears was the calm, quiet hum of the sea. Not a hum. The absence of a hum, and yet, the sound was not empty.

A school of fish with bright blue and silver bands swam alongside her and then abruptly dispersed, still in perfect formation. Sea stars nestled in the sand scattered everywhere. One reminded her of chocolate chip cookies. Another of mustard. There was a whole patch of cobalt blue sea stars, with thin spiked legs moving slowly over the pale sand. A motion caught her attention, and suddenly a penguin swam beside her, his feathers surrounded by bubbles from his dive. His eyes seemed curious and suspicious, the same beady-eyed expression from the animated film where penguins saved the world. She laughed into her snorkel and the penguin sped away.

Ahead a dark shadow moved toward her. Heart racing, breath quickening, she recognized the shape. A shark. A hammerhead, coming toward her, now swimming below her. Ten feet of grace glided through the water. The swish of its tail fanned the bottom as if the shark could write a message in the pages of sand. He swam on, uninterested in her, and continued his quest for plankton.

Rising to the surface, she gathered her bearings. Snorkels dotted the water like little periscopes on submerged submarines. She was a safe distance from the ship, but not too far, and not too close. She lost sight of her friends, but she wouldn't recognize them in their wetsuits and masks anyway.

Noticing an outcrop of rocks nearby, she swam toward it. There might be more penguins there. As she neared the rock, a glint of light caught her eye, as if someone struck a match. It couldn't be a match underwater. Something else. Sunken treasure? She swam closer.

The light flashed again. Not a treasure. A swimmer! A diver fully submerged under the water, snorkel clenched in the mouth. The swimmer dragged a large net bag.

Her eyes widened in the mask. Simon Monforte!

Wrapped inside the bag, the body was as gray as the net that held him, though she couldn't make out the figure. She gulped water and sputtered to the surface.

She started treading, her swim fins holding her aloft while she cleared the water from her snorkel. There were no other swimmers nearby now. Just her and whoever was dragging the body. Adrenaline flooded through her, and she fought the panic that threatened to overwhelm her. What should she do? She could shout out. Her throat felt raw from the saltwater. She should swim back to the boat and tell someone on board. She should. She could. Her curiosity begged her to follow.

Refitting her snorkel in place, she swam forward, keeping a safer distance. She turned her mask toward the swimmer, now thirty or forty feet ahead. The spark of light winked yet again, and she realized the swimmer's jewelry caught the light as hands propelled swimmer and corpse through the water.

She slowed her advance, sculling with her hands to hold herself in one place as the swim fins disappeared. The bag, tugged by its warden, disappeared behind the rock.

Simon was already dead. Rescue would not help. Whoever pulled Simon to his watery grave was dangerous. Deadly. Had the swimmer seen her? Had they recognized her? No. If she couldn't see the face behind the mask, they couldn't see hers.

Turning back toward the boat, she kicked steadily but without panic. There was no room for panic. She needed to stay calm and pace her swim. Glancing behind her, she saw the dark shape approaching. She squealed into the snorkel then clamped her teeth around the mouthpiece, determined not to swallow more water. The dark shape swam close.

A manta ray. The manta glided past, like an underwater bird sailing through the blue. She felt the water shift as it flew by. Her chest eased and the tightness lifted until she saw that, behind the manta ray, another figure swam closer. The gait of the swim told her this was no sea creature, but human. The same person trailing a bag full of Simon? She turned toward the boat and powered her fins, her legs fatigued and ready to cramp. She slowed to let her legs rest, then jerked to a stop as a squeal sent bubbles barreling out of her snorkel. An octopus the size of a small dog swam by her, and she sculled frantically to keep herself from moving forward. She could touch it if she reached out, and she almost did. The giant magenta tentacles gathered water in an invisible hold and then blasted inches in front of her mask like a rocket launching through space.

She surfaced again, sputtering. The boat rocked in its mooring closer than she thought it would be. She exhaled her relief. Her legs were lead, her arms heavy as she followed the periscopes moving slowly toward the ship. There were dozens of swimmers. One of them had been pulling a body in a bag. No one swam behind her now. The swimmer was gone.

And so was Simon Monforte.

A "Do Not Disturb" sign probably still hung from his cabin door. Would Simon remain undisturbed where he rested now? Or would he find some other place to rest in peace, like in the belly of a beast in this deadly sea? She had been right in thinking that Simon Monforte slept with the fishes tonight.

CHAPTER THIRTEEN

Juice and finger sandwiches were distributed when they arrived back on the *Darwinian*. Amy was exhausted. She wrenched the heavy wetsuit from her pruning flesh. Around her, the other swimmers were loud and jubilant about what wonders they found below the surface at Chinese Hat.

What wonders, indeed. Her hand shook on the glass of passion fruit juice.

"I have to tell you something. It may even make you mad. Hammerheads are not vegetarians. I just told you that so you and Zelda would get in the water."

Zelda narrowed her eyes. "You fibber!"

Amy eyed Genna with disbelief.

"You don't regret it, though. Look what you would have missed!"

Amy remained silent.

Rian took a bite of a sandwich. "You look like you saw a ghost. You're the color of this Wonder bread."

Amy sputtered. "I did see a ghost. I saw Simon."

"Simon?" Zelda exclaimed.

"*Shh.*" Amy glanced over her shoulder. "Not here."

"What are you talking about?"

"Not here," she snapped. "Not until we are alone."

The foursome returned to their cabins, changed quickly, and reunited in Zelda and Amy's suite. She detailed the incident breath by breath. At their request, she shared it again.

"And you are sure it was Simon?" Rian asked.

Amy nodded. "Stripped to his skivvies. Besides, what else could it have been?"

"A pile of trash? Leftover sashimi?" Genna suggested.

"I know it was Simon. I didn't see his face, but I knew it when I saw the net bag. I think the swimmer anchored him to the rocks somehow. So the body wouldn't float up."

"And you couldn't tell who dragged it?" Genna asked. "A man or a woman?"

"I couldn't tell you."

Genna prodded. "Were they big? Were they small?"

"That's not going to be helpful," Rian said. "Both the water and the mask magnifies things underwater. They also make objects appear closer than they are. You could have been a lot farther away than you thought. Think of the side-view mirror of your car. But the opposite."

"What?" Zelda frowned. "You'll have to explain that one to me."

"The side-view mirror of your car says 'Objects are closer than they appear.' That's so you can see the whole car beside you. Underwater is just the opposite. Images appear closer than they are. Magnified. Refraction and such."

"That explains the octopus. He was ginormous!" Three pairs of eyebrows arched. She shared her encounter with the octopus that propelled himself just inches in front of her. "He swam so close, I could have touched him, but I guess he was farther away than I thought. But he was huge, magnified or not."

"At least, if you couldn't recognize the swimmer, he couldn't recognize you," Zelda suggested. "If he doesn't recognize you, he can't come after you next."

"That's incredibly reassuring."

Genna didn't give up. "Didn't you notice anything else?"

Amy thought for a moment. "What caught my eye in that direction was a flash of light from a match. I knew it couldn't be a match underwater, and then I realized it must be a ring on his finger."

"Simon's finger?"

"No, I think it was on the swimmer's."

"You just said 'his.'"

"I think it *was* a man." Her eyebrows pursed in thought. "I can't say for certain, but I didn't see long hair. Unless the hair was tucked under a cap."

"So we're back to the bling," Genna said. "Sheila has bling. Wife has bling . . ."

"Bill Forthright has bling," Amy said. "He wears two rings."

"And now we're back to the accomplice." Genna shook her head. "Wouldn't you have to be a strong swimmer to pull a dead body in a net? Do you think he fits the bill? Our Bill with rings?"

Rian nodded. "You'd think so, but once you had momentum in the water, pulling the weight would be pretty easy. Getting it overboard would take some heft."

"You know too much about crime," Zelda said.

"Crime Time TV." Amy hoped Rian wouldn't bring up her Dial-A-Psychic fiasco, too.

"You're either the good guy or the bad guy," Rian conceded. "I like to know how either one sees the nefarious side of things. That way you don't get caught unaware."

"Nefarious. Wow. Is that what we have on board the *Darwinian*?"

"Yes, and a pod of baby whales," Zelda said sullenly. "We all had our blubber squished today."

"Which made a very clever cover," Amy said. "There was a lot of splashing and squealing when we all jumped in the water. That would be the perfect time to pull a body overboard and go unnoticed. No one was recognizable in their wetsuits."

"We're back to the security cameras," Rian said. "Wouldn't a camera catch someone dragging a body in a fishnet?"

Genna nodded. "You *would* have to know where the cameras are so you could be somewhere where the cameras are not."

"Don't you think I should tell the captain? We're supposed to report any further interaction with Simon to him."

"You didn't exactly have an interaction *with* Simon," Genna said. "And honestly, you're not sure *what* you saw down there. Or *who* you saw. I can't imagine explaining that to the captain."

"Who already thinks we are silly American women," Zelda added.

"If the pretty shoe fits," Genna said.

"Here's what I think." Rian steepled her fingers. "Until Captain Chavez finds Simon's body, I say we leave it alone. I am not inclined to volunteer answers to questions that are not asked."

Amy nodded. Rian was right. What they knew put them in a precarious position. They knew Simon was dead when they loaded him into the towel bin. That at least made them suspects if not guilty. They had no proof otherwise. If she told the captain that Simon was now anchored to a rock at *Sombrero Chino*, how would she prove she didn't put him there? She didn't have a swimmer buddy to confirm her story. She didn't have anything but a whopper of a tale.

Whether Amy played her hand to the captain or not, a killer was on board. A killer ruthless enough to put a bullet through Simon's head and then drag him to the ocean floor. And four women ruthless enough to cover it up. She shrugged off the chills that ran up her spine.

Yep. Keeping their silence made sense. They could keep their distance and their eyes open. They could sleuth for things that didn't match up and people who were not who they claimed to be. There were plenty of those things on board.

She thought of Genna's lies at dinner. Amy was not entrepreneur of the year. She didn't sit on any board of tourism. People said all kinds of things when they didn't think there would be consequences. The longer they waited to share what they knew, the better. When Captain Chavez hauled them in for more questioning—and that pretty shoe would drop—they would need answers. The only way to find answers? Keep sleuthing. Keep nosing around in other people's business.

"I'd like to know where those cameras are," Rian added. "I like to know when I'm being watched."

"Why?" Zelda screeched. "Because you brought pot on board? I know you did. How in the Sam Hill did you get that through customs without getting us arrested?"

"I didn't. I wouldn't. I found a connection down on the Jacob Marley Deck when I explored the boat."

"Ship," Zelda said.

Rian ignored her. "The crew decks are down below."

"You are unbelievable. If you get us thrown off *my boat*, I will never forgive you."

Rian smirked at Zelda. "This is a ship."

"While you both argue the semantics of this vessel, I'm going to the lounge for a drink," Genna said in a huff. "A tall fruity one. Care to join me?"

Amy nodded and followed Genna's long strides, leaving Rian and Zelda behind.

"I don't remember seeing Sheila and the rest of that crowd from Maine on the snorkel platform this afternoon," Amy told Genna.

"You were busy swimming with the hammerheads."

"Did you see them?"

"The hammerheads?"

"No . . . the Sheilas."

"I don't recall seeing them, but I do remember noticing a handsome man with a patch over one eye." She grinned suggestively. "His name is Rudy. He's very appealing in a dangerous kind of way. He was checking me out for his dance card earlier. So, I let him. I walked right up to him and introduced myself. He's alone on the cruise and so very engaging!"

"Genna." She reached for Genna's arm. "I didn't tell anyone about this because I didn't want to spoil Zelda's cruise, but I had a snippet before we left Arkansas. A snippet about a man in a pirate patch. He was holding a gun."

Genna turned to listen, giving Amy her full attention. Genna made jokes about her snippets. Sometimes not even behind her back. Genna teased her about forecasting domino plays as if that's why Amy won often. She won because she played skillfully, but Genna didn't want to admit that. She suspected Genna thought of visions, or dreams, or whatever she called them, as a threat. Not a dangerous threat, but something Amy could do that Genna couldn't. An inexplainable gift. Divine gift. Or curse. Or something else.

The courage to tell Genna about her snippets for the first time had taken a long while to rise to the surface. Intrigued, Genna encouraged her to psychoanalyze them and peel back the layers. They proved impossible to analyze. When Genna suggested her snippets could be profitable, Amy joined a physic hotline, hoping to train her dreams into something useful. Something more suitable than picking the right horse or a lottery ticket. Neither experience had gone as they thought it would.

When she shared the snippet about Zack, Genna broke out in chills, rubbing her thin arms and shivering like someone had walked over her grave. She didn't know which side of the fence Genna was on when it came to her weird dreams.

"Tell me about this pirate snippet," Genna said.

They were standing outside the Beagle Lounge.

"The scream woke me up," Amy began, pulling the dream from her memory. "Of course, I was sound asleep. I heard the scream first. It was a loud, piercing scream. And then I heard the blast of a ship's horn. I remember lying still, wondering if I would hear it again. I thought maybe it was real and outside my bedroom window in Bluff Springs.

"The sound was in my head, of course. Snippets are always in my head. The scream and boat horn were followed by an image. A man with a black patch over one eye held a pistol. I knew he pointed it at someone, but I couldn't see who. All I saw was that little bit of him. The patch. And the pistol." Amy shivered. "I didn't want to ruin Zelda's excitement, so of course, I didn't say anything. Not to any of you. What would I say exactly anyway? Other than what I've told you now?"

Genna nodded.

Amy sighed deeply. "Then we came across Simon Monforte

on the deck. Dead with a bullet hole in his head. And now, I watched the killer haul the body to the ocean floor to get rid of it. The killer may have seen me. And your sexy suitor is about as close to pirate as you can get. Does he wear a ring?"

"No, he does not wear a band! I always check if they are married first. I wouldn't ever flirt with another woman's man."

Amy's shoulders drooped from the weight of what she knew. She and her best friends were in the middle of the Pacific Ocean, cruising around the equator hundreds of miles from civilization. They were on a boat, a ship, with a hundred passengers—minus one—and not even half again as many crew. A killer traveled on board the *Darwinian* with the rest of them. The killer—or killers—knew about them, about their foolish attempt to hide the body. If she and her friends had not arrived on deck when they did, they'd never be in this mess.

"We will keep this between the two of us until after Zelda's birthday. Okay?" She wouldn't want it any other way. "And Genna, I think you should stay away from this Rudy."

Genna whirled around so quickly, Amy could feel the wind pass between them. "Just because he doesn't have the hots for you doesn't mean he's a killer. I can't believe you would try to worm your way into my affairs with something so pathetic as your little swami tsunami night sweats. You're not psychic. You say so yourself. You call yourself a tele*pathetic*, for pity's sake. Why would anybody believe you?"

Amy felt her jaw drop open. "What, what did I do?"

"Don't play innocent. You know what you did. You scored yourself a fancy date at the Governor's Conference, that's what. Hoodooed your way into bed with the governor. Rising right to the top of your game."

"In bed with the governor? Genna, what are you talking about?"

"I'm talking about you and Merriweather Hopkins being all chummy and conniving behind my back! I'm talking about you trying to steal something fabulous right from under my feet now!" Genna fumbled for a cigarette she didn't have.

"You're in nicotine withdrawal. It will pass, Genna. Just take a deep, slow breath."

A vein throbbed at Genna's neck. Her poise and polish melted before Amy's eyes, and the calm exterior gave way.

"You better guard your back, Amy Sparks. When you make accusations over one of your sketchy *dreams*, you're making enemies you won't even see coming. And you are a long way from little old Bluff Springs."

Amy took a step back. Genna's reaction was unexpected. Whether Genna's anger was about her or Merriweather Hopkins, the Governor of Arkansas or this new man named Rudy, she couldn't tell. They all seemed related. Amy never saw Genna's confidence wither like this, and yet something foul was caught in her craw.

Genna's angry stride, spine straight as a plank of wood, marched her to the lounge, and she swung open the door and stepped inside. The *whoosh* of pale pink linen at the hem of the skirt disappeared through the door.

CHAPTER FOURTEEN

The island of Santa Cruz lay ahead of them, a bustling port by comparison to the other shore landings they'd experienced so far. Amy read in the brochures that Santa Cruz was the epicenter of Galápagos tourism if cruising the isolated islands didn't fit your budget. Visitors could fly into Santa Cruz, take a boat charter to a nearby diving site for a day's exploration, then get a bird's-eye view of the Galápagos, a tasty meal, and a bucket of beer without spending a generous fortune. Amy couldn't imagine what Zelda had spent on their passage. Zelda made it clear that she should not ask.

Standing now with Zelda at the ship deck rail, the aqua sea lapped right up to the rocky shore. Along the narrow streets, colorful buildings leaned into each other in rag-tag fashion as if the wind had swept them together in a heap.

"Yes!" Zelda said. "Shopping! Finally!"

"How anyone can come to the Galápagos and pine for a shopping mall is beyond me. I want to see Lonesome George. He's the oldest creature on earth."

Amy had read all about the famous tortoise. Galápagos National Park and the Charles Darwin Research Station were on the itinerary for all the passengers disembarking the *Darwinian*.

They had been given a specific time slot so as not to overcrowd the museum. If Zelda wanted to shop when their time arrived, Amy would go exploring on her own.

While the passengers usually left the ship in the rubber pangas, today they walked off the ship in single file. From her vantage point above the gangway, they were ants in a colony, everyone with a job to do. The crew deck bustled with activity as the ship restocked. Boxes of supplies came in; refuse went out. As the passengers left the boat, she watched, wondering who was hiding the biggest secrets. Who told the biggest lies? She had secrets of her own, and all four of them lied to the captain.

A few faces she recognized by now. She would enjoy getting to meet some of them, but she was here to be with her best friends, not make new ones. She liked Piero and his brothers. The two sandy-haired men were Paul and Tobias, college professors from Austria. Not too far off on that guess. They left the ship now, their backpacks bulging with gear for the day.

Amy waved as Sheila and Elaine stepped onto the wharf dock. They both turned briefly back to the yacht, but they didn't wave. A man in a white uniform appeared beside them, grasping Elaine's elbow. She adjusted her hat and sunglasses, and the three of them walked to a car and got in. For two women on a bucket list adventure, they were not very engaged. None of them participated in any of the excursions so far. Or so it appeared.

That made her think about dinner last night. She steered the conversation to their missing shipmate, but Andrew kept dominating the conversation with his enthusiasm about the dive. Amy had given up on any hope of sleuthing. She remembered their conversation.

"You swam right past me, almost as fast as the Humboldt Current herself. Pretty powerful kick. I would say you've had some practice," Andrew said.

"I didn't see you."

"We were all camouflaged in our wetsuits."

"Pod of whales," Zelda said under her breath.

"Elaine, why didn't you snorkel with the rest of us?"

"Oh, heavens, no. I could never swim with sharks."

"Me either," Sheila said.

"We managed." Zelda cast a sideways sneer at Genna. "We swam right past those hammerheads, and they didn't even bat an eye."

Andrew had laughed. "I don't think sharks have eyelids. Or maybe they have eyelids but they don't blink."

After that, Genna seemed distant. She would hold a grudge against Amy for as long as she needed to, but she would eventually forget and forgive. Genna-style. Amy had faith in that. Until then, she would give Genna whatever space she needed.

Zelda tugged at her arm. "Let's go shopping!"

Within two hours, Zelda *oohed*, *ahhed*, and touched everything in the shops along the wharf. She bought scarves and pillows with whimsical silk drawings. "I can sell these in my shop," she enthused as if she needed an excuse to buy them. Amy tagged along as Zelda browsed. In a gallery full of island art created by a woman who claimed to be a descendant of the first colonist family, Zelda, after much consternation, finally chose a small painting. The artwork was stunning. Each piece in the gallery embodied both time and place.

At a clothing boutique, Amy left Zelda on her own and wandered out onto the sidewalk. There were people everywhere. The wildlife had disappeared. So had the quiet of the islands she now missed.

"Hey, Andrew," Amy called as she passed by another shop with its doors wide open to the street. He waved, his face full of excitement. "What did you find that has you so pleased?"

He joined her on the sidewalk. "This." He held up a two-dollar bill.

"Hmm. That's, uh, nice."

"Nice? The Ecuadorians consider the two-dollar bill a good-luck charm."

"Oh! And what did you pay for those two dollars?"

"Only ten bucks! A steal of a deal!"

Amy laughed. "Are you superstitious?"

Andrew eyed her carefully. She understood. The superstitious were often the butt of jokes. Or considered loony. She'd experienced a bit of both. Not everyone understood this obsession, since its logic had no bearing in the physical world. Or the metaphysical world, for that matter.

He didn't respond. "Takes one to know one," she said, and felt him relax. "Always cross the fingers of your left hand, not your right. Don't whistle at the sun. Never sit with your back to the door."

Andrew laughed. "Never sit at a corner table! And knock on wood three times if you don't want to tempt fate."

Birds of a feather flocked together. She knew all of those superstitions.

His eyes were mischievous and serious at the same time. "Never say 'happy birthday' too early. That's *mucho* bad luck."

"That's one I don't know. We do have a birthday coming up."

"I remember. So here's another one: don't raise your glass in a cheer with water, or you'll wish death on your friend."

"I'll keep that in mind."

He rubbed the bill in his fingers. "Bird poop and itchy hands mean money is coming."

Amy laughed. "Bird poop? I've not heard that one, either. How about a rabbit, rabbit, rabbit?"

"Always the first thing I say on the first day of every month."

They both laughed. Who knew she'd find such a kindred spirit in the Galápagos. Without his costume, he appeared much younger. His hair was dark, almost as dark as Zelda's, with a deep part on one side. The cut couldn't be called stylish by today's standards, but instead it struck her as old-school. She remembered he was a teacher in Louisiana. No wonder. The culture there was notorious for being superstitious and fond of the past.

"And . . ." he added with a smile, "don't bring bananas on board a boat. It leads to dangerous and unpredictable situations."

They laughed again. There were plenty of bananas on board the *Darwinian*.

Zelda arrived festooned with brightly colored packages hanging from her arms. "What are you two so tickled about?" Amy and Andrew shook their heads, and Zelda shrugged, then repositioned her packages. She pulled a box of turtle-shaped chocolates from one of the bags.

"Chocolate turtles from the chocolatier who claims these are Charles Darwin's favorites."

"That's a spin," Genna said, arriving as the chocolate box opened. "Darwin's been dead a long time."

Andrew grinned.

"We've got a date with George," Genna said. "He's also been

waiting a very long time."

"Where have you been?" Amy asked.

"Watching the pelicans and sea lions chase the fishermen," Rian answered from behind Genna. "The fishermen clean their catch on the dock and toss the scraps to the animals waiting. What a madhouse of barking and squawking and flopping around."

"Watched from where?"

"From right over there, that bar. We had piña coladas and drank in the sideshow. Money well spent." Rian eyed Zelda's packages.

"To each their own," Zelda replied with a cocky bob of her head.

The research park, when they finally arrived, felt hot and crowded and disappointing compared to the rest of their trip. On the other islands, wildlife roamed free under a vast sky surrounded by an endless sea. The conversation had been hushed as the visitors listened to what the wildlife had to say. The blue-footed boobies croaked and eyed them with idle curiosity. The ever-present seals welcomed them with their loud barking as if they were the watchdogs and welcome committee. In the wild landscapes, the scrubby bushes twittered with the Darwin finch, with its mottled yellow feathers and bright tangerine-orange beak. Here, chatter broadcast everywhere. Human chatter, in a dozen languages. Amy tried to tune it out.

The museum was important. She knew that. Information about the history and conservation efforts of the Galápagos had to be shared to preserve it, and the money from their admission went to this important cause. But it was a zoo with an unrelenting sun beating down on them. She couldn't hide her disappointment any more than she could hide her fair skin.

Lonesome George looked lonesome. He had been found on the island of Pinta in the early 1970s by a scientist studying mollusks. The island's food source had been decimated by feral goats who were far more prolific than the tortoise. Rescued from starvation, George had lived his years since at the research station, where his food and care remained consistent. George was the only tortoise of his breed left on earth.

It made her heart ache. The last of one's kind, isolated from family and friends. She knew how that felt. She wadded bills into the donation box, and they walked to the bus waiting at the curb. Climbing into the seat next to Rian, she hoped the rest of Santa Cruz would be more uplifting. Zelda took up two seats with her packages as she sorted through them like a kid with a Halloween candy haul.

An ancient, repurposed school bus drove them to the top of the island, grumbling uphill for nearly an hour. Their destination was a coffee plantation in the lush highlands, almost two thousand feet above sea level. Amy sat back in the dark-stained, well-worn leather seat, blue pom-poms swinging from the dash above the driver with every bump, turn, and lurch.

The arid landscape at sea level gave way to lush green as they climbed. The bus finally lurched to the curb, and the passengers hustled off, eager to be free of the ride.

Ushered past the entrance to the coffee plantation welcome center—their entrance fees already paid by the cruise—they entered a large room that held benches on three walls. Cubby cubes were stuffed with rain boots, her first clue the day would be a messy one. They emerged, geared up and packages stowed, as gray clouds misted the plantation. Perfect weather for growing coffee—maybe not so perfect for sightseeing with a guilty conscience about when the other boot would drop.

"I don't see the Monfortes," Amy said. "For a tour, they sure aren't doing much touring. Sheila and Elaine got in a cab at the dock. No telling where they were going." She looked for Piero, too, but didn't want to say that out loud. Neither Piero nor his brothers were on the bus. That wasn't surprising. They didn't seem to be tourists, exactly, nor were they crew.

The group sloshed along the narrow muddy tracks, slipping inside their galoshes and the slick mud, where the path had been worn free of grass. Amy lifted her eyes from the rutted track. The vista rose from dark hills of deep green, and a soft, misty cloud hung over the landscape. In single file, they followed the rows of coffee trees laden with bright red beans called cherries. She sloshed along contentedly then rounded a bend in the path. And stopped. The landscape opened to a field of deep mud puddles. In each puddle, at least one giant tortoise snuggled half-submerged in the mud.

"They are huge!"

"They are huge," Zelda agreed.

"They make me think of hay bales. Those big round-backed bales all over rural Arkansas pastures." These bales were alive.

"They are here to eat their fill of grass and other greenery before making the trek down to the sea to lay their eggs," Tobias said beside her. "The journey is more than six thousand meters."

He stood at her elbow, his binoculars raised to his eyes. "Do you want to look?" He pulled the strap from his neck and handed it to Amy.

"Their faces! They resemble E.T.!"

Tobias laughed and accepted the binoculars.

"How far is six thousand meters? In miles?"

Tobias regarded her, his blue eyes quick on a handsome, sun-pinked face. "About four miles. It will take them weeks to maneuver the rough hillsides. Tortoises don't take the highway." He smiled at his humor.

Of course they didn't. And how fast did a tortoise walk, anyway? Too embarrassed to ask, she settled on "slow and steady wins the race."

There were dozens of puddles and dozens of tortoises. Amy stood in awe of these magnificent creatures. They reminded her of hippos in the mud, at least in pictures, but tortoises were gentle. They were disinterested in the crowds as they took their afternoon baths. The tourists were diverging from the paths now to stand closer to the giant beasts, cameras clicking to preserve the moment. Tobias took a picture of the four of them at the muddy pond, two giant tortoises in the foreground, their faces raised to the camera with shags of half-chewed greenery hanging from their mouths.

"That's going to be a nice picture," Zelda said. "At least I'm a few pounds lighter than these two turtles, even if the camera does add a few."

"You are profoundly lighter," Rian said. "A tortoise weighs about nine hundred pounds."

Amy turned to Tobias. "So are they turtles or tortoises? You say turtle. I say tortoise. Which is it?"

"Both," Tobias said. "All tortoises are turtles, but not all turtles are tortoises."

Amy chuckled. "That's a riddle. What's black and white and read all over?"

Tobias laughed. "What has armor but is not a knight, snaps but is not a twig, and is always at home even on the move?"

"A turtle! An excellent riddle! Well, what's the difference? Turtle or tortoise?"

"Both are accurate," he said, "but these are tortoises. The

tortoise is a land reptile. They don't swim. They can't swim. They can float, but their feet are flat and made for walking, not for swimming."

"Could have fooled me," Zelda claimed. "They're all knee-deep in the water. Do they have knees?"

"Well, not in the way we think of knees. The tortoise enjoys the puddles, but this is more about controlling their temperature. Since they are reptiles, they are cold-blooded creatures. Mud either helps cool them down or keep them warm, depending on the ambient temperature."

Zelda beamed at Tobias. "You're a walking encyclopedia."

"That's what I do. I teach the sciences at university."

"Rian studied botany," Amy said. "She's a whiz with healing herbs."

Tobias nodded at Genna.

"No, this is Genna. That's Rian, and this is Zelda. We're on this trip because Zelda is turning fifty. We're celebrating the evolution of the fittest, the smartest, the most fashionable . . ." Amy gestured like in a game of duck, duck, goose. "And I'm, well, I guess I am . . ."

"The most psychic," Genna answered.

Amy groaned. Tobias regarded her closely.

"A psychic?" His eyes filled with interest. "Do you read minds and talk to the deceased?"

Color reached her cheeks. How dare Genna share that tidbit with a stranger? "No, I'm not psychic. She's making a joke. And not a very funny one," she added with a lethal look at Genna, whose anger seemed to be brewing, still, under the surface.

"Oh, my mistake," he said, but the curious look remained in his eyes. "This is my colleague, Paul," he said as the other man joined them at the puddle. Tobias offered introductions again.

"What did you find to take pictures of?"

"*Rubiaceae Coffea.* The coffee bean cherries are a robust color this time of year."

"Paul shares your interest, Rian," Tobias said. "He also is a botanist. His specialization is phytotoxicology. The study of poisonous plants."

"Are there poisonous plants here in the Galápagos?"

"Only one species that is indigenous." Paul pointed to a tree with its limbs weighted by small fruit. "*Hippomane Mancinella.* Commonly called *manzanilla de la muerte.*"

"Little apple of death," Genna said.

Paul nodded. "One of the favorite foods of the giant tortoise. If they can reach the fruit, that is. However, there is nothing about this tree that is not poisonous to us. The sap causes a rash burn similar to the poison sumac. The fruit is lethal to humans. Even standing under one of these trees in a rainstorm can be disastrous."

Rian shoved her fingers into her shorts pocket. "I saw one of those trees on Fernandina. I'm glad I didn't touch it."

"What is your specialty?"

Rian smiled. "*Cannabis sativa.*"

Paul raised an eyebrow in amusement. "Brilliant," he said with a grin.

They returned to the path. Taking a forceful step in the muddy track, Amy's ankle turned in her boot. Lunging forward, she bumped against Zelda. Before either one of them could catch their balance, they both plowed face-first into the mud. The giant bale, half-submerged a few feet away, blinked heavy eyes and stared.

"Oh no!" Zelda cried as she righted herself. Mud dripped from her face, and her décolletage gurgled as mud settled into her bra. Her boots squelched and filled with muddy water as she glared at Amy. "You!" she spat, mud sputtering from her lips. "You did that on purpose!"

"On purpose? I slipped!"

"You pushed me!"

"I didn't mean to. I slipped in the mud!"

"Well don't just sit there. You look ridiculous sitting there. You're a kid in a puddle."

"And you are so grown up yourself!" Mud spit from her lips.

"Well, I am just fifty!" Zelda pushed her Fendis to the top of her head and swiped at her eyes with a filthy sleeve.

Amy grinned despite herself. If she looked as silly as Zelda, they both were a sight. Two tortoises in a mud bath, only not quite as large. She chuckled and then heard Genna's unmistakable snort behind her. Zelda cocked her head, then they sat in the ooze and howled.

"This is not funny!" Zelda screamed, her eyelashes heavy with mud.

But it was funny. And she laughed, mud dripping from her fingers. She put her hands to the ground to push herself up. Sinking up to her elbows, boots filled with mud and weighing her down with the same heft as a stone, she slipped and sloshed and laughed harder.

"Arrggg!" Zelda yelled. "I can't move! We're in quicksand!"

A crowd had gathered around them, including Paul and Tobias. Concern showed on everyone's face, but mostly their amused smiles hid behind polite hands. Rian and Genna stood over them, not trying to hide their mirth.

Suddenly the pirate was standing over them, too, his shadow darkening the sun from their eyes. Rudy. The man who had caught Genna's flirtatious eye. Where did he come from?

"Are you all right?" He put his hand under Amy's elbow. "Let me help you up." His voice was silk. No accent. She studied him, not sure where to look, and her eyes kept moving to the black patch even though she tried not to.

She forced her gaze to his lips. "Where did you come from?"

He guided Zelda to her feet then ushered them both by the elbow to a wooden bench a few feet away. She and Zelda left a trail of mud in the grass behind them. They flung mud from their fingers.

"I came to escort you back to the ship. I can see I came at an advantageous time."

Zelda harrumphed.

"I'm not sure about that," Amy said. "But I'd give anything to be anywhere else but this mud slick."

Zelda indiscreetly scooped mud from her bra.

"Escort us back to the ship? But why?" Genna asked. "Because we're VIPs now? Special cargo? First-class?"

He grinned at Genna, and Amy felt a twinge of jealousy. "Not as fun as all that, unfortunately. This is much more serious."

Amy's heart sank. "This is about Simon Monforte, isn't it?"

"I knew we would never get away with it," Zelda grumbled. "We can't seem to shake him loose no matter what we do. Same as this gooey mud."

"Be quiet," Genna ordered.

"I would prefer that you come without resistance."

"What? Are we under arrest?" Zelda asked.

"What do you mean 'without resistance'?" Rian asked.

"Who are you anyway?" Genna folded her long arms akimbo at her waist.

Rian stepped away. "Are you a cop or something?"

"Or something. Please, I would prefer to discuss this in private. Away from ears that have no business with your own."

"Business?" Genna lifted her arms from her waist then planted them even firmer. "What are you talking about, Rudy? Is your name even Rudy?"

Standing close, Amy heard him sigh. He was drawn to Genna. That much seemed obvious, but if this was his pickup line, it was an elaborate one.

"Please, I don't want to disclose my badge in public."

"Badge?" Zelda's hand flew to her chest. "Oh, no. We are under arrest!"

"No, no," he said. "Come with me. I have a car waiting for us. We can discuss this on the drive back to the dock."

Amy's feet felt rooted to the ground. She pulled off her boots, emptied the mud and then pulled the boots back on. She could have done that again and still not emptied all the mud under the bottom of her feet. It would give her something to do. It would delay having to make a decision. She didn't want Rudy to sense her thoughts. What was she thinking? Thoughts that were scattered all over the place, that's what.

Yes, a ride back in a car sounded much better than a long ride by bus, especially covered in mud. She already felt the cold. No, she didn't want to sit in the back of the bus and sulk. No, she didn't want to talk about anything serious. Especially if serious meant talking about a murder on the *Darwinian*. A murder they put their silly hands in and thought they could get away with. They could be headed for the guillotine. Or whatever punishment Ecuador had in store for them. Did he say anything about murder? No, she didn't think he did. He said . . . What did he say? Escort them back to the ship. A nice, dry ship. Was that sweat dripping down her chest or mud? Mud.

Definitely mud. But he was a pirate. The pirate in her dream had a gun.

"I don't think we should go with you," she said, feeling less bold than she wanted to sound. "I don't think that's a good idea."

"I don't think you have much choice," he said, and suddenly the silk was gone.

"What do you mean?"

"It will be okay." Genna hooked her arm in Rudy's. "We're in safe hands. Aren't we?"

Rudy nodded to Genna and smiled. Roguishly handsome, the patch made him even more mysterious. But still . . .

"Come on," Genna said. "Let's go back to the ship."

Rudy rose from where he squatted beside Amy and started down the path ahead of them. One by one they fell into step behind him, silent except for the sloshing of their boots.

Back at the mudroom, they found their shoes. She and Zelda tidied up in the bathroom, using half the roll of paper towels, but not doing much more than smearing mud from one place to another. Zelda grew grumpier by the moment. Amy felt responsible. If she hadn't tripped in her boots, if they never witnessed a crime, if she did not eat bananas with her yogurt at breakfast!

The black Lincoln idled in the shade, windows rolled up and dark. Amy glanced at Rian. She knew they both thought about running back to the puddle. The car was far more elegant than the rattling old school bus, but the limo stretched before them like a dark ride with danger, like something from a mobster movie setting. The passenger window rolled down a few inches, the driver nodded, and Rudy opened the door for them to climb in.

It was AC cold inside the car. Shivering, she nestled closer to Zelda, while Rian tried to keep a safe distance from the mud.

"What is this about?" Genna demanded. "And who are you really?"

Rudy turned from the passenger-side front seat. "My name is Rudolph Granger." He flipped open a worn leather wallet and flashed a badge.

Amy leaned forward. "Drug Enforcement Administration Special Agent," she read aloud. His hands and arms were tanned from the sun. He probably spent more time out of doors than at a desk. His wrist had a tan line where a watch or a heavy bracelet would be, but Genna was right. He didn't wear a wedding ring, and no tan line showed he'd recently taken one off. Genna leaned back in the seat and crossed her arms.

"FBI?" Zelda whispered.

"DEA," Amy said.

"You ladies have gotten yourselves into something quite dangerous. The less information you have, the better. I can tell you very little. Let's just say I have been monitoring activity in the Galápagos, and it has brought me on board the *Darwinian*."

"Undercover?"

"Your bold little maneuver with the gentleman passenger seemed pretty reckless." He chuckled softly. "You have unwittingly involved yourselves in an international drug operation."

She felt Rian tense beside her. "I knew this was about drug smuggling. I knew it."

Genna glared out the window at the trees passing in a blur. "Why couldn't you tell me that earlier?" she said abruptly without turning her head from the glass.

"Until this morning, I was not convinced you weren't

involved. What better cover than four loud women with empty suitcases on an expensive cruise."

"Loud?" Genna's tone pierced the interior of the car.

"How about effervescent," he soothed, his voice again silk on clean-shaven legs. "You all have such lovely and lively personalities."

Genna unfolded her arms and then folded them again across her chest. "I don't think I've ever been called loud."

"Effervescent."

Zelda leaned forward. "Are we in danger? What kind of danger?"

"When we get back to the ship, you will precede me on board without complaint. You will speak to no one about this. They will probably examine your belongings. They will ask you questions. You will answer them. Do not repeat anything we have talked about here. Remember, no one is above suspicion. Once you have passed the rigors of re-boarding, I will find you and debrief you further."

"Debrief?" Zelda frowned. "That sounds serious. FBI serious."

"Whoa," Rian said. "We aren't cattle. What examination? What rigors?"

"Simon Monforte was dead when you put him in the towel bin. You knew that."

Silence filled the back seat.

"Was Simon smuggling drugs?" Zelda asked.

Those were Amy's thoughts exactly. They had taken his murder in an entirely different direction. No wonder the pieces didn't fit. She thought of the puzzles at Tiddlywinks. At times, some pieces appeared as if they didn't fit the picture. They did, of course, but it was hard to see where. The four of them were confident Sheila and Elaine and Bill Forthright conspired to kill Simon Monforte to get him out of the way. Why bother to bring him to the Galápagos if they were planning to kill him anyway? Why come all this way to stage a murder? And why would they bother with murder at all? He was already dying if what Sheila said was true. Wouldn't they just wait for the inevitable? Why would they take that risk? They wouldn't.

They wouldn't unless narco-assets was a cover. A cover for something even more valuable in the US than a bunch of boats. Like a drug-smuggling ring with Simon Monforte at the top.

How had they gotten a gun on board? That had bothered her since the beginning. It certainly didn't pass through airport securities from Maine to Ecuador.

And why didn't they hear the gunshot?

"You got off easy with Captain Chavez," Rudy said. "I convinced him you were not involved in the death. Other than the obvious. What else did you discuss with him?"

Genna turned from the window. "How can we trust you?"

He smiled suggestively. "You shouldn't. Trust no one but those you know well."

Well, that narrowed the field. Amy snuggled closer to Zelda for warmth and crossed her arms across a soggy chest. The appeal of her soft bed at home beckoned, with its scented sheets and matching walls, and Victor asleep at the foot in a sunbeam, all of it safely tucked above the Cardboard Cottage & Company.

"We told him that Monforte was drunk and lecherous, and we dumped him in the towel bin to teach him a lesson. It got left at that," Genna said.

"And he said nothing more?" The corners of his mouth turned up into a sexy, mischievous grin. Genna was taking that bait, for sure.

"He said he'd be watching us," Zelda added. "There are cameras everywhere."

Rudy nodded. "And what else did you see that night?"

"Nothing," Genna said. "We didn't see anything else."

"And since then. Have you seen anything else out of place? Anything unusual?"

Amy squirmed in the seat. She heard a faint slosh in her shorts. Gross. She needed a long, hot soak in a tub. Should she mention the net bag at Chinese Hat? Genna shook her head and glared at Amy in her reflection in the window. Amy took the hint and chose a question instead.

"Why didn't we hear the gunshot?" Amy asked. "And why didn't the captain say anything about it?"

Rudy turned around in the seat. He studied her carefully. "For many reasons," he said finally. "The captain is better served by keeping this news quiet for as long as possible. News of a murder could easily create panic at sea among his passengers. He needs to be careful. Practical. Discreet. And as for the gunshot, sound travels differently at sea than in the city. A bird call can sound identical to a woman screaming. A subsonic bullet can sound like two pieces of wood slapped together. Think of a deck chair getting knocked over, or a hatch slamming shut. It would be easily overlooked on a busy boat."

"But it was late."

"What time is it now?" Zelda asked abruptly. "I need to get ready."

Rudy shook his head. "I don't have the time." He flipped his bare arm. "What is time in the islands, anyway?" He turned to the driver and spoke in Spanish. The driver nodded.

"Good gawd, Zelda, your birthday is still hours away," Genna said. "You have plenty of time to get ready for your bash."

"Bash?" Rudy asked.

"Birthday bash," Amy answered. "In the lounge. At midnight."

"Midnight? That's an odd time to start a party."

Zelda leaned forward. "You're invited! Everybody's invited to my uh-oh five-oh."

She left a muddy handprint on the back of the seat. "Oops."

"Are you enjoying the Galápagos so far?" Rudy smiled at Genna.

"We are!" Zelda said. "Except for, well . . . that man."

"And how did you find the snorkeling? That's an especially beautiful dive."

"Absolutely beautiful," Genna agreed, giving him the full Gregory grin. "Underwater was peaceful and serene."

"What all did you see?"

"Penguins and starfish. A hammerhead shark." Genna laughed, probably remembering her ruse. "Amy thought hammerheads were vegetarians."

"Because you told me that. That's why."

"No, they're not vegetarians," Rudy said. "They'll eat anything with flesh."

The hair on Amy's arms stood up, dragging dry mud with it. And now they would never find Simon Monforte's body. No body, no crime. Maybe they really would get away with their shenanigans.

When the car arrived at the wharf, Rudy opened the door and pointed them to the gangway without speaking. She glanced back at the limo as the driver sped off down the narrow streets of Santa Cruz, taking with him what little comfort she felt in the confines of the car. Rudolph Granger was now nowhere to be seen.

They boarded without a single question from anyone after they showed their ID. Strange. She had been worried about everything for nothing, after all. She felt almost invisible as they made their way through the ship, and yet, she knew their every move was captured on camera.

CHAPTER FIFTEEN

"I am confused. Simon is dead and missing, and yet the captain lets his passengers get off the boat to tour Santa Cruz?"

Zelda changed into a different outfit, tossing the old one across the bed. "How's this look?"

"Great! You look great!" Amy paced the floor in front of the couch. "Although you might if you were a captain of a drug-smuggling vessel, and you didn't want anyone to know about a murder on board. You don't even have to be a drug boat to want to hide that fact. This is a high-dollar cruise. Who wants to spend a lot of money to get bumped?"

"Are these shoes better? Or these?" Zelda admired the heels in the mirror.

"And now we have Rudy, Mr. DEA, undercover chasing down smugglers while the Monfortes are buying drug spoils. Narco-assets. They are believable liars, this Monforte clan. They didn't miss a beat with all the *is* and *was* language we used at dinner trying to trap them into a mistake. Simon *is* sick. Simon *is* in his cabin. Not *was*. Not once."

"I like them both," Zelda said, still inspecting her reflection.

"Me too," Amy said without looking. "Andrew saw someone helping Simon to his cabin, but I think Simon was already dead by then. I think they fished him out of the towel bin and were hauling him back to his cabin for hiding. Could it have been Bill?"

At the sound of the knock, Zelda hobbled to the door with one shoe on and one in hand. "Room service?"

"Land shark."

Zelda laughed. "No one's home."

"You got that right." Genna's muffled voice came through the door.

"What are we doing for dinner?" Rian asked when she and Genna were in.

"I ordered room service. Cold lobster salad and chardonnay."

"Perfect," Genna said. "Enough for four, I hope."

"We'll share. I'm too excited to eat much anyway." Zelda preened in front of them. "Is this the right outfit?"

"You look fine," Rian said.

"I wonder who Andrew saw with Simon," Amy said as Zelda turned in the mirror.

"Andrew is a poker player. Poker players are prone to lie, cheat, and steal."

Amy was surprised Zelda was even listening.

"That's Genna's MO," Rian said.

"I have never stolen anything in my life."

"Uh, what about your ashtray collection?"

"That is not stealing. They expect you to take their ashtrays. For advertising. Why else would you print your name on the bottom?"

Amy stepped in front of Zelda. "What reason does Andrew have to lie?"

"Maybe *he* was helping Simon to the cabin. Maybe *he*'s

covering his tracks because he saw Elaine."

"But Elaine didn't say she saw him."

"She didn't say much of anything."

"Did you see Bill praying before dinner?" Amy asked.

Rian nodded. "Very hard to squeeze the Catholic out of you. I've tried. It gets stuck. Like gum on the sole of my shoe."

"How do these shoes look?"

"Not a bit Catholic."

Zelda turned to Rian with a quizzical grimace. Rian shrugged.

"Why was Simon even on deck alone?" Genna asked.

"He wasn't alone. Somebody else was there. Had to be because somebody else shot him." Amy plopped down on her bed. Clothing castoffs piled up on Zelda's bed as she changed her mind, one outfit after another. Rian and Genna were on the sofa. "Maybe it was a drug meet-up."

Rian shook her head. "That's a stretch. A sick old man making a drug deal? I don't think so."

"Maybe a not-so-sick old man was there with him? Or his secretary? Or his . . ."

Another knock sounded and Genna stood up. "We're lucky Rudy's watching over us even if it is only with one eye. A very nice eye. And a great jawline, and strong shoulders and nice lips, and a firm tush, and . . ."

Rian chuckled. "Somebody is in the throes of rapture."

Zelda smiled as the steward delivered their meal to the table. "At least he's managed to keep the captain off our tails. We walked on board without so much as a whistle."

Under the cloche lay a generous mound of lobster salad surrounded by carrots, gherkins, and pickled pearled onions. Zelda divvied the food onto plates and poured the wine.

Genna accepted a plate and eyed it eagerly, picked up a fork, and dived in. "I think we're safe to presume that whoever swam with Simon and the hammerheads didn't see you," she said between bites, her eyes on Amy. "And as to any other transgression on board, I'm putting my trust in Rudy. He won't let anything happen to me. To us," she added with a coy smile.

"Genna, why didn't you want me to tell him about the body in the bag?" Amy asked.

"When?"

"In the limo. Returning from the mud."

"I didn't say anything."

"No, but your vibes sure did. I thought you were reading my mind."

"That's impossible."

"I'm glad I didn't." Genna didn't seem angry at her anymore, either, but she wouldn't push her luck by bringing it up. Maybe the sight of her dripping in the mud had appeased Genna's anger like some sacrifice at the altar of an ancient Incan idol. "I assumed that if I told him about the body in the bag, he would march us right to Captain Chavez for more answers. We don't have any. We need answers before the subject comes up again."

"Time to change the subject altogether," Zelda demanded. "It's my birthday, my cruise, and I'm tired of talking about that blowhard. Can't we just have some fun?"

Zelda had a point. They were on the cruise to have fun, celebrate, and discover the Galápagos and its wonders. As cold-hearted as it sounded, Simon Monforte meant nothing to them. He was someone who crossed their paths. Somebody else's husband someone wanted out of the way. *Vamoose!*

Unfortunately, they did what they did—tossing him to the towels.

Whoever dragged Simon to his rocky resting place did not see her swimming nearby. And whatever the Monforte clan was in Ecuador to buy—legal or not—was of no concern to them. They had a birthday bash to get to, and neither an inconvenient murder nor a handsome undercover cop would derail Amy's dedication to Zelda.

She had spent weeks making the party plans, corresponding with the ship's social director by email to create a party that would make Zelda proud. They all had a hand in the plans, from the DJ playlist to their secret gig scheduled for midnight. Rian had been the hardest to convince about that part, although she thought Genna would be the one to bail.

"I still don't understand why we have to do this midnight thing," Rian said, draining her glass of chardonnay. Amy shook her head. She wouldn't spoil the surprise, would she? "I mean, why do we have to celebrate your birthday at midnight?"

"Because I was born at midnight. It's a family tradition that got started and stuck. My parents always woke me up at midnight to wish me a happy birthday. When I was a kid, my parents would drag us all downstairs for cake and ice cream."

"At midnight?"

Zelda nodded.

"It's almost time to go," Amy said, wiping the dregs from her plate with a crust of bread.

Zelda clapped her hands.

By the time the four friends made it to the lounge, the festivities were well underway, even though most of the patrons were unaware they were at a party. As with most evenings, the passengers shifted from the dining room to the lounge as part of the evening's entertainment.

Balloons and streamers greeted Zelda at the door. The DJ was already spinning Zelda's favorite dance tunes. It was only ten thirty. Amy grinned at Piero and the Perudo gang, who were slamming their cups of dice with fervor. She could join them, but she chose to stay close to Zelda. Rian appeared with a tray of shot glasses and a plate of limes.

"To Zelda!" they cheered and downed the chilled tequila. Rian went back for another round.

Bouncing the crowded dancers through the eras, the DJ blasted the playlist from disco *Brick House* to *Love Shack*. The *Darwinian* was underway on calm seas, but the Beagle Lounge was rocking and rolling, shaking and grooving, with Zelda at the epicenter of attention.

Piero appeared at Amy's side, grabbed her, and twirled her on the dance floor until she was breathless and dizzy. She liked the way his hand felt against her back, the way he led her through the crowded dance floor. She liked his confidence, his bravado, the way his hips moved. A flutter tickled her belly and she grinned.

Wobbly, tired legs told her to take a breath, so against her wishes, she begged off the next dance and returned to the bar for a glass of water, surveying the room the way a party hostess checks on her guests. There was plenty of lighthearted spirits, loud laughter, and bodies in motion. She smiled. All of her hard-earned plans were worth it. Zelda would never forget her big five-oh!

Genna was toe to toe with Rudy, his hand comfortably at the small of Genna's back. Sheila danced with one of the Perudo twins. She couldn't tell which one because she couldn't tell them apart. Paul and Tobias, stripped of their birding gear and expensive linen blazers, were dancing with two of the women she recognized from their panga.

The poker table seemed almost too quiet for a crowded bar, but then poker players were always intent on not losing the chips in front of them. Andrew sat next to Rian. No doubt with his lucky bill tucked into his pocket. Rian checked the time then reached for the bottle and the bowl of limes on the table in front of her pile of winnings.

Bill Forthright and Elaine were at the other end of the bar. Elaine stared at the dance floor with what seemed like a mixture of envy and contempt holding the curve of her mouth downward. Poor woman.

Bill slid off the barstool and strode to the poker table. He stood briefly behind Rian, as if rooting for the winner, but then he stepped behind Andrew and laid a hand on his shoulder. Andrew shrugged it off. What just happened? There were no empty seats at the table. Bill had gotten there too late for a seat in this game. Was that a signal of some kind? Was Bill giving Andrew a message about Rian's poker hand?

Rian's chips were on the line, not hers, and Rian was doing fine with her poker face bluffs.

Piero appeared at the bar beside her. He pulled a barstool closer to Amy's. "Please say you have not tired of the dance floor? Or of me."

She blushed, hoping he didn't notice. His dark hair curled behind his ears, slightly wet with sweat from dancing. His eyes were dark and shiny, chocolate melting in a pot. Shorter than most American men she dated, Piero was trim and muscled with a patch of dark hair that curled from the open collar of his shirt. She felt her cheeks grow hot. Her thoughts strayed, and she raised the glass to her lips to hide them.

"This is your friend's birthday?"

She nodded. "We've been planning her birthday bash for a long time. I find it hard to believe we're finally here!"

"Bravo! You created a festive occasion for everyone. Usually, the Beagle Lounge is quieter at this time of night. Nothing more than poker or Perudo in play. This is much better."

She smiled. Yes, this was better. "The party doesn't start until midnight."

"Midnight? Is this an American custom?"

Amy laughed and drained her water. "No, not an American custom, just a Zelda tradition." She eyed her empty glass, and Piero nodded to the bartender without comment. She could get used to this.

"My friend was born at midnight. So it became a tradition in her family to celebrate at the stroke of twelve. It may not make sense outside of our circle, but Zelda is one of a kind. Her birth certificate claims her birthtime is midnight, but technically midnight belongs to neither today nor tomorrow."

Piero shook his head. "*No comprende.*"

Amy laughed again. "I enjoy riddles and conundrums like this. Technically, ante meridiem means before noon, and post meridiem means after noon. Not to be confused with antemeridian, which has to do with geography."

She sipped the wine that magically appeared in front of her. "Anyway, twelve a.m. and twelve p.m. are ambiguous times. Noon is neither before noon nor after noon, and midnight is both. Which means her birthday is neither today nor tomorrow. Her birthday is at midnight. For one whole minute. So we celebrate in that limbo because it's different. A silly tradition!"

"Most interesting." His eyes were focused on her lips.

She felt her cheeks color. Why had she nattered such

gibberish about Zelda's birthday riddle?

He raised his glass, his dark eyes scanning the room and then returning to her.

She pointed to his right hand. "I noticed your ring earlier."

"This?" He covered her hand with his. His palm felt warm and surprisingly soft, his fingers tanned from the sun. The ornate ring glistened in the light above the bar. "This is the ancient Peruvian signet," he said without moving his hand. She eyed the ring while imagining the weight of his hand elsewhere. Could he read her thoughts? "It has been passed down to the eldest son in my family for generations."

"Then you are the eldest?"

"The eldest living. The firstborn died early in life, at which time it passed to me."

His fingers twitched as if to close a little tighter over her hand. "This is the original coat of arms of Peru. The one General José de San Martín created. The great liberator of Peru from Spain, our San Martín." He leaned in to show her the emblem carved into the flat gold surface.

"Here, we have *Inti*, our sun, rising from the great Andes, as seen from the great sea." He paused as if reflecting on the magnitude of his words. She felt his pride in his heritage. She felt his breath on her cheek.

"He was not born in Peru, San Martín, but he was a devoted protector. He was a career soldier who built armies and led the fight against many oppressors. He helped free Peru, Chile, and Argentina—even Ecuador."

She loved the way he said Ecuador. It was all soft vowels and tongue.

"As with our politics, the crest has changed since then. This ring was first presented to Bartolomé Chavez to honor his service to the general."

"Chavez? Are you related to the captain?"

Piero smiled. "He is a cousin."

"And the other men at your table?"

"Other than my brothers? Long-time friends and business partners."

"What business are you in?"

"Such questions!" Piero lifted his beer to his lips, his dark eyes twinkling with humor. "We are in the business of fun," he said and laughed.

His laugh was so charismatic—the pied piper of enthusiasm. "Fun? What kind?"

"Fun that requires more dancing." He offered his hand.

Eleven forty-five. One more dance with Piero, and then . . .

"I am gliding a swan through the air," he whispered into her ear and then raised her arm to twirl her around. Her pulse quickened as he pulled her back toward him, his hand now on her hip. Their eyes met, and she surrendered to this time and place, and the longing. Until Genna and Rudy danced by.

"Almost time," Genna announced.

Amy caught Rian's attention just as she pressed another lime to her mouth.

It *was* time.

She let go of Piero's hand and Genna let go of Rudy's, and the three of them—Amy, Genna, and Rian—made their way to the tiny stage. The DJ stilled the music as they had planned, and the room soon fell quiet enough so they could speak. "It is our friend Zelda's fiftieth birthday," Amy said to the crowd. "You only turn fifty once! So, Zelda, we have a once-in-a-lifetime surprise for you."

The DJ laid down the first notes for them to follow. Zelda

beamed at them from the dance floor. The first guitar chords and drum strokes sounded, and The Beatles' "Happy Birthday" song filled the room. She and Genna and Rian launched into their much-rehearsed dance routine, prancing about on the tiny stage. They played air guitar in the right places. They wiggled their hips. They sang off-beat and low-key and full of love as they belted out along with Paul, George, John, and Ringo. Zelda twirled in her Jimmy Choo ankle-strap sandals.

By the time they got to the stanza "I want you to dance," every passenger in the Beagle Lounge rocketed to his or her feet, Zelda in the middle, with everyone singing along whether they knew Zelda or not. No matter where you lived, no matter what era you were from, everybody knew The Beatles. Everyone knew their songs by heart. Everybody could sing and celebrate Zelda's big five-oh with a song that didn't sound like an off-key birthday dirge. It was a magical moment.

The clock struck midnight, and Amy smiled at her friend through the dancing bodies.

The bartender poured champagne into glasses at the bar as the birthday song came to its boisterous close. The song had only lasted two minutes and forty-five seconds. The gift would last a lifetime, just like The Beatles music itself.

"To Zelda!" Amy raised her glass. "Happy birthday to you!"

The passengers cheered. The Beagle Lounge roared and then quieted as the thirsty crowd drank their champagne, toasting to Zelda and each other.

And then a woman screamed.

CHAPTER SIXTEEN

Amy and Genna were among the first to exit as the passengers in the Beagle Lounge scrambled through the door, all rushing in the direction of the scream. Piero stood behind her. Rudy stood behind Piero.

Elaine Monforte stood with trembling hands to her mouth, not far from the lounge, at the base of the stairs to the Moon Deck. A large mass lay at her feet. The body had tumbled from a closet door at the stairs. It was Simon Monforte.

Zelda gasped and grabbed Amy's hand. "It's Simon!"

"It can't be," Amy said. She felt herself being pushed aside.

"Hold on!" Rudy said with authority. "No one touch him." He rushed to the body and kneeled beside it. Simon Monforte lay face down on the deck. His bathrobe bunched around his legs. The terrycloth ties trailed out from under him as if they were snakes trying to escape. A pair of long-poled boat hooks lay beside him, the curve of one of the hooks still caught in the folds of his bathrobe collar. His bald head was partially covered by a towel, jauntily thrown over his shoulder as if he were coming back from a swim.

It was a blue towel. There was an entire bin of them on deck, and she and her friends had dropped him into the middle of it.

Her hands flew to her cheeks as the heat of shame rose, and her breath caught in her chest. The crowd of passengers grew tighter, pushing her and Zelda and Elaine closer to the body. Elaine let out a shuddering, hitching breath and then a moan and then a sob.

Rudy rose and stepped into the closet, straddling the body, his eyes sweeping the small space. He bent down, and their eyes met briefly as his hand emerged from his pocket. He dropped his gaze to the corpse at his feet. Kneeling once again, he touched the sleeve of Simon's bathrobe, then the folds of the cloth as he untangled the boat hook from the collar. He pressed his fingers to Simon's neck, but it didn't seem necessary. The color of the body said it all.

A thick scent rose to her nostrils as the wind blew across the deck. At that moment, a shiver ran through her, and she was back in Arkansas in the little trailer in the woods and its rotten egg smell. She turned her head away, pushed through the crowd to the rail, and heaved.

Now, looking back at the throng gathered in the ring of light, Rudy was gone. In his place were Piero and the crewmen in white uniforms, pushing through the crowd with authoritative Spanish. The rest of them stood in silence. Mascara tears streamed down Zelda's cheeks.

In what seemed like minutes, two crewmen lifted the body to a stretcher, covered it with a blanket, and disappeared down one of the interior corridors. Bill, Elaine, Sheila, and Andrew trailed behind them.

~ ~ ~

"That was definitely not Simon in the net underwater," Rian said when they were in the privacy of Zelda's cabin.

Zelda curled into a rumpled wad on her bed, tears dragging the rest of the mascara down her cheeks. "Why?" she yelped. "Why do these things happen to me? And on my birthday! I'm cursed," she said between sobs. "Cursed!"

Amy patted her friend's sunburned arm and handed her a tissue from the nightstand. Zelda smeared more mascara and blew her nose.

"I agree," Genna said, and Zelda sobbed louder. "I meant about Simon. Not about you being cursed. That's hoodoo. Pure bunk."

Amy sighed heavily. "I was so sure that was Simon underwater."

Rian shook her head. "Drugs. You heard what Rudy said. I think that was a drop point. I think they were anchoring drugs to that rock, not a body."

Genna gasped with excitement. "I overheard a couple of the crew the other day talking about dropping anchor for a rendezvous."

"You and your eavesdropping," Amy said.

"It comes in handy. I'm working on my fluency."

"Which means your eavesdropping skills are circumspect."

"Are you mad because Simon wasn't in the bag? Or are you just being cantankerous for the sake of it?"

Amy shook her head. "I was so sure it was Simon."

"What I heard when I was eavesdropping was something about a rendezvous, then he said some numbers—I'm not so proficient with numbers after twenty—but he did say '*latitud*' and '*longitud*.' Both sound enough like English to recognize. Even if they do go by very quickly."

"And you are just now remembering this?" Rian asked. "Are you sure you got that right?"

"Well excuse me for being the *Spanish for Dummies* guidebook. One of them said, 'Blah blah blah *la chiva está en la cita.*' And then the other one said, 'Blah blah. *¿Cuanta coca?*'"

"*Coca*," Rian said. "That means cocaine. So does *chiva*, in slang."

"Maybe he said Sheila," Amy said. "Chiva. Sheila. They sound alike. What if Sheila and Elaine paid them to rendezvous Simon with that rock?"

Genna shook her head. "What? Then bring him back on board? Hang him up in the closet as if they were hanging up clothes? You saw the boat hooks. Whoever put him there propped him up with those hooks to keep him wedged upright in that closet. You have to give up that notion, Amy. It looked like a body. Underwater it looked like Simon. Somebody stuffed him in the supply closet and not under a rock."

Zelda let out another loud wail.

"Interesting how Amy's snippet fits this scenario. She heard the scream."

"What snippet?" Zelda sprang up from her pillow.

"The one I had before we left Bluff Springs. I didn't want to ruin your fun by telling you about it."

"But you told Genna?"

"Not until yesterday. Not until I saw Rudy and his—"

"Where did Rudy go?" Genna interrupted.

"And what about him?" Zelda asked, her tone perplexed and annoyed at the same time.

Reluctantly, Amy told Zelda about her dream. She told her about the scream and the horn, and the man with the pirate patch and the gun.

"Are you saying Rudy killed Simon?" Zelda asked, her eyes wide.

"That's just crazy talk. He's DEA undercover. He's the good guy on this boat. Did you appreciate how he took charge of the scene? Impressive command and authority."

Genna was smitten. Her feelings were written in her bright smile and the crinkle of her eyes when his name got mentioned. "We're lucky he's tight with the captain and has already explained how we were not involved."

Amy couldn't keep the disbelief from her voice. "Not involved? How can you say that?"

Genna defended herself with a look. Amy plopped down on the bed beside Zelda, grabbed the glass from Zelda's hand, and swigged the last of the Cognac.

"Woof," she breathed and handed the empty glass back. "Tomorrow, while we are cruising to the next island, we need to do some snooping. We need to find some answers."

"Now that everybody is aware that *señor Monforte está muerto*, we are not going anywhere. No more islands for us."

"We're going to the ship's clink. They'll lock us up and throw the key to the hammerheads," Zelda whimpered.

"Drama will get us nowhere," Genna said. "We need to decide what we tell the captain when he questions us again. And you can be sure he will."

"We could just tell him the truth," Amy declared. "What's wrong with that?"

No one answered, and the room fell silent. Rian twisted a curl between her fingers, and Zelda covered her face with the pillow. Genna, tapping her fingernails silently on the polished teak, peered out the window to the sea and the horizon. "Tomorrow is already today. We will be arriving at Bartolomé sometime after lunch."

"And we haven't slept yet," Zelda said. "I'm exhausted."

"They'll search all the cabins for the gun," Amy said. "Although I can't imagine that the gun is still on board. There's a gazillion miles of ocean floor to toss it to."

"Uh-oh," Rian said. "I need to do some tossing."

"Oh, my gawd." Zelda's voice sounded muffled from under the pillow. "Don't tell me. I don't want to know."

"They don't need a search warrant," Genna added. "The rules are different at sea."

"What will they be looking for"—Zelda sniffed—"exactly?"

"Stuff like this." Rian pulled her hand from her pocket and held up an old-fashioned silver box lighter.

"Simon's lighter! You took his lighter? Rian! What is wrong with you?"

"Before you get your panties in a twist, I didn't take it from his pocket. I put it back with the rest of the stuff. One of the crew on the Jacob Marley Deck had it. He lit a smoke, and I recognized it. I couldn't help myself. I collect lighters. This one is from the seventies or eighties. *GulfStar*. I think that's an old boat manufacturer."

"This is evidence!"

"It's a souvenir."

"Rian, this links you to the crime. And maybe even the criminal!"

"I am aware of that now," Rian said pointedly, "which is why I need to do some tossing."

"Let me see it." Rian laid the lighter in Amy's outstretched hands. The small square had a flip-up top, the vintage kind before disposables were invented, back when everybody smoked cigarettes and refilled their lighters with little cans of fluid. The flat surface of the lighter was scratched from years of mingling with coins and keys in a pocket, but the logo, a compass star, was visible.

Amy dropped the lighter in Rian's palm. "The only old boat manufacturer I know of is *StarCraft*. My daddy had a little twenty-footer. He bought it so I could learn to water ski. I wanted to work at Cypress Gardens as one of those ski ballet babes."

Genna grinned. "I can picture you getting dragged behind a boat."

"They wore cool costumes," Amy returned.

"Ha!" Zelda snorted. "I've seen those postcards. They were trolling pretty girls for gators."

Amy laughed. Zelda was not that far off. "Did he say where he got this lighter?"

"Poker game."

"And what did you trade him for it?"

"My MC Hammer pants."

Holy cow. How did the lighter get into a poker game? Andrew.

To be fair, Andrew wasn't the only poker player on the ship. Not by a long shot. There were tables full in the Beagle Lounge every night. The game was probably popular with the crew, too. Could that be synchronicity at work? Hard to imagine.

Her intuition told her that Andrew was connected with the Monfortes somehow. She was beginning to sense that his place at the dining table was not by accident. And yet he acted as if he were an innocent bystander. Maybe he was. Maybe he wasn't. Andrew was a poker player. Andrew saw Simon after they did. There had to be a connection and it was a shot worth sleuthing.

"What are we going to do with it?"

"We? *I'm* going to hide it on deck. If the lighter is still there at the end of the cruise, it's mine. A souvenir for my collection."

"That's creepy," Zelda said.

Amy glared at Rian. "You need to stop going down to the crew deck."

"You need to stop minding my business."

Amy stood up and paced the floor between the bed and bathroom. "We need to figure this out. The body gets moved to the cabin. Then it's moved to the closet. And then it falls out right at Elaine's feet. Isn't that convenient?"

"On. My. Birthday."

"Welcome to fifty, sister," Genna said.

Zelda threw a pillow and hit Genna square in the head.

"Good night, my friends," Rian said and stepped toward the door. "We need to get some sleep, or we will be zombies for the rest of the day."

"Zombies," Zelda echoed and laid her head back on the pillow. Genna grinned at Amy. Back in Arkansas, they had an unfortunate experience with a zombie named Zack.

CHAPTER SEVENTEEN

Amy fell asleep holding the peridot gemstone necklace at her throat. When she awoke, she still held the charm in her fingertips. A gift from her grandmother, the necklace with its tiny diamond and peridot gemstone always hung from her neck. In the same way the chain connected the silver Celtic knot, the necklace connected her to the one person she loved, admired, and understood more than any other. The charm connected her to the one person who loved and understood *her* more than any other.

After her death now more than two decades ago, Grandmother's warm embrace was a single touch away. She had only to feel the cool silver to remember the warmth of their love shared, her calming voice in her ear.

She heard the voice in her head. Not like a snippet, but rather the remnants of fond memories. The comfort was real, as true as anything she knew. And more so than the visions that plagued her dreams. Snippets offered a glimpse into something forthcoming, but she never knew what. Grandmother Ollie understood them. She used them to help others. Secretly, away from ridicule.

Why was she so inept at understanding them? Had the

pseudo-psychic gene faded from the family tree, skipping a generation until it was nearly gone? Not gone completely. She saw what happened to Zack in a snippet. She saw what happened to Simon. And what good had come from either one of those visions? Nothing. Nothing at all.

She touched the faded burn scar along her hairline, barely visible now to anyone but herself. She thought of that night often, as she did now. A kid at a summer camp bonfire with Fourth of July sparklers and the taste of charred grit in her mouth. This gift, this necklace, endeavored to keep her close and out of harm's way. Had it ever done its job? Had she done hers?

Stop! She rolled over and punched the pillow into a cradle for her head. No time to hunker down into self-pity. This was a bucket list trip of a lifetime. They were celebrating her best friend's landmark birthday, on a ship in a sea full of beauty and wonder. If she didn't snap out of this glum frame of mind, she would never be able to snap Zelda out of hers. She had to get herself right-side up. Determined to be the lighthouse on the jetty, the buoy Zelda could cling to, she had to put her gloomy mood aside. Buckle up, buttercup.

She squeezed her eyes shut and fingered the knot, lightly tracing the pattern with her fingertips. As if reciting a mantra, her mind emptied.

She fell asleep dreaming of Victor and the fresh cream Sammie would feed him while in her care. She dreamed of Piero with his dark chocolate eyes and warm fingers brushing a stray curl from her cheek. His lips parted as if to speak, then, reaching for her lips instead, he parted them as well.

The PA system in the cabin jolted her awake with its gibberish in Spanish and static. She and Zelda bolted upright in their beds.

"What the . . ." Zelda jerked the night mask from her eyes.

"Passengers attending the birding workshop will kindly join us in the Science Center on the Azure Deck in thirty minutes. Thirty minutes on the Azure Deck," the voice intoned in English before repeating the message in Spanish. She recognized the voice as one of the naturalists. There were eight of them spread throughout passenger services, although she had only met four.

Amy grabbed the daily bulletin slipped under the door. "They're shifting our itinerary. Today is another sea day, it says. The shore landing to Santiago and Bartolomé are both moved to tomorrow afternoon."

"Why?"

"Weather conditions are more favorable for a shore excursion tomorrow," Amy read aloud. "Oh, and the captain sends his regrets."

"Hogwash!" Zelda settled the mask back over her eyes and pulled the covers around her shoulders.

"I'm going to get some breakfast and check out what's happening." Amy grabbed her clothes from the nightstand drawer and headed to the shower.

She agreed with Zelda. She didn't think they were changing itineraries because of the weather. They were keeping everybody on board. And that included a killer. Maybe plural. She let the stream pound her shoulders with as much water pressure as possible, the temperature cranked to hot. Her shoulders felt bunched up around her ears with stress. Tension had her jumping at every sound, every shadow. She wanted to get out of the cabin and into the fresh air.

The breakfast station, with pastries and breakfast tamales made with olives and raisins, carafes of juice, coffee, and tea were still warm when she arrived on the Sun Deck. Usually one

of the busiest, the deck seemed quiet today. Most of the
passengers were probably at the birding workshop. Or nursing
hangovers. No one soaked in the hot tub. Only a few of the deck
chairs had occupants. A whiff of sun lotion took her back to
childhood as she sat dreamily in the chaise with a cup of tea
with two lumps and a generous pour of cream. Almost as
satisfying as Sammie's Irish brew.

The Cardboard Cottage would be in high gear and humming
with the chatter of tourists. She had entrusted her business to
the most qualified people she could find, trained them for more
than a week, and left the keys in their hands. She could only
hope all went smoothly at Tiddlywinks. With no cell phone
service in the middle of the ocean, she felt the disconnect. Out of
sight, out of touch. Out of control. Reaching out to knock the
arm of the deck chair for insurance, she thought of Sammie's
crumpets and cinnamon buns hot from the oven and gooey in
her fingers. She licked her lips and tasted sunshine.

Adjusting her hat and glasses to shade her face and eyes, she
drank in the rays. They had slept the morning away. The sun
had glowed on the horizon when the four friends parted ways,
and she finally fell asleep.

Amy focused on the deck at the end of her feet. Simon had
been in the chaise lounge not fifteen feet from where she sat.
Now it was occupied by a gentleman in a European-style
bathing suit, obviously oblivious to what had happened in that
chair. His skin was already deeply tanned, unlike Simon's. The
woman beside him had a sunbathed glow. Rings on his fingers
glittered gold. Hers sparkled above well-manicured nails. There
certainly was no lacking for bling on board the ship.

Glancing at her pale legs, she wondered how many freckles
she would earn on this trip. Maybe they would all blend to

make a tan.

Something glittered from the deck, catching her eye. Curious, she rose to investigate. A watch! Caught in the deck, nearly out of sight, one end of the heavy rubber strap had broken loose from the lug. She pulled the strap from the boards, returning to her chair and tea. She had never seen anything like it. Probably expensive, and someone would be sorry they lost it. The entire watch was black except for the bezel and case and the pusher buttons on the side. When she touched one of the buttons, the dial lit up with a map and a GPS. A map of what? She tapped the button again, and the face loaded a compass and gyroscope. It had to be worth quite a bit of money. She tucked it into the pocket of her shorts, grabbed another cup of tea, and headed toward the stairs.

"Hello, Amy!"

She recognized the deep, silky voice. Rudy leaned against the rail, the epitome of tall, dark, and handsome. His muscled and well-tanned arms showed below the rolled-up sleeves of his amber-collared shirt. White linen trousers were cuffed to his shins with stylish swagger, and his brown leather deck shoes look well-worn, too. His dark hair blew gently in the breeze coming across the deck, held down slightly by the band of his eye patch. Today he wore shades and a tiny gold hoop earring. He grinned, and her heart thumped. No wonder Genna was smitten. He might be twenty years Genna's junior, but she could tell they would make a fun and fitting match.

"Where are you going all by your lonesome?" he asked.

"I'm going to lost and found." She pulled the watch from her pocket. "I found this on the deck. It was wedged between the deck planks. Someone is missing this."

He took a step forward, glancing at the instrument in her

hand. "Expensive dive watch. Looks like the spring bar on the strap got sprung. Some guy is going to be very happy to get this back."

Fingering the dial, the current time and day popped up. "It's still ticking."

"Takes a licking and keeps on ticking. And it's not even Timex. Where are your friends?"

"Still in bed, I think. Although, I haven't seen Genna and Rian since we parted ways this morning. Not since . . ." She let her words trail away.

He turned his head as a couple entered the lounge. She and Rudy were standing only a few yards away from the closet door. A heavy lock now hung from the clasp. "Yeah," he said, turning back to face her. "That was a surprise."

"No kidding."

She wanted to tell him about the bag in the water. She wanted to share just how big of a surprise it was seeing Simon Monforte fall out of that closet. She wanted to unload everything onto his sturdy shoulders, but that wouldn't be the right thing to do.

"Where is lost and found?"

"Down on the Azure Deck. At the stern by the medical center."

Amy looked at him, at the lock on the door and then shoved the watch into her pocket. "Thanks," she said and moved toward the stairs.

"Take care," he called. She could feel his gaze on her back as she descended to the deck below.

Although much smaller than a cruise ship, the *Darwinian* still seemed like a maze of corridors that would get you lost if you weren't paying attention. She felt like a rat after cheese. She passed by their cabin, decided not to check on Zelda and then descended another set of stairs at the stern. Here, she found it. Lost and found, with a desk bell attached to the counter at the passthrough window. She plunked the clapper, and a smiling face emerged from behind. "I may help you."

She held up the watch. "I found this on the Sun Deck."

The man took the watch from her. He smiled, and his narrow eyes disappeared into the crinkles of his face. He rattled off a litany in fluent Spanish she didn't understand, which surprised her, too, because he appeared to be more from the Far East rather than Latin South. Maybe he was from one of the Pacific Island nations. He handed her paper and a pen.

"You fill this out if you please," he said, pointing to the blanks. The instructions were in Spanish, too. "Passenger name, cabin number, description of item, location found." He put the date at the top for her, with the typical day, month, year format not common in the US.

"*Bueno*," he said when she returned the completed form. "You will check back when we return to port. If the owner does not claim the item, the item can be yours!" He smiled as if they were conspiring in a game of strategy or planning a jewelry heist. "Diver's watch. Very expensive." He slipped it into a plastic bag along with the carbon copy of the form.

"So, uh, how would I locate a passenger's cabin?" Wild goose chase, maybe, but worth the effort. "One of the passengers invited me to come to his cabin, but I forgot which one."

It was a lie, and he probably knew it.

"What is the passenger's name?" He woke the mouse of an ancient PC and stared at the screen.

"Piero."

"And the last name?"

What was Piero's last name? Piero Perudo was how she thought of him in her mind and her dreams. She shrugged. "What about Andrew Broderick? Or Simon Monforte?"

He looked up from the computer, eyebrows raised. How many cabins was she planning to visit tonight? She saw the question in his eyes. He grinned.

"We're having an impromptu party," she added quickly.

"Broderick? I do not have that name on board."

"Broderick. B-R-O-D-E-R-I-C-K."

"Yes, yes," he said with impatience. "I am spelling the name correctly. I have no Andrew Broderick listed on the manifest."

That didn't make sense. "What about Simon Monforte? M-O-N— "

"Yes, yes. I am spelling it. Monforte's cabin is on the Moon Deck. A balcony suite. Cabin fifty-one. Oh, yes, and a Monforte in Cabin fifty-two as well."

"They have two people traveling with them. Where are their cabins?" She crossed the fingers of her left hand behind her back.

"The Monforte Company has three cabins booked. Two balcony suites on the Moon Deck and a junior suite on the Gaia Deck." He appeared puzzled.

"What? What is it? Can you tell me?" His eyes narrowed. "We're having a cocktail party and want to invite them all. We can't leave anyone out."

Boy Howdy, wasn't she joining Genna in the ranks of the liars club, and it wasn't difficult to get a place at the table, either. Open your mouth and out it comes, a big fat lie by Amy Sparks, thank you very much. She stuck her hand in her pocket, and his eyes lit up, no doubt thinking she would pay him for the information, but her pocket held only a tube of lip balm and the button found on the stair.

"I understand if you can't help me," she said, casting her eyes to her feet.

"The name you want is Andrew Forthright. Not Broderick. Andrew Forthright and Bill Forthright are in Cabin twenty-two. Gaia Deck."

Her brows bunched. Andrew Forthright? Bunking in Bill's cabin? Not Andrew Broderick bunking with a friend.

"Thank you for your help," she said and turned away.

Forthright. Bill and Andrew were related? Were Sheila and Elaine aware of this? Why the incognito? What was going on with these Monfortes and Forthrights and passengers "also from Maine"?

Zelda and her friends were on the Gaia Deck, too. Cabins were on either side of the corridor that ran through the middle of the yacht. Balcony suites were located on the uppermost Moon Deck, probably costing more than a small diamond on this boutique boat. The Monfortes seemed to have more than their share of diamonds, so why did Bill not have a cabin on the Moon Deck, too? Sheila would have made the reservations, of course, and she wouldn't put Bill in a lesser suite. Would she? Not unless they were hiding the fact that Bill had a bunkmate named Andrew.

Only three cabins for four people. Interesting. That meant Sheila and Elaine were bunking together, or Elaine had lied about having the key to Simon's cabin.

Up two flights, she found herself back on the Sun Deck, but at the stern. She had gotten turned around. Her cabin stood all the way forward of the Gaia, one deck below. On the Sun Deck, the jogging track ran along the perimeter from fore to aft, leading in either direction to the Beagle Lounge, the terrace, and the hot tub, and the breakfast bar she had just left. Looking up at the stairs now, the Moon Deck went one flight up, and whether rat and cheese or cat and mouse, her curiosity led her to climb.

CHAPTER EIGHTEEN

Amy climbed the stairs to the Moon Deck, opening the door to the corridor that led to the balcony suites, hoping she gave the impression that she had every right to be there. She wasn't breaking any rules. All decks on the ship were open to passengers. The Moon Deck at the top of the ship offered the best views for moon gazing, hence the name, but its interior was devoted to the balcony cabins. If someone questioned her, she would claim to be passing through.

The corridor seemed much shorter than on the Gaia Deck. Maybe because there were fewer cabins and the doors were spaced farther apart. Even the scent of this deck smelled rich. Or maybe she smelled expensive perfume wafting from beneath one of the cabin doors. She thought of the couple on deck with their dark tans and glittering jewelry. They were probably in one of these suites, their balcony looking out over an expensive ocean view.

She touched the little brass plaque on the door of one of the cabins. Forty-one. Simon's cabin would be at the end, forward. Fifty-one would be on one side and fifty-two on the other. Were Sheila and Elaine staying in the cabin across the hall? She was almost certain Simon had bunked alone. Sheila told her point-blank he liked his privacy.

She stepped forward tentatively. What was she doing here? What did she hope to see? A look inside Simon's cabin. Pure curiosity. No other reason than because she was a nosey parker.

No, Simon never made it back to his cabin. He'd hung in that closet the whole time. It was the only thing that made sense. Whoever pulled him out of the towel bin attempted to get Simon to his cabin and lock the door. Their plans were derailed along the way, and Simon was propped up by his bathrobe with a shepherd hook. The *coup de gras* was the pool towel thrown over his shoulder. The rolling of the boat must have shifted things inside the closet enough to dislodge the hooks, the weight of the body pushing the door open.

The image of him face down on the deck sprang to mind. She shook it away.

Why was he on the Sun Deck in the middle of the night anyway? The Moon Deck was the place to be for stargazing. Plus, the Moon Deck was but a few feet from his cabin door.

Simon wasn't stargazing. He was meeting someone. The note drew him to the Sun Deck to meet with someone with clandestine intentions. But whom?

Wasn't that the $64,000 question?

Whoever wrote that note, that's who.

If what Andrew said was true, whoever pulled him out of the towel bin was trying to dispose of the body when they were interrupted. Andrew was near the stairs, the same stairs with the closet behind it. She would ask Andrew for more details at dinner. She'd take them with the proverbial grain of salt, of course, because as Zelda said, poker players were liars. Andrew proved that true. He was no Broderick, famous or not. And somehow he and Bill were related. She had an inkling of that at dinner, although it had passed without much notice. Their hair had the same dark brown shade to it, and they both parted it in the same way. If she had played her game of genes, she may have noted other similarities. She'd look for those later. The gene pool rarely lied, not the way people did.

With their age differences, Bill and Andrew were most likely father and son. But why the incognito? Why the espionage? Why were they hiding their relationship from Simon? Strange, these people "also from Maine." Andrew may not even be a schoolteacher from Louisiana. Now that she thought about it, this was probably a lie, too. No telling what he did for a living, but narco-something might be involved.

Bill put a hand on Andrew's shoulder at the poker game. Andrew shrugged it off. Now that gesture made sense. Not a cheat signal, as she thought at first. This was a gesture of another kind—the protective hand of father to son. A warning sign that it was time to lay down the cards and walk away. The first rule of poker.

Know when to run.

Standing outside the cabin door, she wished for Superman's X-ray vision. There was no "Do Not Disturb" sign on the door of either Cabin 51 or 52. There was no reason for one now. Not really. But someone had put the sign out that night. Someone who didn't want anyone going into Simon's cabin.

The pieces were still scattered on the table, but the puzzle was taking shape. Whoever killed Simon hung him in the closet. They also had access to Simon's cabin key. They would have burgled what they could, or found what they came for. The idea was a lightning strike of thought. With access to his cabin and his body hanging in the closet, they could take their sweet time hustling his cabin for as long as needed.

A cabin door opened, and she turned to hide her face.

"And to what do I owe this pleasure?" Piero said, coming toward her with surprise in his eyes.

"I, uh, I . . ." she stammered, turning to face him.

"You were looking for me, no?" His grin was contagious, too. "You were looking for your Piero."

She couldn't help but smile at that. Her Piero.

"You must come in now that you have found me." His smile widened. He motioned for her to enter his cabin, which was midway in the corridor. Their eyes met for a moment, and her pulse quickened.

"Your cabin is up here?"

He shrugged. "Luck of the draw. Please. We will have libations on the balcony. It is a view unparalleled by any other."

What was she doing? Maybe the lost and found clerk was right in raising his eyebrows at her.

"*Por favor. Para mi. Por favor.*"

Now, how would she say no to that? She stepped inside, and her eyes widened in surprise. The room opened to the sea. Instead of the navy and marine motif of her cabin, even though luxurious, this suite was all cream and gold, teak, and class.

"Wow, gorgeous!" She grinned with country bumpkin awe.

"I agree." He was looking at her.

Her cheeks colored. Her hands flew to her face, then she tugged at her hair.

The door to the balcony already stood open to the sea breeze, and Piero guided her through with a warm, gentle hand on her back. The Pacific Ocean hung before her, a canvas painted with cerulean blue in broad brush strokes with streaks of cloud. Only the thin line at the horizon parted the sea from the sky with a shade somewhere between indigo and plum. The creams and golds of the interior created a striking contrast to the background. Zelda would be in décor heaven. Piero appeared with a glass of wine in each hand. Accepting the glass, their fingers touched briefly, then she turned to the rail and everything beyond.

"It is spectacular, is it not? Even for someone born to this sea, it still brings me joy."

He pulled a deep breath of salt air into his lungs and his chest expanded. The outlines of strong muscles expanded beneath his shirt. She turned her gaze back to the horizon.

"I am so glad to have you join me. What a pleasant surprise." He turned to face her. "Tell me now about you. Tell me about this Amy Sparks who is from Arkansas."

He made it sound like applesauce.

She took a sip of wine instead. "Oh! This is delicious! What is it?"

"It is called *Tacama Blanco de Blancos*." He took a sip and she followed, then he poured more into her glass. "I am glad you appreciate a fine wine."

She nodded and smiled. "White of whites?" She took another sip. Add a bit of wine to her infatuation, and she might never get off the Moon Deck!

Piero nodded and swirled the glass in his hands. "It comes from the Ica Valley of Peru, which lays at the foot of the great *Cordillera de los Andes*. We are quite proud of this wine, as we are the oldest South American vineyard in the New World. Ah, but here I am speaking about me. I want to learn about you."

"You own this winery? Your family owns this vineyard?"

He shook his head and wagged a finger. "You will not divert my attention. We will speak of you now."

For a moment she shared Genna's *glossophobia*, feeling

tongue-tied with the fear of sounding stupid when it mattered most. Genna's fear was the very reason her political path had derailed from her plans. Although a politician at heart, Genna could never stand in front of the podium to speak. She couldn't do it. Amy felt that way now.

Piero sipped his wine and Amy found her courage.

"I live in a cute little tourist town in Arkansas. In the mountains. We have our own *cordillera*." She made a valiant effort to roll her *R*. His smile spurred her on.

"Ours is the Ozark Mountains, and they are considered the oldest range in North America."

"You were born there? In this Ozark?"

"No." She shook her head. "I was born and raised in Florida."

"Ah, Florida. I am familiar with this state. She has much to offer. Where do you come from? From where did your family originate?"

She gazed at the sky, at a frigate bird riding the wind. "I have no clue."

"No clue of your heritage? How can this be?"

"My family was . . . well, they were . . . well, we moved around a lot. We didn't have big family reunions with cousins and aunts. We didn't have big family holidays with traditions and all that. We were a small family. We stayed to ourselves."

Piero's dark eyebrows were raised high on his forehead. She laughed at his surprise.

"My grandmother, Ollie, always said we were Scotch-Irish from way back. My mother didn't believe her and my father didn't care. Most Americans are not as heritage conscious as other cultures abroad. We're a true melting pot."

"I think I understand." She heard a trace of sadness in his voice.

"Now I am an *Arkansawyer!*"

His brows shot up again.

"You say Peruvian; we say *Arkansawyer.* Personally, I prefer *Arkansasian*, but no one agrees with me."

Piero threw back his head and laughed. The sound was a melody in her ears, pulling her somewhere she could go without much effort. She needed to drain her globe and get out of there fast, but Piero emptied the bottle, splashing the last sip into her glass.

"You have a similar note to this wine. Full-bodied and full of character. Crisp on the tongue, I would imagine as well." His head tilted toward her.

She stepped back quickly. His eyes searched hers for a moment, curiosity and puzzlement under the dark lashes. He straightened and leaned an elbow on the rail.

"You were not here for me."

His abrupt change of tone startled her. Confused her. Her cheeks burned. What did he think? That she came up here to have sex with him? Just what exactly did he think of her?

"No—yes, I—I didn't, I—" The words wouldn't form. What did she want? What could she say? "Piero, I didn't come up here looking for you to, to—well—if that's what you thought. But I'm glad I found you here. I enjoy your company. Maybe we can play more Perudo. Maybe we . . ."

"Maybe we will have another dance." His eyes were composed now. "Maybe even a slow dance." He grinned, and the wrinkles around his mouth deepened. His wrinkles said he was a man who liked to laugh. He was also a man used to having his way. What kind of danger was she flirting with?

Capital *D*? Weren't all men danger with a capital *D*? Heartbreakers, at least. Capital *H*.

He touched her elbow lightly. "I am sorry. It is my mistake. I hope not to offend you. Customs among American women are still a mystery to me. Not that I have many occasions to—"

"No offense taken." It was only a little lie.

"Then tell me, why were you in the corridor? Who were you looking for?"

Amy drew the glass to her lips, hoping the globe would hide her expression. What in the world would she tell him? *I came to snoop around. I came to prowl in Simon's cabin. I came to nose around in other people's business.*

"I hoped to find Sheila and Elaine." A little lie. "I wanted to express my condolences. About Simon Monforte. I wanted to see if I could be of help."

"Yes, yes." He cast his eyes briefly to the floor. "A sad occurrence for this ship. Miguel has considerable regard and concern for this circumstance."

"Miguel?"

"My cousin. The captain. Miguel Chavez."

Amy nodded. "And what is your last name?"

"I am Piero Belaúnde."

It put her in mind of a dish you would order in a Michelin star restaurant. Or a greeting among the best of friends. Be-LOUN-de. His name rolled through her head like a wave rolled onto shore, leaving little bubbles behind in the sand.

"Belaúnde."

He smiled. "*Bueno.* You have the pronunciation."

"I've heard that name."

Piero's eyes widened. "You have heard of Fernando Belaúnde Terry? He was a very great man. A great politician who did many great things for the people of Peru."

"And you are related?"

He waved his hand as if to brush the comment aside. "Distantly. Only distantly."

"Genna will be so excited to hear about this! She's really into politics, and—"

He held up his hand to interrupt. "I am not a politician. That is not my calling."

"What is your calling? What is this business of fun you mentioned?"

He grinned, and again the wrinkles around his mouth deepened. His dark eyes twinkled in the reflection from the sea. "Ah, you are devious. You are determined, are you?"

"Determined. Absolutely determined."

They were standing close now, at the rail. Their wine glasses were empty and set aside. She could feel the heat coming from his arm micrometers from hers. She told herself to step aside, but she didn't. She let the hairs of his arm brush hers as he raised his hand and raked it through his hair. The wind picked up across the balcony, and his dark locks lifted with the breeze.

"Are you going to tell me?"

He sighed deeply. Why was he so reluctant? She took a step back, now more afraid of what he might say than no answer at all. He touched her elbow and pulled her back to the rail.

"My family owns this ship."

"Oh."

"We also own a small fleet of boats that explore our view of the Galápagos. The *Isla Ballestas* of Peru, where people not as fortunate to travel in this manner can still enjoy the wonders of the Galápagos."

She felt herself relax.

"My family is diligent in their efforts to conserve these fragile ecosystems threatened by the tourism companies of the past. Many did not have the same regard for nature. Many are ruthless and see only money to be made. *We* see a responsibility to protect. Miguel—Captain Chavez—has inspired many ecological standards throughout the archipelagos. He is impeccable with his commitment for preservation."

"And you own a vineyard, too?"

"Only five hundred hectares." He grinned.

She thought she would melt on the spot. "And what else?"

He raised an eyebrow and cocked his head. "Is this not enough? You want more?"

"I just think there is more."

He laughed, and she joined him. "Yes, okay. We own several tourism centers throughout the region. We have a sandboarding and dune buggy enterprise in the desert."

"Sandboarding?"

"Not my thing. Too gritty. It is difficult to remove the Peruvian Desert when you have returned from a ride. It seems to collect everywhere!" She could imagine. "And . . ."

"There's more?"

"We have a beautiful old riverboat that takes passengers deep into the Amazon rainforest so they may appreciate the indigenous villages and wildlife. They will discover pink dolphins and three-toed sloths, and monkeys by the tree-full! You have been to the Amazon?"

She shook her head. She was overwhelmed. What did his family not own in Peru?

"And?"

"That's it. We are a large family. We have many cousins and many aunts, as you say. We have family members throughout

Peru. And in Ecuador, too. Family is important to us."

"Why were you hesitant to tell me?"

He didn't answer, and she wondered if he would. He pulled the salt air again into his lungs and let it escape in a long, slow exhale. He smoothed his hair. "We are Peruvians. We must remain of the people. A republic. We were taught to use our good fortune for the betterment of the people. We were taught that boasting of one's position or power is not proper custom. We are passionate people, yes. Even a bit loud." He smiled. "All in the heat of the excitement. Of the game."

"The game of Perudo."

He nodded, and an impish grin widened his mouth. "People can easily get the wrong idea when you have wealth. We prefer to show humility, even in such luxury like this." He swept his arms through the air, motioning to all that surrounded him. "Wealth can draw evil from people. It can make honest men resort to ruthless behavior. We have found this true."

"Yes." She focused on the bird soaring overhead. Yes, she had found that to be true. "Money is at the root of all evil, isn't it? No matter where you go."

As for ruthless behavior, the *Darwinian* had plenty of that on board, too.

CHAPTER NINETEEN

"I have information you don't," Amy said.

"What?" Zelda was still pouting in her PJs, her hand stuck in an ice bucket. Another Zelda tradition.

"Piero owns this boat. Or at least his family does."

"Oh, he's Piero now, not Perudo man."

She ignored the snub. "He owns a vineyard, too. And he's humble and he's . . ."

"Somebody's smitten," Genna chided, poking Amy with her fingernail.

Amy flicked Genna's finger like a bug on a bowl of chips. "I wouldn't call the kettle black."

"No, I guess I can't. And he is a tall, dark, and handsome kettle, at that. I think that eye patch is super sexy."

A knock on the door sounded, and Rian, as the closest, opened to find a steward with an ice bucket and a bottle of wine.

"Compliments of the *Darwinian*. May I, if you please?"

Rian stepped aside, and he set the gift on the table. He handed a note to Amy then flipped open a corkscrew. "I will open for your pleasure?"

Amy nodded, trying desperately to hide her glee behind the

folded note.

"Oohhh," Genna cooed when the steward left and they each had a glass in hand. "A love note. From Perudo man?"

Amy nodded.

"Tell us. You have to read it to us," Zelda urged.

"I don't and I won't."

"I'd read it to you if it were mine."

"He wants me to join him for dinner."

Rian chuckled. "We are going to stare at you from our table among the Monforte clan."

"We'll make ogle-google eyes at you from our table," Zelda said, "until you snort wine out of your nose."

"Oh, please." She read the note again. "We aren't going to the dining room. We're having dinner on the Moon Deck. Dinner under the stars!"

"Under the *stars*!" Zelda threw a pillow at Amy. She dodged it and saved her wine from spilling.

"This is the wine from Piero's family vineyard."

"So you already had some," Zelda teased.

She ignored the innuendo.

Zelda folded her arms. "That's just rude. If you aren't going to tell us, you should just keep quiet."

"Okay, okay, but I hoped to question Andrew and the Monforte clan at dinner."

Genna snorted with contempt. "You can't be serious. Dinner with us and droopy Elaine or dinner with a Peruvian ship magnate? What kind of decision is that?"

"Listen to this," Amy said. "Andrew's real name is not Broderick. It's Forthright. He's Bill's son. At least, I think that's their relationship. I could be wrong, but it fits."

Rian shook her head. "Poor Andrew, he's got so many

poker-tells, I can't imagine he ever wins a hand."

"Did you see Andrew's reaction when Bill put a hand on his shoulder at the poker game?"

Rian shook her head. "I missed that."

"He shrugged it off faster than a hot rock."

"Yeah, he was down to his last chips and betting with the tells of a lunatic. He kept putting a hand in his pocket. I thought he was trying to sneak out an ace, the way Genna does when we're playing cards."

"I imagine he was rubbing his two-dollar bill in his pocket. That's what I would be doing. He's superstitious, too. The Ecuadorians say the two-dollar bill is lucky."

Rian shrugged. "Lucky wasn't working."

"Superstitious *compadres*," Genna interjected.

"I tell you what else isn't working," Zelda whined. "This ice bucket. I still have a headache."

"You're supposed to put the ice on your head," Rian said.

"Oh, that's just silly." Zelda shook the water from her fingers, drying them on the duvet.

Another knock sounded. The four exchanged glances before Rian opened the door to find the steward yet again. This time he held out a note.

"The note's for Genna," Rian said.

Genna tore open the envelope and unfolded the paper. "From Rudy!"

"This is just not fair. This is my birthday cruise, and everything fun is happening to everybody else but me."

"I think it's just you and me for dinner, kid." Rian winked at Zelda. "We'll take on the Monfortes by ourselves."

"Why don't you ask Rudy to join us at our table? He can take Amy's seat since she's dining *under the stars*," Zelda said, feigning contempt.

"That's a great idea," Amy replied. "He can get more information out of the Monfortes."

"The note says he needs to talk with us. All of us. Urgent, it says."

"What does that mean?"

"I guess we're going to find out."

She knew she had a bit too much wine a bit too early in the day when the corridor began swaying at her feet. She needed a nap to help catch up on lost sleep, but she was intrigued by Rudy's note and compelled by his request. This didn't seem like a ruse to get Genna alone on a dark deck.

They made their way to the stern, then up the aft stairs to the Sun Deck. The sun was low on the horizon, and Rudy waited at a table in the shade. She couldn't read his expression with his face in the shadows. He wore the amber-collared shirt from earlier and the white linen trousers cuffed to his shins. His feet were propped up on a table, crossed at the ankles, but he dropped them to the floor as they approached and sat down. Genna took the chair closest to him. A bucket of beers sat on the table, which he offered with a nod, but she didn't take one, and neither did the others.

"What's so urgent? Why lure me out with all my chaperones in tow?"

He smiled briefly. "Our situation is a bit more complicated." He looked at Genna, his mouth in a thin line.

The shadow of his beard seemed even darker, if that were possible, giving him a more sinister look. He certainly was suited for his job. He wouldn't stand out as a clean-cut desk agent in any circumstance, but now he looked like he was ready to slink into the belly of the underworld. Amy didn't know what DEA agents did, precisely, but she suspected they had power and privilege.

"I wouldn't involve you, except you are already involved. I am concerned you are in more danger than you suspect, and I want to make sure you don't say or do anything that could put you in harm's way." He drank from the beer bottle and set it back on the table in front of him.

Zelda squirmed in her seat. Rian sat back and steepled her fingers. Genna lounged comfortably, her long silver ponytail swung over her shoulder, which was now inches away from Rudy's.

"The captain's security team will begin interviewing passengers about the death of Simon Monforte immediately. I will be assisting."

His voice held a cadence that captured their attention. It was deep enough to carry if he wanted to. She remembered how he took command as he stood over the body on the closet floor. Still full of authority, he spoke softly now, as if to imply that what he said would go no further.

"I intend to determine the identity of everyone and their whereabouts between the time Monforte went to the Sun Deck and when he was left in the closet. Now that's a tall order, as you can understand. Since you were in such close proximity, I want to start with you. I want you to disclose everything from the time you found the deceased on the lounge chair to the time you dropped him in the towel bin." Slowly, deliberately, he studied each of them, ending with Genna. He turned slightly to face her, the corners of his mouth turning up in a sexy grin.

Smitten kitten. Both of them. Genna had to be disappointed this was no party for two.

"Genna, you start."

"I didn't see anyone else."

"You did not see or hear anyone on deck?"

"No."

"Did any of you?"

They all shook their heads.

"So you happened upon Simon on the deck chair and you . . . what? What made you pay attention to him?"

Genna answered. "He didn't say anything when we arrived on deck. I asked him for a light, but he didn't respond. I thought he would make some self-important remark, but he didn't. That's when Rian shined her flashlight on him. He had a bullet hole in the middle of his forehead."

"Rian found a lighter in one of his bathrobe pockets. And a cigar," Zelda said. "Amy found his cabin key and the note in the other."

"You went through his pockets?"

"Not a proud moment," Amy said, with a look at Rian and a twinge of guilt. She would give anything to put distance between them and the scene of the crime. To take back what they had done. "I was encouraged in the heat of the moment by someone I trust."

Rian rolled her eyes.

"This note? Did you recognize the handwriting?"

"No, of course not, but it was on ship stationery. Something about meeting on the Sun Deck. It sounded like blackmail or something."

"Blackmail?"

"'You pay, you get.' What else could it mean?"

Rudy nodded. "Whose idea was it to put him in the towel bin?"

They fell silent.

"I don't remember," Genna said finally. "It happened so fast. One minute we were talking about the wife and mistress and who had killed the husband, and the next minute he was in the bin, and we were back in our cabins."

"It's our 'no body, no crime' theory," Zelda said. "We didn't want him to spoil my cruise. We thought if we could at least hide him out of sight, we wouldn't have to go home for as long as he wasn't found. That was stupid."

Rudy didn't respond, but she imagined what he was thinking. What they had done was pretty stupid. There was a long pause in the conversation. "And then what happened?"

"We spoke to Captain Chavez," Amy answered. "The next morning. They had a video of us dumping Simon in the cart. Genna told him that Simon was drunk, and we were teaching him a lesson about being a lecherous old fool. We told you this already."

"We told the captain it was just a joke," Genna added. "And we're sticking to that story, so don't blow our hoax."

"Chavez believed you."

It wasn't a question, but Amy heard the doubt in his voice.

"They didn't spot the bullet hole in the video, because the hole wasn't all that big," Zelda continued. "The captain said Simon wasn't in the cart, then, so Rian figured that out."

Rudy lifted the bottle to his lips and took a swig. "Figured out what, exactly?"

"Rian said that if the captain believed Simon was drunk as we said, why would he think otherwise when the camera recorded whoever pulled him out? If he was drunk going in, he would be drunk coming out. If he didn't believe that to be true, we would be in bigger trouble than we were."

"Who do you think pulled him out? Rian?"

"I have no idea."

"And neither does the captain," Amy added. "He admitted they don't have that on video. It seems the cart was out of range of the security camera."

Rudy sat back. "That's unfortunate. And you have no idea who did this?"

"We were banking on the wife," Genna confided. "I mean why wouldn't she want to get rid of that supercilious fool? We were going on the premise that the wife shoots him, hears us coming, and hides in the shadows, observes us put Simon in the bin, waits until we leave and then pulls him out and carries him to their cabin. And then she hangs the 'Do Not Disturb' tag on the door."

"But then we decided that he was too heavy for just one woman, so there had to be at least two involved. Or maybe even three," Zelda said.

"Elaine, Sheila, and Bill," Amy added. "We were not aware of Andrew's true identity at the time."

"What about Andrew? And who is Bill?"

"Bill works for Simon. Andrew is not who he says. I think Bill is his father, but for some reason, they were keeping that a secret from Simon. The clerk at lost and found told me Bill and Andrew share a surname *and* a cabin on the Gaia Deck."

"How did Simon get the gun on board?"

"Simon? No, the gun had to belong to one of the others."

"You think one of them smuggled it on board?"

Rian perked up. "That is a good question. I wondered that myself."

"Any ideas?"

They shook their heads.

"The Monfortes buy narco-assets," Amy said. "Maybe that is

part of it. We learned about that at dinner the other night. They sell yachts up in Maine and buy narco-asset boats down here cheap. Narco-jewelry, too. You should see the bling they wear."

Rudy leaned forward. "Narco-assets? You are familiar with Monforte's business in Ecuador?"

"We are now. Bill gave us quite the primer. He claimed they have a system that keeps them safe from the revenge of pirates."

Yikes. She regretted using the term. He didn't notice her discomfort. He was probably used to people looking at his patch. People often stared at the scar that ran along her hairline. She never forgot it was there, even after all these years. Maybe he felt that way, too. Maybe he didn't. Men behaved so differently from women. Mars and Venus, always circling in close orbit and never aligning for long.

Zelda piped up. "Rian also figured out that Simon was not in the net bag after all. The one Amy saw swimming with the hammerheads. It was a drug drop. Isn't that right? Genna heard the crew talking about attitudes and latitudes. Isn't that right?"

Rudy stared at her. "A drug drop. You better tell me about this, Amy."

"Just what Zelda said. I saw a swimmer pulling a bag through the water. I thought it was Simon. I thought the swimmer anchored him to a rock so he wouldn't float to the surface."

"What did you see?" he growled, and Amy was surprised at how quickly he moved through his roles. One moment he was chatting with friends; the next he was a hunter on the prowl. "Tell me. This is very important."

"It is?" Zelda's eyes widened. "Tell him about the ring," Zelda urged.

Rudy sat forward. "A ring? In the closet?"

"No, in the water. I think it was a ring. It was a flash that caught my attention in the first place. I assumed it was a ring reflecting sunlight as they moved through the water."

"Did you see who it was?"

"I was too far away. I was afraid the swimmer might come after me, so I swam back to the boat. We've been looking at everybody's hands. A lot of people wear rings."

Rudy followed Amy's eyes.

He didn't wear a ring.

"We decided I didn't see Simon in the bag," she continued, "and the proof was when he fell out of the closet at Elaine's feet."

"On my birthday," Zelda complained.

Amy and Rudy had been front and center when Simon's body crashed through the doorway. She was there when Rudy touched the sleeve of Simon's bathrobe and pressed his fingers against Simon's neck. Their eyes met briefly. "It sure was a convenient discovery, especially if you were the one who put the body in there."

"Who put it in the closet? You saw them?"

Amy shook her head. "It fell right at Elaine's feet. That's weird timing, not just bad luck. The captain was looking for a lost passenger, Simon, and lo and behold, he falls out of the closet at his wife's feet. I would never have believed her insomnia story if it wasn't for Andrew. He's the one who saw someone helping Simon to his cabin."

"Did he recognize this person?"

"No. He said he couldn't see the other person clearly."

"And did you tell the captain all of this?"

"No! We decided to leave well enough alone," Genna said. "When you told us who you were, we decided to stay out of the captain's way and off his radar."

"Good," he said. "That's for the best."

Genna smiled at him. "We thought so, too. We can trust you to keep us off the captain's radar, right?"

"I will share this with the captain," Rudy said. "I'll reiterate you're not involved in this matter any deeper than the bin."

He grinned, and Amy recognized his amusement. He was tickled that four women from Arkansas would drop a dead body in the towels and then go off for cocktails.

"As I told you before, the danger that exists here is real. We have our suspicions about who is involved in the drug trafficking aboard this ship, and how they are making their drops. Monforte may have gotten in the way. Make sure you do not get in the way." He looked directly at Amy. "We have not removed anyone from suspicion in this smuggling enterprise. *Anyone*. You understand? From the top down."

Was he talking about Piero? Her Piero? It sounded as if he was.

"We?" Rian asked. "There are more of you on board? DEA?"

Rudy shook his head. "I can't comment. It could jeopardize everything."

Rian was probably thinking about her weed connection down on the Jacob Marley Deck. Genna was probably thinking about when Rudy would finally get her alone. She was thinking about dining with Piero Belaúnde under the stars. And Zelda was determined to have a good time. Girls just want to have fun. And dead men kept getting in the way.

"Why don't you join our table at dinner?" Genna asked. "That way you can determine for yourself what this Monforte clan is up to."

"Yeah," Zelda said. "Amy's having a private dinner with

Perudo man under the stars tonight. There's an empty seat at the table."

Genna smiled at Rudy. "You can help figure out who's who and who's lying. We thought Sheila was Simon's mistress at first, but now we aren't so sure about that. Her bling is big enough to be the mistress but says she's the company secretary. She and Elaine are sharing a cabin. Now that Amy's discovered Andrew may be Bill's son, we have to consider the possibility that all four of them are in on this little plan to take out poor Simon during his last-ever bucket list cruise."

Amy shook her head. Such a way with words. "Genna thinks Sheila and Elaine are lovers. I think they are close but not in that way. There's something there, but I'm not certain what it is. Rian claims it's none of our business, and Zelda doesn't care as long as no more wasbunds drop like flies at her feet."

"If the pile fits," Genna snipped.

She could tell Genna regretted the outburst.

Rudy frowned. "Wasbunds?"

"Never mind," they said in chorus and smiled.

"I'm going to dinner with Piero Belaúnde." She let the name roll to shore. "And y'all"—she motioned with a sweep of her hand—"can dine and grill the Monfortes."

"Be careful," Rudy said. "Remember what I told you. From the top down. Don't disclose anything you shared with me or anything I shared with you. Got it?"

"Got it."

A motion caught her attention, and she raised her eyes. Captain Chavez stood like a sentinel at the deck above, the same pressed white uniform, the familiar dark mix of curiosity and concern set firmly in his jaw. He was listening to their conversation, or attempting to listen. She glanced back to Rudy.

Rudy was gone. How quickly he disappeared. Genna was gone, too.

CHAPTER TWENTY

"How do I look?"

Zelda smiled at Amy, her hands on her shoulders from behind. She added the final touches to Amy's hair. "You're stunning. Beautiful."

She dared to look in the mirror. Yes, she was. She admitted it. There was a sparkle of her hazel eyes that were now on the green spectrum in this light. She had a sun-blushed glow to her cheeks, along with a scattering of freckles. Her smile, always a little lopsided, was a pale mauve-pink, and full of hope. She felt hopeful. Not that she could hope for anything more than dinner under the stars with a man whose name sounded like a drumroll. The prospect of time alone with an attractive man had her feeling buoyant. Especially since he thought she was beautiful, too. It had been a long time.

Zelda skillfully swept her copper curls into a loose knot on top of her head, with soft tendrils dropping around her neck and ears. They wouldn't stay soft for long once the salt air got to them, but she'd make a sizzling first impression.

She smoothed her hips and studied her reflection in the mirror. The slit of the long dress was deeper than she'd normally wear, rising to mid-thigh, but the drape of the material made it more mysterious than revealing. It was more cloak than dagger. Zelda encouraged the purchase, and now she was glad she had splurged. A dusty purple, the way lilac blooms appear in morning dew, the gown reached nearly to the floor. All folds and flare, the skirt draped alongside a deep V-neck bodice front and back before gathering at the waist. Surprised at her reflection, Amy realized her waist looked like an hourglass in the accents of this band, a big difference from her tomboy T-shirts. There was no lace, no fringe, no bling anywhere on the dress. It was simple, soft, and flowy. She wished she had something more striking to wear at her neck, thinking of the amethyst necklace Sheila wore on costume night. She fingered the peridot at her neck. Of course, she would never take this off.

It was enough. She was enough. She twirled in the mirror, and the dress floated as if it were cotton candy spun at the fair.

Zelda helped her into her shoes. The rose gold ankle-strap sandals were perfect. Although far more heel than she felt comfortable with, Zelda promised Amy could make it work.

"Just hold on to the rail as you walk. And go slow. Slow is sexy. Remember that."

Amy grabbed her clutch with the "necessities" as Grandmother Ollie called them, and the cabin key, then disappeared through the door.

"You're beautiful and I love you, my friend!" Zelda called as the door was closing.

Amy stopped abruptly in the hall. The steward was waiting. "Sorry, miss." He offered her his elbow. "I am to escort you, if I may."

She took his arm, and they floated through the corridor.

Piero rose when she reached the stairs of the Moon Deck at the bow of the *Darwinian*. He waited at the top in a white dinner jacket, the shirt collar open at the neck. He was pleased to see her.

"*Que guapísima estás*," he whispered, taking her hand, his smile wide. "*Como una estrella caída.*"

Whatever that meant. It was flattering whatever it was.

"You are beautiful. A star that has fallen from the sky."

Hopefully, he wouldn't notice her cheeks flush with color, and she fought the urge to clasp her hands to her face. Instead, she held his hand as they walked toward a table set for two. White linens and sparkling wine globes danced in the candlelight. Piero gave a quick nod, and a cello in the shadows began to play.

Her favorite instrument! How did he know?

Mellow notes full of warm sea breeze floated by on silky butterfly wings. A solemn, sweet melody surrounded them. Had she fallen through some divide in the universe and landed in another dimension? She felt as if she had. He made her feel like a star. The sky overhead looked like ink flowing in all directions. Pinpricks of light broke through by the billions. She had never noticed so many stars.

Piero tugged her hand and she glided toward him. A warm hand on her back guided her closer, while the other hand gestured her into both rhythm and meter as the cellist's bow teased the sound from the strings.

"We are at the equator." She felt his warm breath on her earlobe. "Zero degrees latitude. Halfway between one world and the other. As with your friend's birthday. We are the same here. Suspended in time and place."

The tempo changed, and he guided her to one of the chairs, his hand brushing her shoulder lightly as he settled her into place. A steward appeared from nowhere and poured the wine.

She gazed at the black water off the deck. The equator must be some magical place where dreams transcended reality. She felt as if she were drifting in those butterfly notes dancing around her in the dark.

"I have never met anyone who favors you," Piero said.

"But you don't even know me."

"Ah, all the more reason. A mystery is irresistible and impossible to ignore."

She laughed lightly. She wanted to be coy and glamourous and amusing all at the same time. Her heart swelled. "I am no mystery. I live an ordinary life."

"I do not believe that."

She watched him, then. He was more charming than handsome, which made him seem real, rather than some bodice ripper romance hunk. He had a strong chin, a straight nose. Eyes that danced in the candlelight. His mouth caught her attention; his lips parted slightly, like a secret door ajar waiting to swing open. And for her to explore.

It was as if by looking at him, she could see herself.

"Yes, I have an extraordinary life. I live in a beautiful community. I have remarkable friends who make my life meaningful. They helped me make my dreams come true. My little cottage industry at home in Arkansas, for one. This trip, too."

"And me. Do not forget to add me to this list of dreams come true."

She laughed again. "Yes, you are on the list."

"Well, at least I have accomplished something on this passage. I was beginning to think I had wasted my time aboard. I have yet to win at Perudo!" He threw back his head and laughed, and again, she found the sound irresistible. A loud laugh that could be disarming if not so full of delight. Delight. That fit. He laughed because he savored life. He seemed thrilled to be suspended in this time and place. On this boat. On this sea.

They let the music take over the conversation for a moment. She felt lavished by the silence that held nothing more than the churn of the water below the bow and the chords sustained by the cello. A cloche appeared, again as if from nowhere. With a flourish and no words, the waiter presented fresh lobster ceviche and a silver cone of crisp taro chips.

"Delicious, as usual." She drank from her wine. "So, why are you on this boat? What is the purpose of your passage?"

One brow rose above the other. "You are a woman with a direct manner. And a curious mind."

"I didn't mean to be rude."

"I didn't take it to be rude. All the same, I must reply that my presence on this boat is a business matter that really cannot concern you."

She nearly sputtered into her wine. A business matter? Something so private he couldn't answer? Wouldn't answer. That's what he meant. None of your business, Amy Sparks, in proper Spanish form. She emptied her glass and set it gently on the table, deliberate in her movements, hoping time would speed forward, away from wounded pride.

Their place settings and discards disappeared by waiter-magic, and beneath another cloche, a steak fillet sizzled in a plate of green peppercorns, capers, and wine. It smelled wonderful. But her appetite had disappeared, too.

Piero pierced his steak and examined it. "I hope you enjoy it rare. It is most flavorful at this temperature."

She nodded and carved a bite.

"You have improved greatly at Perudo."

She could tell he tried to regain his footing. He smiled, his lips inviting. She smiled back and chewed her food.

What was this business of his? Did it have to do with drug smuggling? Could he be the suspect from the top down as Rudy suggested? Her heart crumbled. Why had he invited her to dinner? Why was he so attentive to her? Not because she was a fallen star.

No. To gather information. He was hunting information! He was pretending to like her so he could gather what she knew. Of all the low-down dirty tricks to play on a person who wore her heart on her sleeve, this was the worst. She stared at the signet ring with its ancient history. He could be the swimmer. Had he seen her swimming, too?

A peppercorn caught in her throat, and she coughed.

He started to rise. "Are you okay? Are you well?"

She nodded, motioning him to sit, a napkin to her mouth.

Perudo man. Piero Belaúnde. Winemaker. Ship magnate. Fun producer. *Drug smuggler.*

Was he a *killer*, too? Had he killed Simon Monforte and hung him in the closet like a pair of yesterday's pants? How would she get through this dinner? How were they all going to get off this yacht alive?

He poured more wine in her glass, and she drank it down in one long gulp.

He folded his hands over his plate. The gesture reminded her of Bill Forthright praying over his meal. To what deity would she pray to get out of this chaos? She felt as if she were in an escape room that had no exit. A maze in the middle of the ocean, hundreds of miles away from anywhere civilized. There was no place to shelter from the storm.

His eyes, dark in the candlelight, now flickering wildly in the wind, studied her from across the table. "I can tell I have upset you." He paused. "Although I do not understand, I regret that we have ended our meal on such a sour note. I want nothing more than to enjoy a quiet evening with you. I hoped we would find our common ground, I think you Americans say. Is that not a possibility? Can we return our temperament to when we began this beautiful evening?"

Confused. Rejected. She couldn't respond. Could she shake all these doubts loose after they piled up like the lizards on the rock? The cold-blooded seeking a warm, safe place. Is that what he was? A creature on the hunt? Like his Perudo dice in the cup, where truth stayed hidden from view. Liar's dice and deceit. ¡Dudo!

"I don't feel well," was all she could manage.

CHAPTER TWENTY-ONE

"This is Rudy," Genna said to no one in particular at the table. "He's taking Amy's place tonight."

Sheila and Elaine sat together. They were never far apart from one another. Friends, lovers, or codependent? Genna was determined to disclose the truth. They both smiled at Rudy, and she felt a flutter of jealousy.

Sandwiched between Rudy and Andrew, Genna knew she was in the perfect position for an inquisition of the Monforte clan. She was particularly interested in overhearing the conversation between Elaine and Andrew, given what Amy shared about his incognito status in Bill's cabin. She'd need to direct an inquiry in that direction at some point in the evening's meal. Rian sat on the other side of the table between Bill and Sheila, and Zelda sat between Bill and Rudy. The seating arrangement couldn't have turned out better if she'd set out place cards at the plates. Rian could engage Sheila and Bill on either side of her. Zelda could talk to Bill about money. The Monfortes and Andrew introduced themselves around the table to Rudy.

"Where is your friend, Amy?" Andrew asked, his smile bright. Genna remembered the pair were chummy on Santa

Cruz. She called them superstitious compadres.

"She's having dinner under the stars." Zelda beamed. "A date on the high seas!"

Andrew looked annoyed.

"Have we met before?" Bill asked.

"Not likely," Rudy responded. "Of course, we've both been on this boat several days."

"You look familiar to me. I saw you in Ecuador at the auction. But I don't remember your . . . the . . ." he stumbled. "The eye patch. I must be mistaken."

Rudy nodded. "Easy mistake." He didn't seem phased by the mention of his patch. Genna wiggled a little closer to him.

"Our condolences to you all," Genna said to Elaine and Sheila, with a glance at Bill. "That must have been quite the shock."

Elaine, eyes droopy as ever, nodded to her soup.

Sheila touched Elaine's hand briefly. "Thank you. Yes, it was a shock, and we are *in* shock. We still can't believe it, nor can we wrap our heads around why."

"Has the captain shared any details with you?" Rudy asked.

Sheila shifted her gaze. "A few. His security team is conducting the investigation—at least while we are at sea." She glanced at Elaine. "We've already talked with them. We've gone over every detail that could be significant. I even shared how strangely Simon acted that night. We were in the lounge for a while after dinner. He kept looking around as if looking for someone. I didn't ask him about it at the time, because I didn't put too much stock in it until . . . later."

Again, she turned to Elaine. "As best we can discern, Simon went to meet someone much later. He knocked on the door of our cabin to say he was going out for some fresh air. He was dressed for bed. I thought it odd at the time, but I felt too tired and a bit too tipsy to bother with his details." Her voice faltered. "Now—Now, I wish I had. Maybe I could have prevented this."

"This is not dinner conversation, is it?" Bill said. "This is not your fault, Sheila. No one could anticipate this. We have all been preparing for Simon's transition. I've laid the necessary groundwork for the company's future, but I did not plan for such an abrupt and sinister end."

"We are all very sorry for your loss," Zelda comforted. "No one can ever prepare for this. I had an unexpected death in my family, too. My husband was killed in a hit-and-run accident. It was a tremendous shock. I couldn't have gotten through it without my friends."

"You're a widow, then?" Bill poured wine into Zelda's glass, then into his own.

Zelda nodded and caught Elaine's eye. "I understand your distress. And your confusion. There's a numbness that settles over you at first. For a long time, I felt as though I were looking through a window that desperately needed to be cleaned. I knew I needed to wipe off the grit and get on with it, but I was stuck. I stared at the streaks and the cobwebs and wondered how did I not see it before now? Right there, in front of my nose."

Elaine met Zelda's eyes. "This, too, shall pass?"

"It will. I promise you."

"I am a widow, too," Genna divulged. "Twice. And Zelda's right. The grief will pass."

Rudy glanced at Genna.

"I will be there always," Sheila said, then reached over and tenderly kissed Elaine's cheek. "My sister and I have been through a lot together and we will get through this, too."

"Sisters!"

"Yes, Elaine is my younger sister."

"But you don't look anything alike!"

Sheila chuckled lightly, fluffing her hair. "No, I guess not. We are from a mixed marriage. I am the spitting image of my father, and Elaine resembles our mother."

Genna forked a mouthful and chewed. There was something undisclosed in their relationship, but not what any of them expected. They shared a mother. She sipped her wine, then turned her attention to Andrew. He had plowed through the steak and now mopped the juices with a wedge of crusty Spanish bread. Bread crumbs sprinkled the front of his shirt, and she fought the urge to swipe it clean.

"And how are you related to this clan?"

Andrew coughed. "I, uh . . ." He glanced at Sheila and then at Elaine, his eyes finally settling on Bill.

"We are not related," Sheila said, and an uneasy silence settled over the table.

"This is my youngest son," Bill said, his voice on the edge of emotion. "We have not spent much time together, and I hoped this trip would be a new beginning."

Andrew shifted in the chair beside her. The question hung in the air, but no one seemed willing to ask it. Why had they hidden this relationship from Simon?

"My father and I have a strained history. We are hoping for a new start, and I've always wanted to explore the Galápagos."

"Father-and-son relationships can be difficult," Rudy said with a direct glance at Andrew. "You're lucky to have an opportunity to start fresh. Not everyone does."

Andrew nodded.

Rudy seemed to enjoy the heartfelt game of show and tell

around the table. His expression held the amused grin Genna was beginning to recognize. If Amy were here, she would be giving them both her I-told-you-so look.

"Especially when money and vice are involved."

Bill regarded Rudy. "What are you implying?"

"Never mind. I speak about myself more than anything. Poker is also a vice of mine. Sometimes I win and sometimes I lose. That's the nature of the game, but when Lady Luck is holding out, you can get in deep. Not that my old man was there when I needed help."

Andrew stiffened with unease. He looked down, noticed the crumbs on his chest, and brushed them away as if they were cinders on fire.

"Of course, *my* father was no accountant for a wealthy firm. He ran a dive shop down in the Keys. We lived on lobster and beer."

"Lobster?" Genna asked.

Rudy nodded. "Down in the Florida Keys, lobster is easy to catch, free for the taking, and pretty tasty grilled with a squeeze of key lime juice. Lobster is a poor boy staple. The Florida version of mac and cheese."

Genna laughed. "Now lobster mac and cheese is all the rage on gourmet menus."

Rudy grinned at Genna and then turned his gaze to Bill. "The old salts taught me how to play poker. They also taught me there are many ways to settle a debt." Rudy glanced at Andrew. Bill's fist dropped to the table with a muffled thud, which drew everyone's attention. "You mentioned auctions. Is that your interest here in Ecuador? Narco-assets? Do I have that right?"

Bill's eyes widened and then narrowed. "Yes, our company

does acquire assets from auctions from time to time. That is not our only source, of course."

"Of course not. Too dangerous."

Bill regarded Rudy with interest, fingers working the black stone of his ring.

"Elaine and I are not interested in running the company, and we're fortunate to have Bill's sound business sense." Sheila was used to keeping the peace between Simon and Bill. Genna could tell it came naturally.

"That must be a comfort," Rudy said. "And now with a power of attorney in hand, Bill can keep things running smoothly. He can keep business as usual as if nothing has gone awry."

Sheila's eyebrows drew together as she frowned. "I'm not sure what you are alluding to here. Bill is a loyal member of this company, as am I. While Simon may not have been the most humble of souls, he was a smart businessman. He trusted Bill. Simon made these decisions months ago. He already decided Bill would take over when . . . when the time came. I was in charge of preparing those documents."

"How do you know about the power of attorney?" Bill said.

Rudy shrugged. "Just a lucky guess. I overheard him say he was settling his affairs."

"When did you talk to Simon?"

"I was a bystander listening in. I shouldn't have, I know, but it was hard not to listen. Hard not to hear. He was shouting."

"What did he say? Who was he talking to?"

Rudy studied them, his expression veiled in the somber light. His shoulders were relaxed as he leaned forward, elbows on the table. And yet, Genna felt the tension beneath the cool façade. Elaine, Sheila, and Bill watched his every move. Rian and Zelda, too.

"I didn't see who. I was eavesdropping as I said, but I understand he wanted a gun for protection from someone he feared. Something easy to smuggle on board. A twenty-two caliber. Maybe a Ruger. Nothing fancy."

The table grew eerily silent again. Genna wanted to know what they did with that information. She didn't know what to do with it, herself. Rudy had not mentioned this before now. Of course, he would know more than she and her friends did, but what he just revealed could drag the Monfortes down like a bobber on a fishing line tugged by a whopper. Would she and her friends sink with them? The Monfortes kept their thoughts to themselves, but their eyes were dark in the fake flicker of the candlelight. Elaine focused on the plate in front of her. Sheila gripped the globe of her wine glass, her eyes on Rudy's. Bill, too, looked at Rudy with a thin, poised smile, but his heartbeat was visible above the collar of his shirt.

"This is preposterous," Bill said, dropping his fist to the table, quieter this time. "You are insinuating that we had something to do with his death!"

"I'm just repeating what I heard," Rudy said, now sitting back. Genna felt him retreat, his undercover persona pulling him back into the shadows. She could tell he liked leading people where he wanted them to go, drawing them in, gaining their trust. His was not a job all that different from her own, but with danger and risk. She knew all about biasing others with words. Manipulating them, even. Rudy was leading them toward a confession. Or a slip-up. One of them pulled the trigger.

She knew it.

Andrew cleared his throat. "When I saw Simon, it must have

been minutes before . . ."

"How did you confirm it was Monforte?" Rudy interrupted. "Did you talk to him?"

"No, I just assumed . . ."

"And you didn't talk to the other person, either. What made you think this was a man?" Rudy turned to Sheila. "It could have been anyone. Anyone strong enough for him to lean on."

Sheila set her glass down with such force, the stem snapped, spilling her wine everywhere.

"Oh no!" Elaine dabbed her napkin at the wine pooling on the table. "Are you all right, Sheila?"

"I've had enough of this nonsense," Bill said through clenched teeth. "I don't know what you're trying to pull, but your implications are out of line. I was not involved in Simon Monforte's death. *None of us* was involved, and we will not rest until we have given him a proper farewell and brought his killer to justice."

"Justice?" Rudy growled. "Might as well ask for the moon."

"Why do you say that?"

"Because matters are handled differently at sea. Captain Chavez will want nothing more than a cursory investigation on paper and a chance to sweep it all under the floorboards of one of the lower decks. Down where they keep the carrots and cargo no one else ever sees. If you want justice for Monforte, you're going to have to beg for it."

Bill jerked his chair back from the table. "My apologies to you ladies," he said brusquely and strode from the room. Sheila and Elaine jumped up and followed.

"What is this about?" Andrew asked, his dark gaze on Rudy. "If this is about the money I owe you, I told you I have it. You don't need to upset my father to get at me. Or Sheila and Elaine, either. Her husband's dead for heaven's sake!" He rose, tossed his napkin to his empty plate, and sped from the room.

"Well, that was a Led Zeppelin," Zelda said.

Rian and Genna burst into laughter.

"Sorry, Rudy," Genna said between giggles, "we are not as ruthless as we sound. You caught us in a private joke."

He nodded curtly. Genna sensed there were many sides to Rudolph Granger, DEA. He was the kind of mysterious she felt drawn to, the kind she couldn't predict. Rudy had a nugget of husband number one in his enigmatic core. A charismatic politician, Daniel showed one face to the world and another behind closed doors. He was an exceptional orator, a thing of beauty to watch. But he was also unpredictable. Extreme. Risky business, these risky men, she thought now. But exciting. Rudy had that same appeal as Daniel, although with much rougher edges, much more scrappy. She suspected he would be charming in a bow tie and tux. The thrill of taming such a beast was a powerful draw.

And yet, she knew more than their age kept him out of arm's reach. Just barely out of reach. She couldn't explain it away, and she didn't want to. Not yet. The thrill of infatuation was electrifying. His attention made her feel younger than her sixty-plus years, and desired, even if it was for a short while. Not forever, never forever, but ten days was better than none. None was safer, but not as much fun.

Was she playing with fire?

Sure she was. Blaming Amy for warning her about Rudy was histrionic, but it had burned a hole right through her psyche. Rudy wasn't Amy's type. The Perudo guy was Amy's style, all swoony and proper. Rudy was Merriweather's type. She was glad *she* wasn't on board.

"Sometimes the past floats up from the bottom when you least expect it," Genna said as if speaking to herself.

"The past always catches up," Rudy agreed. "But you never know when."

CHAPTER TWENTY-TWO

Zelda burst through the door of a darkened cabin with Genna and Rian on her heels.

"*Eek!*" she screamed when she flipped on the light and a tear-stained Amy sat up in bed. She was still in her gown, hair lopsided and hanging loose from where she had buried her head in the pillow.

"What is the matter with you?" Zelda squawked, running to her side. "Are you sick?"

Amy shook her head.

Genna and Rian joined Zelda at Amy's bunk.

"What's going on?" Rian was cool, collected, and concerned.

"What a disaster," Amy choked out, fighting back her sobs.

"Didn't you have fun? A wonderful date under the stars?"

She nodded at Zelda's remark. "He said I am a star fallen from heaven. He even had a cellist in the shadows. I love the cello." She buried her face in her hands.

"Out with it, Sparks," Genna ordered. "You're a mess, and no cello did this."

Rian poured a Cognac from the bar cabinet, handed the glass to Amy, then went back for the bottle.

Amy's eyes burned from the fumes, and the gulp burned her

throat. "It was so romantic. He was so romantic. We were at the equator, and we danced, and the cello was in the dark playing this wonderful somber melody, and . . ."

"And?" Genna demanded. "That all sounds perfect. Did he hurt you?" She anchored her stance, ready to spar with an invisible villain.

Amy shook her head. "No. No, he was a perfect gentleman."

"Then what? What? Tell us."

"Be quiet," Rian said. "If you keep going on and on, we'll never learn what happened."

Genna's mouth snapped shut.

Amy blew her nose on the tissue Zelda handed her and held her glass out to Rian. "One more." She'd sip it slowly this time. "Everything was perfect, then I asked why he was on the boat. He called me a curious woman. He said his business wasn't any of my concern."

"So what?" Zelda shook her head. "Explain this to me."

"Don't you understand? It's just as Rudy said—from the top down. This drug-smuggling operation he's been watching. Piero must be involved. What else could it mean? What could be so private, Piero can't tell me?

"I could have died right then and there. It was horrible! I wanted to be somewhere else so badly, I didn't even finish my dinner. And I felt like Cinderella running from the ball in those shoes!"

"Wait just a minute," Rian said. "Tell me again what he said. Slowly."

"We were talking about dreams coming true. Not my kind of dreams, but dreamy dreams. This cruise for Zelda. And the Cardboard Cottage. He said he hoped he was on my list of dreams come true. I said he was. And then he laughed and said,

'At least I have accomplished something on this passage.'

"So I asked, 'What *is* the purpose of your passage?'

"And he said, 'My presence on this boat is a matter that doesn't concern you.' Or something like that." Amy sniffled and took a sip of her Cognac.

"I think you made a big jump," Rian said.

"That is exactly what you'd say to someone who asked about the Pot Shed. Or what's inside the Pot Shed. You would and I know why."

Rian rubbed her chin and then twirled a curl around her fingers. "Because it's none of their business, that's why."

"Because drugs are illegal."

"No, because it's none of their business."

"You want to hear the earful we got tonight?" Genna asked.

"I do." Anything to get her mind off Piero and how stupid she felt.

"Where should we start?"

"Start with Elaine and Sheila," Zelda suggested. "That was a big surprise."

Another round of Cognac, and the three friends filled Amy in on their dinner conversation. Elaine and Sheila were sisters, half-siblings, sharing the same mother but not fathers. She knew they had some connection other than the one Genna kept putting forward, but the gene pool game had not worked its usual magic.

Andrew, as they guessed, was Bill's son. They were hoping to mend what appeared to be a strained relationship. That Andrew had a poker-slash-gambling problem probably didn't help the relationship, and it appeared he owed Rudy money.

"He's a teacher in a Catholic school," Genna added, "and that makes a double *whammo* for daddy. Maybe Bill is cleaning up Andrew's debts. Maybe he was embezzling from Simon to do it. Maybe Simon caught him with his hand in the till. I think Rudy thought so, too."

They relayed what Rudy said about overhearing Simon being frightened and smuggling a gun on board to protect himself.

"A twenty-two caliber," Rian said. "I was right."

"Rudy was a cannon. *Boom, boom, boom*"—Genna pumped her fist with the words—"a pro in action."

"With Simon out of the way, Bill is the big chief now, power of attorney and all," Zelda said. "Bill gave me his card and said to give him a call anytime I needed advice."

"How did Rudy know about the power of attorney?" Amy asked.

"Well, duh," Genna said. "He's a federal agent. He's privy to a lot of things."

Amy wiped at her eyes. "That's a pretty specific document, isn't it?"

"Maybe, but common enough to be a lucky guess," Genna answered. "When Rudy implied that Sheila was strong enough to get Simon back to the cabin—or back to the closet if that's where he went—you'd think the earth moved and the globe shattered. She broke her wine glass right on the table. *Crack!* Big-boned girl from southern Amarillo."

"Wow! I missed a lot!" Amy eyed Genna. "And you said, 'What kind of decision is that? Droopy Elaine or dinner under the stars?' I would have rather been with y'all."

"At least we're together now," Zelda said, "safe and sound and full as a tick on a hound dog." She patted her belly. "Bill's not the kind of guy I'm drawn to, and I'm not at all unhappy with my accountant back in Bluff Springs, but you never know when you need a second opinion or another pair of eyes. Especially when it comes to keeping the government out of your wad of cash. It may be a long way from Arkansas to Maine, but the world has gotten smaller these days, hasn't it?"

Amy groaned. "You're not on the hunt for husband number five, are you?"

"Oh, heavens, no," Zelda said, shaking her head. "Oh. Heavens. No. Not even if David Cassidy got down on one knee."

"Zelda," Amy said. "He's been RIP for a while."

"No! Keith Partridge is dead?"

Amy reached out and hugged her friend. "People are a box of chocolates, and you're a crunchy nut!"

"Chocolates! That's the answer. I have turtles from Santa Cruz. Let's have one with a nightcap!"

"We've already had our nightcap," Genna said. "Amy's had three."

"I get her share, then," Zelda replied as she passed the box of turtle-shaped confections that promised to be Charles Darwin's favorites.

CHAPTER TWENTY-THREE

They arose early and went for coffee and nibbles at the stern, near where they had met Rudy yesterday. There was something about watching where you've been that offered some reprieve from struggle, and the stern gave them a full view of where they had been. The water swelled and frothed in the wake, and the islands slipped behind them over the horizon. The overcast morning sky turned the water a charcoal gray. Amy pulled the collar of her hoodie tighter and was grateful for its warmth.

The pang of the all-too-brief evening with Piero still tugged at her thoughts. She felt angry. Then silly. Then angry once again, all in the span of a single cup of coffee. Had she overplayed her emotions? Yes. But so had he. She felt disappointed in herself for falling into a sophomoric fit full of drama and imagination. His business was not her business. She had no right to think it was. Sighing into her cup, she tried to make peace with herself. It had been fun for whatever tiny slice of time their flirtation had lasted.

Rian stood next to Zelda, their hands cradling their cups, forearms against the rail as the gray wake rose behind them. Genna stood as if caught with her hands in a pickle jar, a sour look on her lips.

"I am loath to say it," she said, breaking the silence and swinging her ponytail behind her shoulder, "but we put our foot in it when we dumped that body. Had I been able to plot the scenario more carefully, we would have walked away as if there was no dead husband on the chaise."

"I believe I suggested that," Rian said. It was hard to miss the I-told-you-so attitude.

Zelda shook her head. "Well too late now. We're all headed for the pokey as soon as this ship docks."

"Rudy said he could smooth things over with the captain, and I choose to believe him," Genna said. "But we need to make sure we have our stories straight between the four of us. Can we still get away with that lie? That we thought Simon was drunk when we put him in the towels? Can we all stick to it?"

"No," Amy said. "I can't. I'm ready to come clean." Her heart sank. Was she always going to be the weak link in the little clutch of friends? It wasn't about the lie itself. The world was crammed full of lies and liars, and no one seemed to mind very much.

Amy's reticence was about something else. If she tried to share her thoughts with her friends, she'd struggle. And yet, she needed to tell them. They were looking at her expectantly.

"Out with it, Sparks."

"Aren't y'all just a little embarrassed for the way we disrespected the dead? He may have been an obnoxious being. He may have already had one leg in the grave as Sheila said, but he deserved more than our blatant disregard. Our reasoning was rash and reckless and motivated by nothing more than our selfish desires."

Tears stung her eyes, but she was determined not to let that show. Biting her lip helped. "When we moved him, we committed a crime. We have to face that fact."

Rian shoved her hands into her cargo pockets. "If we aren't careful, we might dig ourselves further into a crime we *didn't* commit."

"I agree," Zelda said firmly. "And this is my fault. I didn't want it to ruin this cruise, and I've ruined it anyway. I'm the one who wanted to hide him."

Genna put her hands on her hips. "What's the matter with y'all? We're not going to take this lying down. Look, the captain had a dead body on board for two days and couldn't find it, so their investigative team can't be the brightest bulbs on the boat. You know they searched Simon's cabin. You know they questioned Elaine and the rest of that gang by now. If they had evidence, we would already be in the pokey, just as Zelda says!"

Rian nodded to the railing above them. "Too bad we didn't search Simon's cabin when we had the chance."

"I tried. I got caught."

"When did you play nosey maid?"

Amy told them about finding the watch and about her trip to the Moon Deck, glossing over most of her impromptu visit with Piero.

"Back to the question," Genna said. "If we maintain that we thought Simon was drunk and not dead, could they prove otherwise? What do you think, Rian?"

"There has to be a doctor on board who has examined the body by now. I'm guessing he has an idea of the time of death. You should ask Rudy about that."

"How does that help us?" Zelda wondered.

Rian pulled at a curl. "It doesn't help us. He was still warm when we found him. At least, warm enough. He hadn't been dead long."

Zelda turned to Rian, her perfectly arched eyebrows raised as far as they could go. "Are you sure he was dead? Maybe he just wasn't breathing."

"If you're not breathing, you're dead."

Zelda scrunched her nose.

"Our only alibi is each other," Rian continued. "I think we happened upon the scene of the crime just minutes after it happened, which means any post-mortem examination is not going to give much time lapse between the murder and us."

Zelda giggled. "Well, aren't you *Magnum, P.I.*"

Genna snorted. "More like *Barnaby Jones*."

"Old Jed Clampett reincarnated." Rian laughed. "The Clampetts were from the Ozark Mountains, too."

"We know!" Genna said. "Arkansas has been trying to dig out of that hillbilly hee-haw reputation ever since. We're never going to break that rap."

Zelda broke into song in a slow southern drawl. "*Gloom, despair, and agony on me.*" She had a beautiful voice even when she twanged it up.

They were still laughing when the crewman approached.

"I will be escorting you," he said solemnly. "You will follow."

They did as they were told. They knew why, and Amy envisioned the angry countenance of Captain Chavez in their near future.

"Here we go again," she said as they were ushered into a brightly lit room with no windows, one door in, and one door out. The door clicked shut behind them.

"I am *Oficial Iza*. I am the vessel security officer, lead investigator charged with crime aboard the *Darwinian*. You will answer his questions."

His questions? There was no one else in the room with them. They settled in chairs similar to the ones in the Beagle Lounge and waited.

"State and spell your name." His dark eyes landed on Amy first, his thick mustache moving slightly with his lips.

"Amy Sparks. A-M-Y. S-P-A-R-K-S."

He pressed the pen to paper. "*Ah, eme, i griega*. Correct?"

"Not Emmy. Amy. A-M-Y."

"*Si, i griega.*"

"No, my last name is Sparks."

"*¿Qué?*"

"Sparks. S-P-A-R-K-S."

"This is what I said." His tone was curt, his impatience already thin. "*Eh-seh . . .*"

Amy frowned. "Essay? No, just Amy. Amy Sparks."

He twirled the paper around so she could see he had written her name correctly. The crisp letters were from the same alphabet. How different they sounded in Spanish. She nodded and folded her hands in her lap.

"Genna Gregory." She gave him a full-on polished smile, spelling her name in Spanish. "*¿Comprende?*"

He nodded and turned to Zelda.

"Oh boy," Zelda said.

"*O, beh, o, i griega.* Correct? Oboy?"

"Jeez Louise." Amy covered her grin with her hand. Officer Iza looked up, his brow puckered with either confusion or contempt. He exhaled, the point of his pen heavy on the page, and tension mounting in his jaw. She suspected they were not the first to be interviewed today, and they would not be his last scrambled vowels and consonants.

Genna chuckled. "No, her name is not Oh Boy or Jeez Louise.

Zelda Carlisle. Rian O'Deis." She rattled off their names with these foreign letters.

"*Bueno.*" He nodded at Genna.

Thank goodness for Genna's so-called rusty foreign language skills and her talent for taking control.

"What is your profession?"

Genna cleared her throat. "We are business partners in the United States. Of America."

It was the shortest elevator pitch Amy ever heard Genna give, completely lacking the verbal trappings she was prone to pile on.

"What is your business in Ecuador?"

"We are celebrating a birthday and our lifelong dream to see the wonders of the Galápagos."

"What is your business with the deceased?"

"We don't have one."

"That is not accurate," he said, pouncing on the statement as if he were a dog with a ball. "You attended his table at dinner. You attended him afterward. We have the security footage. How do you explain this if you have no business with him?"

Amy felt Zelda tense in the chair beside her. They were at a crossroads. Genna, taking the lead whether they wanted her to or not, would either take them down the path of truth or the other road. God only knew where that would lead. Both could be a dangerous dead end. Rudy said he told the captain their story, and he was probably in a room similar to this one, interviewing other passengers. Would their stories match? Not if Genna went awry with her tale. Amy's chest ached, and she realized she was holding her breath.

"*Business* is the operative word, here," Genna scolded. "We had no *business* with him, just the unfortunate occasion to dine at his table and later to find him dead."

Dead. So there it was. Genna had decided to take the high road. The truthful road. But, somehow, it didn't feel any less dangerous than the other.

The man laced his fingers and leaned forward. "Ah, so you admit he was deceased when you carried him away."

"We didn't carry him far," Zelda blurted. "He was too heavy."

His dark eyes landed on Zelda. "Describe the scene as you encountered it."

Zelda glared at Amy, who nodded for moral support. Zelda began telling the story from her point of view. Her account was as accurate as Amy could remember, and she was surprised Genna did not interrupt, correct, or chime in. There was little left to chance. All could easily be confirmed with the video footage. Anything they said now that conflicted with the evidence would bear badly on their character. As if their character wasn't a bit thin already. They weren't gaining a reputation for being sweet little ladies from Arkansas.

Zelda inhaled and tucked her hair behind her ears.

"Did you remove anything from his person? From his pockets?"

"What was missing from his pockets?" Rian asked.

His eyes narrowed with suspicion. "Did I claim items were missing?"

"I assumed so. You wouldn't be asking that question otherwise."

"You took something from him, yes?"

"No, I did not."

"But there *is* something you choose to share?"

"Not particularly."

He eyed Rian with greater suspicion, if that were possible.

"So, was something missing?" Rian asked.

He nodded curtly. "Upon examination, he had in his pockets a cigar and a guillotine, and so we have concluded he went to the deck to smoke. Although this is not permitted on the vessel." He looked at Genna and back at Rian. "He would have little success igniting the cigar without a lighter. He would have little success reentering his cabin without the key. Did you see these objects?"

"It was too dark to see much," Rian said.

That much was true. It *was* dark. And things had happened so quickly. They were caught up in covering up a crime, busy rolling the bin into play, too fraught to notice too many details. But they had seen those items. Wouldn't that also be on the camera feed? They knew she and Rian picked Simon's pockets. They had to see them!

"Yes. We saw those objects," Amy said.

The man's eyebrows rose. "Explain, if you please."

"The cigar, the lighter, and the cigar cutter were in one of his bathrobe pockets," Amy said, her eyes downcast. "His cabin key and a note were in the other. We put them back in his pockets."

"A note? A piece of communication?"

Amy nodded.

"Do you remember its contents?"

"The note said to meet on S Deck. I guess that meant Sun Deck. It mentioned money."

"There is more?"

"I remember noticing the *Darwinian's* stationery. We have the same stationery in our cabin."

He nodded. "Continue."

"I remember thinking the note had been written by someone

whose native language wasn't English."

"The exact words? You will recall?"

"Not exactly. We were rattled."

"Not rattled enough to interfere with a crime scene, thereby committing a crime of your own."

"It's all my fault," Zelda muttered. "You can just blame this on me."

His brow rose again. "You shot the gentleman?"

"No, of course not," Genna said. "Don't be ridiculous."

"Ridiculous," he repeated slowly.

Amy had the feeling that *ridiculous* was exactly what he thought of them.

"What is your experience with the scuba?"

"The what?" Genna asked.

He laid an item on the table in front of them. "You have experience with this?"

"Is that a guitar pick?"

"A Superman guitar pick," Zelda added. "With the big 'S' on his cape."

The item resembled a large guitar pick about three inches long with three sharp corners, a piece of fishing line knotted at one end.

"Is it a prop from the costume party?" Genna asked. "I don't remember anyone dressed as Superman."

He shook his head and turned the object end over end in his fingers. "This is a line arrow. It is used to mark the direction a diver must follow to find his exit. It is an essential navigation tool for divers who explore caves."

"Caves?" Amy asked.

"Yes." He lowered his hand over the item, and the arrow illuminated in the darkness made by his palms. "As you see, the arrow glows in the dark. And you say you are not familiar with this item?"

"No," Amy answered, and the others shook their heads.

But the line arrow made sense. If whatever was anchored to the rock also needed to be found later, an item such as this would make the task easier.

"Where did it come from?" she asked.

"The arrow jammed the door of the closet. The one in which we discovered the deceased. This was a skillful maneuver. Once the arrow caught in the kickplate, the line was cut from the outside to deter detection."

"Smart."

He eyed Amy, brows furrowed. "Smart is not how you describe an evil endeavor. This man suffered even under the eyes of God. In death, he did not find mercy. We also will have none. We will find this evil-doer and we will have no mercy!"

What drama! She expected him to make the sign of the cross against his chest. He tapped the plastic marker on the table.

"Have you determined the actual time of his death?" Rian asked.

"I am the one asking for information!" He paused and then looked at Rian. "I am asking now your whereabouts at the time of death."

"We wouldn't know one until we knew the other."

He missed that trick. Where Genna pushed for information with gusty determination, Rian fished with patience.

Did Amy have a superpower? Tenacity? Loyalty, maybe. She didn't feel that brave. She didn't consider herself as cunning as Genna, but she did enjoy keeping track of the cues, clues, and tidbits. This riddle was still unsolved, with no proof of their innocence.

"Explain your whereabouts between eleven p.m. and three a.m."

"We were together," Zelda said. "We were together all evening."

"Of course you were." His grin made her stomach lurch. They had not been together all evening. Rian disappeared after dinner and returned to their cabin for only a few minutes before they found Simon. Rian never said where she was, and Amy had assumed Rian was playing poker with the crew, but they had no proof of that, either.

"Who else can account for your whereabouts during this time? What proof can you offer as to your position on board?"

Genna tapped her fingernails on the tabletop. "You can account for our whereabouts. You have us on video. You have the exact time we arrived on deck, and the exact time we moved him to the towel cart."

The grin surfaced again. "We do. We have this documented."

"Even the murder?" Zelda asked.

"We do."

Rian leaned back and steepled her fingers, her dark eyes narrowed against the bright light of the room. "But you don't know who pulled the trigger. That is not on tape for some reason. You didn't see who killed him."

"But we will! Make no mistake, I have not concluded this investigation. If you are hiding details, I will succeed in uncovering them. I will detain all of you here until we find the evidence we require."

"You can't detain us," Rian said. "We have rights."

"Not at sea," he said simply. "Not on this ship."

Amy's flesh prickled. They might be eating rodents in jail after all. She eyed the man seated in front of them, and then he looked at the door, as if to make his point, since the door remained firmly closed. How were they going to get out of this? How would they lift the veil of suspicion from their heads? They had no proof that they didn't kill Simon Monforte. They had no proof that someone else did.

None.

A knock sounded on the door, and the man rose. Cracking the door open, he spoke in hushed Spanish and then accepted something. Amy couldn't see beyond the door. She didn't recognize the voice or the words. The conversation ended with an impatience she recognized, a self-satisfied grin pulling at his mustache as he returned to the table.

"And so you removed the note, you say, read it, and replaced to his pocket. Is that correct?"

Amy nodded.

"Then you will tell me why this was found in your cabin. In the trash receptacle." He pulled a piece of paper from his lap and placed it on the table. Amy's eyes widened. It was the note, the same note they had pulled from Simon's pocket. *Darwinian* scrawled across the top in ornate script. The paper was folded in half when she first removed the note, read it, and returned it to Simon's pocket. Now, it appeared crumpled and then smoothed, as if ironed flat with the weight of a fisted hand.

He turned to Rian. "Your cabin, I am told." He pulled another piece of stationery from his lap and laid it alongside the other. It, too, appeared crumpled and smoothed, but with one big difference.

Only part of the message appeared on the second note as if whoever attempted the message aborted their effort and started anew.

"Holy, moly," Rian said.

"*Nach a Mool.*"

"Yes, we have the evidence." His mustache stretched into a foreboding smile. "You lured el señor Monforte to his death. You wrote this blackmail note to bring him to your rendezvous. It was you who killed him!" He turned his dark eyes to Rian. "You!"

CHAPTER TWENTY-FOUR

The door opened and two men entered, walked the few feet to the table, and stood on either side of Rian's chair.

"No!" Amy yelled, but a moment too late. Rian, already on her feet, was thrust through the open door.

Amy glared at the man sitting smugly across the desk.

"You're going to regret this," she seethed, surprised by her venom. "We had nothing to do with Simon Monforte's murder, and you are not going to prove we did. Something else is happening on this ship, something even more sinister than murder, and we're going to find out what that is!"

The man squared his shoulders and smoothed his mustache with his thumb and finger. "You are free to go." He motioned to the door with his chin and eyes. "For the time present."

They stumbled to their cabins in disbelief. Her stomach clenched with anger. She had not seen the punch to the gut coming. Sucker.

"Now what?" Zelda flung herself onto her bed with a heavy sigh.

Amy curled up at the end of the sofa. She felt like curling herself into a little ball, like an armadillo putting up her armor. But that wouldn't help Rian. They had to keep their heads on tight, their wits in place. Someone framed Rian for Simon's murder by planting those notes in the cabin trash. But who? Who would have access to her cabin? And who knew about the note? The killer, or killers—plural—that's who. And what would she and Genna and Zelda do about it?

"Why was that Iza guy so forthcoming with all those details? Why didn't Rudy mention the line arrow and the lock? Or the items missing from Simon's bathrobe pocket?"

Zelda propped herself up on her elbows. "Maybe Rudy doesn't trust us as much as Genna thinks he does."

"Oh, hogwash," Genna said. "There has to be another reason. We are as trustworthy as the preacher and choir on Sunday."

Double hogwash. They were as unreliable as any suspect.

"What if they are setting a trap to snag us," Zelda mused. "He could be giving us information so we will lead him to the buried treasure."

"What buried treasure?"

"The package in the water."

"You're right, Zelda. We know it wasn't a body drop. It was a drug drop. Or . . ."

"Or buried treasure."

Amy nodded. "Something valuable *and* illegal. That must be why Rudy thought we were in danger. He had suspicions, and he warned us about the captain's culpability. The Monfortes are involved in some way, too, I think. Whoever put him in the closet is in cahoots with the diver who hid the treasure in the rocks."

"Makes sense," Zelda said, "and they used the glow-in-the-dark thingies to mark the position."

"Along with the coordinates on the watch."

"What watch?"

"I told you about that. The diver's watch I found not far from where we found Simon. It was a sophisticated piece of gear. When I showed it to Rudy, he agreed it was an expensive diver's watch."

"What did you do with it?" Genna asked.

"I took it to lost and found."

"Could it have been Simon's?"

"I don't picture Simon swimming, do you?"

Genna shook her head.

"I don't picture Simon getting into a wetsuit, that's for sure," Zelda added.

Amy agreed. Simon didn't strike her as a swimmer even if he was dressed like Poseidon at the party. "The detective didn't mention a watch, and I don't remember seeing one on Simon's wrist. It could belong to whoever dragged him to the closet."

"He was really heavy," Zelda replied. "It took all four of us to lift him."

"There are four of them," Amy said. "Bill, Andrew, Sheila, and Elaine. One on each limb."

"Right," Zelda said, "so who pulled the trigger?"

"The one who hated Simon most," Genna answered.

"Which one was that?"

"That's what we need to find out."

CHAPTER TWENTY-FIVE

They had no idea where Rian was being detained, but they decided she was safe somewhere on this cushy ship and that nothing untoward would happen to her. Well, nothing more than what happened already. The only way Amy could help Rian was to figure out who pulled the trigger. Evidence. She needed to present evidence to the captain and had no plan on how to find any. An island excursion might free her mind enough to come up with something, and *that* idea struck her as Bartolomé rose from the sea beside them.

"Today we will finally land on the island of Bartolomé, one of the most popular of all the islands in the archipelagos," the naturalist guide explained. "Bartolomé has the most photographed scene in our evolutionary history—Pinnacle Rock."

Groups of ten and twelve were gathered throughout the deck, each with their itinerary for the day's excursion. As usual, they would explore in groups, staggering their time ashore, snorkeling, or scenic motoring.

Happy to find Tobias and Paul in their panga group again, Amy squeezed in beside them. They were such gentlemen, so full of life, so open to sharing what they knew about the archipelago history and species. She imagined their lives in Austria, sharing their enthusiasm for the world that lay at their doorsteps in the Alps.

Shoelaces tied, backpack stowed with plenty of water, and passengers balanced on the gray rubber sides, the panga motored off.

The naturalist continued. "Our first outing is to climb to the top of Bartolomé. The island rises one hundred and fourteen meters above sea level. That is three hundred seventy-four feet from the ocean. We will climb three hundred and *seventy-two* steps to reach the top. From the top on a clear day, you can view more than ten islands. If we are lucky, we may see whales. Climb at your own pace. We will not leave anyone behind!"

Zelda groaned behind her. "Three hundred and seventy-two steps? That's three hundred and seventy too many!"

She turned her attention to the guide, who said, "We have encountered many sea lions in our exploration so far. They welcome us to every island. We are still in the breeding season, however. I caution you against reaching to touch them, even if they are directly in your path. It is not only illegal but very tempting. Beware—sea lions bite!

"Yesterday someone asked if the Galápagos sea lions, or sea wolves, as we call them here in Ecuador, are the same as the California sea lions. The simple answer is no. While our sea lions also belong to the seal and walrus family, the Galápagos sea lion is a distinct species that migrated two million years ago."

Standing beside her, Tobias seemed so engrossed, a horn could have blasted behind him and he wouldn't jump.

"The females are called cows. Their offspring are called pups. A full-grown male is called a bull and can weigh as much as five hundred fifty pounds. That's about two hundred fifty kilos if you prefer metric measures. Not a sumo wrestler to tumble with on either scale." He gestured wide and laughed.

"You will recognize the bull by the bump on his forehead. It helps defend his harem against intruding suitors. We are the intruders."

He shared how Pinnacle Rock formed and expanded on the creatures that lived there. His narrative was perfectly timed to the trip from the ship to shore. The panga thrust onto the sand with a soft hiss as it hit the beach before the incoming waves helped push the raft farther on land. Amy scrambled out of the boat in what the crew called a dry landing, but it seemed nearly impossible to keep her shoes dry when landing anywhere on these uninhabited islands.

"Be sure to pick up the first rock you see," the guide said. "Choose a big one. I will not spoil your surprise."

The arid landscape *was* surprising. The island was a desert of black and orange and every hue of brown spreading out before them like a walk on the moon. Tall spires of volcanic cinder and spatter cones and tumbleweed-looking plants covered the landscape.

"Take a picture!" Zelda called, hefting the biggest rock she could grab. She lifted the rock over her head. "This rock is as light as a beach ball and about the same size!" Zelda struck a pose for the camera.

Tobias held a large rock in each hand. "The lava fills with gas and hardens before it falls to the ground," he explained. "This geological process makes these rocks so deceiving!"

The wooden staircase of the Summit Trail started with a large platform then inched its way toward the top step by step. "I'm not sure about this," Genna said. "I'm wheezing already."

"Climb as high as you want, but you'll miss a beautiful view if you don't climb to the top," Amy suggested.

"Take lots of pictures," Genna said.

"Yeah," Zelda agreed, "take lots of pictures."

Amy began the climb, leaving their friends to walk at their own pace, and wishing Rian could climb with her. Rian would be disappointed to miss this walk, the very pinnacle of the trip.

Strategically stopping along the way to let them catch their breath, the naturalist highlighted geological interests, native flora, and island beasts. Amy's heart beat so loudly in her ears that she could barely hear him. The steps yawned on and on. And then, finally, they were at the top.

The view was worth every ragged breath.

A 360-degree panorama surrounded them. A turquoise-and-azure-blue sea sparkled beneath them, and neighboring islands rose from the water in the distance as if they were imaginary giants sleeping in the sea. The sharp-shaped Pinnacle Rock loomed in the foreground below them, and the *Darwinian* rocked patiently off the coast. A steady wind kept Amy close to the rail at the landing.

The islands that lay before her had not always been a place for bucket list tourism or even a living laboratory for the likes of Charles Darwin. Often translated as the *enchanted islands*, they were more aptly translated as the *bewitched islands*, where thick mists rolled over the water and made the islands appear and disappear before your eyes.

In its early days of discovery, pirates and buccaneers patrolled the coast, raiding Spanish galleons for riches stolen from the Inca Empire. Pirates of that time took refuge in the craggy coasts and calderas, hiding in the coves, lying in wait for their next big haul. She imagined them in hiding, although now, there were no traces left of the pirates who had clung to these rocks. And yet, she could feel their presence.

She studied the horizon. A dark band clung to the water's edge—a frothy swirl of gray rolled toward them in the distance, like a bank of fog. She shivered when the wind brushed against the hair on her arms.

"Want a peek?" Tobias handed her his binoculars.

It took a minute to adjust her eyes to the view. The *Darwinian* appeared huge in the glass. She swept the deck and recognized the ship she had been calling home.

Something caught her attention. Bill and Andrew! They were on the tiny balcony outside what must be their cabin on the Gaia Deck. Bill pointed angrily to something in Andrew's hand. Andrew shifted slightly, and the glitter of jewelry winked in the sunlight. She trained the binoculars to his hands. Bling! Narco-bling. A big shiny piece of expensive. Bill reached out and swiped the necklace from Andrew and disappeared inside the cabin. Andrew leaned against the rail, his expression in the binoculars like a kid caught stealing from the local five and dime.

She moved the glasses upward and found two men standing on the top deck. The captain and Piero. She recognized them easily. Piero gestured wildly. The captain shook his head and Piero gestured again. She shifted the binoculars away from Piero, and there she found Rudy. He seemed to be watching the captain and Piero, too, then he pulled something from his pocket and glanced at it. Were Piero and the captain arguing about Rudy, or someone else? She swung the field glasses back to Piero, then back to Rudy. Rudy was gone.

A wake of frothy white caught her attention, and she panned the binoculars to find its source. A smaller boat approached the

Darwinian at a clip fast enough to draw a deep wake. *Policía Nacional.* The letters were painted on the side of the boat near the bow as it sliced through the water. The boat slowed, approached the hull of the yacht, and a crewman threw a line as it came alongside the cargo door near the waterline.

A man stepped from the boat, and he and another exchanged comments. Two men appeared from the dark cargo door carrying a gurney that held a black body bag. Simon! It must be the body being moved to another non-final resting place. Only after the bag was loaded, papers signed, and the boat moving away, did she move the lens.

Through the binoculars, she followed the path from the chaise where they found Simon dead to the towel bin and then to the closet not far from the Beagle Lounge. It wasn't far. Twenty, thirty feet at most. How long would it take to drag a body to the closet, if that was how it got there? Why not throw it overboard instead? She peered at the deck through the lens. Unless you threw it out several feet from the deck, it would likely land on another deck below, not in the water. With something as heavy as Simon, at chest level, it would be impossible unless you were Hercules. The only place to get a body in the water was from the diving platform at the stern, or the cargo bay.

She shivered again. The wind gusted up as the dark horizon boiled forward, clouds gathering in the distance. It was impossible to tell how far away the storm might be. And yet, a storm was brewing.

She lowered the glasses and turned to return them to Tobias, realizing then that she was the only one left on the platform high above the sea. The others were already descending to the beach. Even Tobias was halfway to the bottom of the stairs.

She hung the binoculars around her neck and began her descent. It was easier going down, taking less breath, but her knees creaked and grumbled with each steep step. She paused at a landing and raised the binoculars to her eyes. The passengers were already seated in the panga. They seemed so far away.

The *whack* on the back of her legs sent her sprawling. She flew forward, hands outreached to break her fall. She landed hard, then turned to look behind her. A bull faced her, his mouth wide and threatening, a row of sharp teeth poised as tiny weapons. The sea lion's heavy bulk covered the platform in a threatening stance, and the growl from his throat sounded too much like a tiger's to ignore. She screamed, and the growl grew louder. He lumbered toward her, his whiskers spread wide. She scooted away from the bull, jumped to her feet, and launched herself forward, taking the steps as fast as she dared. The growling fell away behind her.

Her chest ached. Her knees screamed. She ran, backpack flopping against her shoulders, binoculars bouncing against her chest. She jumped the final few steps, stumbled in the sand, and then, breathless, reached the beach. She didn't stop to catch her breath. She reached the panga and flung herself into the raft, flopping like a fish hauled in from a net. Tobias accepted the binoculars she held out to him, and she hoped they were not damaged in the fall.

Amy trembled beside Genna.

"What happened to you?"

She didn't answer. She didn't have enough breath in her lungs to answer. What happened? Bewitched islands happened. People who appeared and disappeared. Bodies. Boats. Strangers. Arguments. Seals bigger than Arkansas cows. Dark, threatening storms brewing on the horizon.

The whitecaps whipped around them as they motored back to the ship. All Amy could think about were her fingers in a death grip on the side of the raft that bounced in the waves, the puzzle coming together before her, and the pieces finally falling into place.

The danger Rudy warned them about was real. And this time Rian was in the trap.

CHAPTER TWENTY-SIX

The note on the door of the cabin requested her presence on the captain's bridge. She took a quick shower and changed, hoping the delay wouldn't add fire to the captain's fuel. If she could delay this meeting forever, she would.

She climbed the curved stairs the four of them had taken before. That morning seemed so many days ago when they had faced the captain with their lies. He knew what they did, and she dreaded the inevitable. She entered the bright room and stopped abruptly.

Piero stood next to the captain. Now shoulder to shoulder, their likeness was easy to see. They shared South American heritage, but there were also telltale signs of family DNA in their handsome looks. Their eyes were deep-set in the same way. Their stance was similar, too. And like a criminal before a judge, she stood before them, sweat beginning to form beneath her bra.

"Ms. Sparks, this is my cousin Piero Belaúnde. I believe you are familiar?"

She nodded and glared at Piero but didn't speak. Piero nodded and smiled, but not the engaging, draw-you-in smile that drew in her before.

"We continue to unravel the circumstance of passenger Simon Monforte, who, I regret, has met an unfortunate end. You are well aware."

She nodded.

"When we spoke last, I believe you and your friends implied Simon Monforte was intoxicated when you landed him in the towel cart. In truth, he was deceased at the time. A bullet wound to the head." He shook his head. "I am most curious to understand why this took place. Please, enlighten me."

His manner felt like steel—hard, smooth, and impossible to see through. He didn't seem angry, only perplexed. Was he asking why Simon was killed? Or why they put him in the cart?

Piero seemed to enjoy her discomfort. He didn't speak to her but glared as if she was a loony goon. She remembered the outfit when her friends sprang her from the hospital in Hot Springs. She was something loony to stare at that day, too.

Her heart sank. How many lies had they told? What was the last one? Liars didn't keep to the same story, as she knew firsthand. Her marriage with a pathological liar had taken her down a dark path that felt like crawling through a tunnel on your knees. She had crawled slowly. Painfully. Emotionally battered. Liars were skilled at faking the tells that gave them away. The best liars didn't even have to fake it. They believed their lies. And if you could believe your lie, you could make anybody else believe it, too. What did she believe?

"To begin," he said as her silence grew, "this note was found in your friend's cabin." Captain Chavez held out the piece of paper she was now all too familiar with. It was the page of stationary with the handwritten block letters of a short message in the upper half of the page. She knew it instantly. It was the note she had pulled from Simon Monforte's pocket. The one they blamed on Rian.

"This was found in the trash receptacle of your fellow traveler's cabin, la señora O'Deis. Found crumpled as if she had not been satisfied with the message she was writing to lure el señor Monforte to his death."

"It says, 'We must to meet en S Deck 23:00. You must pay, you get.'"

Amy nodded. She did not know what to say.

"La señora O'Deis convinced us this evidence was *planted* in her cabin to draw the suspicion of murder to her. She is quite persuasive, your friend. She exposed the two different hands of this letter. See?" He pointed to the letters. "With closer inspection, the letter *ehmeh*—M—is different in this one ..." He shook the letter. Piero handed him the other page. "Compared to this one. The time is scribed differently, as well. A slight difference, yes, but discernable."

He folded the letters and placed them in his jacket pocket. "Why was this put in her possession?"

"I, I can't say why." Who was trying to frame them for murder? Sweat pooled at the base of her bra. She felt humiliated by Piero's eyes. Contempt? Distrust? Something along those lines.

"Cannot? Or will not? This note is one of two possibilities. This is the note that lured el señor Monforte to his death. Or this is a message of extortion intended for someone else. Who would you blackmail?"

"No one!" The heat of panic filled her instantly. Her feet turned cold and heavy, while her cheeks burned hot. "I'm not blackmailing anyone! I don't know anything!"

"Ah, but you do." These were Piero's first words. His tone grabbed her heart and squeezed. "Either you committed the crime or you witnessed the crime. Which you then attempted to cover up so you would have time and opportunity to benefit."

His words cut her to the core. "No! Yes!"

Captain Chavez raked a finger through his hair. "Yes?"

"No, we didn't see it happen. Yes, we tried to cover it up. But not to benefit. Not for *money*!"

"Then for what reason?"

Words failed her. Someone was trying to frame them for the murder of Simon Monforte. Someone had targeted Rian, and now blame was spilling over onto her. Her heart raced.

"Piero! You have to believe me! This note was in Simon's pocket when we found him. I read it and put it back."

"This was not in the pocket when the deceased was recovered."

"Well, of course not! Someone is trying to frame us! Someone is deflecting the blame!"

"What is your explanation?"

"I, I don't have one."

"Then perhaps it is time for you and your friends to be detained until the close of the cruise, at which time a formal investigation can take place."

"No! Piero! Please! Someone is framing us. Can't you see that?"

"Then this will be for your own protection," Captain Chavez declared. "To keep you from further danger."

How had it come to this? They told Rudy what happened. Did he not share those details with the captain? Couldn't Piero see they merely happened upon a crime and had been foolish enough—no, stupid enough to think they could postpone the inevitable? And now what? Facts and fiction were tangled like fishing nets on the prow.

A third possibility struck her, too, and one she didn't want to let form in her mind. And yet, it was taking shape like a monster forming in the shadows. What if Piero and the captain were at the top of the drug-smuggling ring as Rudy had insinuated? What if they killed Simon to get him out of the way, like some pesky fly? What if Piero planted the evidence as bait? How could he?

Was she that bad at picking men?

Piero watched her closely. "We only ask you for the truth, Amy. Nothing less." His voice was quiet, softer than the captain's had been.

Hope sprang to her heart. He could have put his arm around her shoulders, such was the effect of his words. Her name sounded like a caress on his lips. She felt herself being pulled again to him in the moonlight, a body memory that landed like a butterfly, then flitted away. Where was the truth? How could she tell fact from fiction in this horrible game of murder?

"Zelda was so upset that a murder would ruin her birthday cruise that we acted without thought. What we did was wrong, very wrong, but yes, he was already dead. We checked his pockets. He had his cigar stuff, the note, the cabin key. We put everything back in his pocket. We saw no one and heard no one. And yet, we are sure someone watched us. Someone moved him from the towel cart when we returned to our cabins."

"You have suspicions?"

Amy nodded, looking from the captain to Piero and back again. Biting her lip didn't help. She was ready to unload it all. "We thought the wife killed him. Or the mistress. Or maybe the wife, the mistress, and the accountant. We didn't know about Andrew at the time. He is not who he says he is.

"I thought they anchored Simon to a rock at Chinese Hat

when we swam with the hammerhead sharks, but then he fell out of the closet instead, and I knew I had seen something other than a dead body underwater. Drugs. I saw drugs being anchored to a rock. Rudy was right about the smugglers. *Trust no one.* Not even at the top."

The captain's eyes narrowed. "Rudy? Who is this Rudy?"

Amy gulped. Had she blown his undercover cover? "He's just some guy who's been flirting with Genna."

"That is a lie," Piero declared. "I would call this bluff in a game of Perudo."

Amy dropped her eyes. Rudy must have more than one name. He would give one name to four loud women from Arkansas. He would give another to the ship manifest. It was impossible to determine who was investigating who. "He wears an eye patch," was all she thought to say. "Like a pirate."

The look Piero and Captain Chavez exchanged felt full of meaning. This subtle swap of information between the two, the give-and-take of those who were close, was telling. Although, as an outsider, she couldn't decipher the language. But something had changed. Something felt different. Her heart raced. What had she done? Single-handedly tipped Rudy's hand? If they were not aware of a drug sting before, they were now.

The captain signaled to the crewman at the console behind him, and a video feed began to roll forward. She gasped.

Simon, still very much alive, reached into his pocket and withdrew a folded wad of cash, talking to someone whose back was to the camera. Only part of a dark head showed on the film as if the person knew how to shield himself from the camera lens. In the next frame, Simon was holding a gun.

That's why he had gone to the Sun Deck. That was the meaning of the message. The purchase of a gun had been his goal. Not drugs.

Simon reclined in the chaise, a towel rolled up behind his head as a pillow, and she recognized the smug, satisfied expression as he studied the gun in his hands. He put the gun in his pocket and pulled a cigar from the other. He snipped the butt with the guillotine, lit the end, and enjoyed the last cigar he would ever smoke.

Piero spoke. "A crewman disclosed he brought the weapon on board at the request of Monforte. This note is of his doing. This original note. The other is a copy he does not claim. It is a forgery, written to deceive."

The captain nodded. "We will deal with our crewman accordingly when we arrive at the mainland, but he insists he left Monforte alive on the deck, and it would appear this is true. Monforte's family has no idea why he wanted a gun."

"But I do!" she blurted before thinking.

The captain raised a brow. "Proceed."

"Simon thought he was in danger, that he needed the gun for protection. I think his wife was going to kill him!"

"How do you know this?"

"Rudy overheard Simon talking about it. He told the Monfortes that. At dinner. The night I—the night we—" She let the thought hang incomplete.

Captain Chavez turned again to Piero. "We will talk with this Rudy. We will hear the full context of this conversation."

A motion caught her eye again. The video feed, still rolling slowly behind them, looked pixelated with a thin layer of illumination that showed a silhouette as it moved in front of Simon. The figure blocked the camera with a white blur, surrounded by the dark edges of the night. She saw a quick burst of light, and the white blur moved away.

She stared in horror. She had just witnessed Simon's murder. The burst of light was the muzzle flash splitting the darkness. Piero studied her, his gaze intent on her face. She wanted to hurl herself at him, wanted to feel his arms wrapped around her in a tight embrace. But that was nonsense. He was involved, wasn't he? He and his business that was of no concern to her. Glancing back at the screen behind him, the four of them were just arriving at Simon's side. Amy turned her head. She didn't want to see any more.

The floor swayed beneath her feet as the boat rolled in a wave, and she reached out to grab at anything to steady herself. Her hand brushed Piero's. The boat rocked again, and he put his hand under her elbow.

She studied the feed. The video showed the towel cart moving against the rail. Someone pulled the bin, then the bin disappeared from the video altogether. No wonder the captain believed their drunk-Simon story. They never saw him leave the cart. They never saw the bullet hole.

"Neither the gun nor the cabin key has been recovered," Piero said, his hand still on her arm. "From the state of Monforte's cabin, we assume it was searched before our knowledge of his death. The 'Do Not Disturb' sign proved effective in diverting our attention. The family determined certain items were missing from the cabin, including several pieces of jewelry purchased recently at auction in Ecuador. The briefcase was empty. We must presume the weapon was disposed overboard at the scene."

"That's Andrew!" Amy pointed to the screen on the video still rolling as Andrew appeared on camera. He stood at the deck rail, where the towel cart had once been, forearms leaning forward, apparently focused on the inky water in the black landscape of the sea. He raked a hand through his hair and then smoothed it over. The chaise in the foreground where Simon had lain was empty. The corner of the towel bin had shifted to the edge of the video frame as if someone knew how to keep it out of the camera's range.

Who would know how to do that? Crew members would. Someone who knew the layout of the cameras. Or someone who just got lucky.

"Andrew Forthright," the captain said flatly. "What is your concern about him?"

"Andrew said someone helped Simon to his cabin that night. He may be lying. He lied about who he was. I saw him and his father arguing when I was on Bartolomé. Andrew was holding a piece of jewelry."

"You saw this from Bartolomé?" Piero cocked his head, one eyebrow raised. He rubbed the back of his neck. "You have the eyes of a hawk in the sky!"

Amy glared at him. "I was using binoculars."

"Oh, I see."

"Oh, I did see." Her cheeks grew hot. "I saw quite a bit. Like the police boat that came alongside and took the body away." She glared at Piero now with as much mettle as she could call forward. "I saw the two of you arguing. Oh, yes, I did see."

"*El capitán*," a crewman called. He turned at the request. The bow of the *Darwinian* swayed again, like a finger pointing toward danger and the dark storm cloud ahead. He studied the instruments, and in Spanish ordered his crew. He turned back to Amy.

"We will assume that you have been honest and forthcoming. I believe the notes were planted to cast further dispersion on you and your friends. You have an enemy, Ms.

Sparks. Take care. Dismissed."

Before she approached the stairs, she turned back to speak to Piero as the bow of the *Darwinian* rose and fell in the giant swells of the darkening sea. But she didn't have anything to say. She turned and descended the stairs as the ship tossed in the waves, now more violently than only a few minutes ago. The storm she saw brewing from Bartolomé was now upon them.

Stumbling down the corridor like a ball in a penny arcade pinball machine, she flumped into the cabin and threw herself across the bed. She felt exhausted. Mentally, emotionally, physically. She had climbed seven hundred steps, give or take a few, and narrowly escaped a bull seal protecting his harem. The worst part was seeing Piero, seeing the distance now between them. He was still tender—his concern for her was real—but the wedge driven there was a dull maul in a tree stump. She couldn't retrieve it, couldn't revive the infatuation. Passion had dulled as quickly as it sparked.

The boat rolled in the waves, and her stomach roiled in her ribs. Lunch was out of the question. Dinner, too, probably. She wanted to shut her eyes and sleep, but her thoughts tugged at the threads of the mystery at hand. The ends that would make sense of it all seemed so tangible, completely within her grasp. If she could just find the right lead; if she could then yank and pull, she could unravel it. Yes, she could. She knew it.

She rolled over and stared at the ceiling. The cabin seemed dark even in midday as the storm overpowered the equatorial sun.

Where were her friends? They parted ways after returning from Bartolomé, and she assumed they detoured for refreshments, aka cocktails, while she returned to the cabin. Where were they now? And where was Rian?

234 · JANE ELZEY

Glad to be alone for a moment, without girlfriend chatter in her ears, she tried to think. The dread that enveloped her at the summit of Bartolomé grew, just as the storm mounted its full wrath from the sea.

Enchanted. Disenchanted. So closely entwined.

Piero was arguing passionately with the captain. But about what? Rudy, she guessed, or whatever name they knew him by. They might all be DEA agents undercover—Rudy, Piero, the captain—the whole lot of them! Or maybe Rudy was drawing too close to the center of the ring. With Piero at the top. What did Rudy pull from his pocket? And why did Andrew have jewels that belonged to Simon? Did he steal them when he stole the cabin key from Simon's pocket? Did he kill Simon and throw the gun overboard? In a moment of remorse, maybe he had tried to exorcise the evil deed by casting the gun to the water.

Murder didn't work that way. The guilty burned in their soul. She witnessed that in Hot Springs when Zack's killer was handcuffed and led away by the police. Yes, the guilty burn in their soul. Unless they are beyond ruthless.

Something didn't fit. What did Andrew have to gain by Simon's death? What did any of them have to gain? Simon was a dying man anyway. What was she missing?

Her head whirled and her stomach churned. The boat rocked violently in the waves, rain pelting the windows as if tapping out messages in Morse code. SOS. Danger. Capital D. Zelda, Genna, Rian, and herself on board with a killer and thieves and smugglers on the high seas. A deadly sea. And they were at the center of it, dancing around the danger like naïve little pixies from Neverland.

Amy lurched from her bunk. She needed to find them. Genna, Rian, and Zelda were somewhere on this boat in the storm. They could be in danger. They were all in danger.

She knocked on Genna's cabin next door. Flouncing down the corridor, she stumbled into the concierge center. He had not seen them since morning. She checked the library.

At mid-ship, she altered her course, landing in front of Bill Forthright's cabin, banging with her fists. Andrew opened the door abruptly, his eyes wide with surprise.

"What are you doing here?"

"I'm looking for my friends. Have you seen them?"

"No. Why are you looking for them here? Where are they?" His eyes narrowed as his body swayed in the door.

"If I knew I wouldn't be looking for them," she snapped, then regretted it. Careful. She might be standing toe to toe with Simon's killer. He might still have the gun. He might . . .

He stepped into the corridor beside her and the door swung closed. "I will help you look. We can split up. We'll cover more ground that way."

She eyed him warily. He seemed too eager to offer help.

"Hey!" the clerk called as he climbed from the stair below. He carried an arm full of life vests. "It is you! Señorita Pricey Watch!"

"What do you want?" she snapped.

Recoiling as if slapped, his chin jerked up. "*Hunh*," he said with a haughty tilt to his jaw. "I do not want anything, now. I did want to say the watch and owner have been reunited. I did want to say what a nice thing you did. But now, I *do not* want to say this." He squeezed behind her in the corridor, bumping her with the life vests. She rocked into Andrew.

"So sorry you will not enjoy that pricey watch as your own," he said in the sing-song tone of a kid on a playground.

Amy untangled herself from Andrew's grip. "What did you

steal from Simon?"

"What? Nothing!"

"I saw you on the balcony! You were holding a necklace. You stole it from Simon!"

He held up his hands, palms out. "Amy, you're off the rails. I stole nothing from Simon."

"Then where did you get that jewelry?"

"I won it in a poker game."

"A poker game?"

"My father doesn't believe me, either. I swear on my mother's grave." He crossed himself quickly. "I won it fair and square."

Amy took a step back and stared at Andrew. No Catholic would swear on his mother's grave with a lie. "Why does Bill not believe you?"

"Because he doesn't want to. Because he's embarrassed by my gambling. He's embarrassed by the son he never had time for. Honestly, I don't play beyond my means."

He sounded as if he were defending himself to someone other than her. Birds of a feather. What had Genna called them? Superstitious compadres. There was no slope more slippery than defending yourself to someone who wanted you to be guilty, whether you were or not.

"Why are you hiding who you are? Why did you lie about your name?"

Andrew leaned his head back against the cabin door, his hands braced in the doorjamb to steady himself against the rocking ship.

"Tell me!"

"Right now?"

"Now!"

His eyes widened. "I'll give you the CliffsNotes version then."

Amy nodded.

"My mother left my father when I was nine. She was not well. I am the last of five to come along. She took me and went to live with her father in Louisiana, but he would not allow her to get a divorce. He was a devout Catholic. Nor would he let her use the Forthright name in his home. Broderick is her maiden name, the name I'm accustomed to using. I don't think of myself as a Forthright. Never have. I didn't realize I had a living father until Mother was near death."

Amy's chest sagged. "Wow." This was not the explanation she expected.

"My grandfather despised Bill—my dad," he continued. "He told me stories that were not true. I grew up believing my father was a cruel man who had no time for his son."

He would not swear on his mother's grave and lie. And Amy needed his help.

"I believe you."

His smile ran deep. "That means so much to me. I like you, Amy, and I . . ."

She shoved him gently toward the stair. "Find my friends. You search the top decks. I'll search below."

He took off down the corridor.

Amy descended the stairs the lost and found clerk had come up. The Azure Deck had two doors aft and two doors forward that led to a deck at the stern and bow, respectively. She remembered seeing the short U-shaped decks on the wall diagram, and the two decks did not connect from the outside.

As she stepped onto the deck near the stern, she felt the squall in full swing. The unsheltered deck felt slippery under the pounding rain and wind that threatened to blow her off course. The lights from the porthole windows above shone like beacons on a buoy. She made her way carefully to the stairwell that led down one more flight, and something thumped inside the closet near her feet. Her heart thumped with it. Was someone locked inside? Another body?

She threw open the door before her fears led to panic. The boat rocked violently, and losing her balance, she was thrust headfirst inside. She screamed as the closet door slammed, drowning her in darkness. Something heavy rolled outside and jammed itself against the door.

Bracing herself against the wall, she kicked until her legs ached. A splinter of light seeped through the metal louvers in the door, the boat rolled again, and the sliver of light disappeared. Pounding with her fist, she screamed into the roar of the wind. The wind screamed back, howling through the cracks.

She willed herself to stay calm. She would wait until the storm passed or someone found her. She would scream and yell and kick at the door until they did, but for now, her voice was no match for the keening wind. With her back against the door, she waited in the dark as the boat rolled and pitched and groaned around her. Lulled by the dark captivity, she closed her eyes and listened.

The sound of metal scraped across the door. Scrambling to her belly to peer through the louvers, she saw that a heavy barrel had come loose from its mooring and rolled back against the closet. The boat rolled again, the barrel rolled with it. The door flew open and she tumbled to the rail. Rising to her feet, slipping on the wet wood, hands gripping at anything for stability, she stood and peered over the rail.

Wind and rain whipped her face and the churning water below. A panga rode alongside the yacht, the boatman holding tight to the tiller as he steered it close to the side of the ship. A dark hoodie covered his head, and from this angle, she couldn't see his face. From at least another deck below, someone tossed bags into the boat from the *Darwinian*.

It had to be a drug drop. Whether this was a scheduled rendezvous with bad weather timing or some frenzied effort to ditch the cargo, the drugs were moving on. Who was behind it? Piero and the captain?

Did it have to be Piero?

If she found her way to the cargo drop spot, she could come face to face with this smuggler and his maneuver. She would have her answer once for and all. She could also be a bystander in the way. Like Simon. Someone to toss to this churning sea. What chance did she have to survive that?

Where were Genna and Rian and Zelda? Her gut ached with fear. The bottom of the panga was filled with bags, billions of dollars of drugs on their way to a worldwide market. The motor revved, and the panga turned from the ship and sped away, bow bouncing dangerously in the waves. The dark blob disappeared into the veil of rain.

Someone moved toward her. A dark shape, no, two dark shapes, both covered in rain gear and life vests, climbed from the stairs below. She squinted as Paul and Tobias careened toward her in single file, their eyes focused on their feet and the slippery deck, their hoods pulled low over their eyes.

"Tobias!" she yelled as they stumbled forward. "What are you doing out here?"

"What are *you* doing out here?"

"I'm looking for my friends. I got stuck in that closet and . . ."

"You need to get below," Tobias growled, and she was taken aback by his tone. "You shouldn't be out here. Didn't you hear the alarm? Everyone should be in their cabins. This storm is too dangerous!"

"Have you seen Genna? Or Rian and Zelda? I can't find them!"

Paul looked panicked. "We have not seen anyone."

"Where are you going?"

"Going?" Paul's blue eyes were huge.

"Are you coming or going?"

"We are seeking shelter," Tobias said. "We're trying to get back to our cabin. We were turned around and found ourselves on the wrong deck." His blond bangs were dripping from where the hood of his rain slicker slid back on his head. "Come with us." He grabbed her arm and pushed her forward, gently but urgently upward.

Inside was a contrast of night and day. Dry, quiet, and well lighted, the corridor felt how rescue must be to a shipwrecked crew. Tobias pulled the hood from his head. His hands were shaking. Her hands trembled, too, her cuticles blue from the cold.

"I have to find them!" She left them standing there, dripping from the storm, and ran down the corridor to the forward deck and raced down the slippery stairs. No one there. Back inside, she moved mid-ship and stopped. How did Rian get to the deck below? She flung open one door and then another to find a set of stairs, finally. Tumbling against the steel as the boat rolled, she descended until she landed on solid ground.

So this was the infamous Jacob Marley Deck. A dark hole of a place where the captain kept his crew. It smelled faintly of men kept in close quarters, and something else.

Popcorn?

The sound that reached her ears was as sweet as honey in hot tea, as warm and as welcome. Zelda! Somewhere near Zelda giggled, then she heard Genna's unmistakable snort. Following the sound like a coonhound on the hunt, she turned a corner, and there they were.

"Amy!" Zelda called. "Where have you been, girl?"

Dripping wet, she stood at the edge of the table where they were seated—Rian, Genna, and Zelda—playing Perudo with the Perudo twins, a large man in a white T-shirt and toque, and Andrew. She had forgotten about Andrew.

"What a great game." Genna grinned as Amy joined them. "Liar's dice. Right up my alley. Why didn't you tell us this was such a fun game?"

"I'm winning!" Zelda said. "Imagine that! I am a better liar than Genna!"

"¡Dudo!" Genna shouted and they all howled. Paco and Juan, too.

"Pisco sours." Rian lifted her half-full glass. "I'm celebrating getting sprung from boat jail."

They were not on their first round. Not by a long shot.

Amy squeezed the water from her hair. "What are you doing down here?"

"First of all, Big Al here is the chef delighting our palates this week. He makes a mean drink, too." Genna lifted her glass in salute. "Paco and Juan are looking for a wife. No, they are looking for two wives. Wait. They are each looking for one wife. They both want American girls. Tall, blonde, and lanky. Right?"

The twins nodded. They were not on their first pisco sour, either.

"And we're going to help. They're coming to Arkansas, and

we're going to help them find wives. We're going to find them some southern roots stock."

Zelda smiled. "We are! We are going to make them a match, yenta!"

"All this while I've been running around the ship in the rain looking for you! And you"—Amy turned to Andrew—"you were supposed to help me find them."

Andrew shrugged. "I did."

Amy burst into tears and then burst into laughter. One segued right into the other. "Of all the places to go on this ship, this is where you landed?"

"This is the safest port in the storm," Rian replied. "The closer to the water, the smoother the ride. We came down here to—"

"Oh, I know why you came to the Jacob Marley Deck."

"We came down here because we were told to . . ." Rian started, emphasizing each word slowly as if trying not to slur, "by Piero via Paco and Juan because he was concerned for our safety. And no one could find you."

"We brought them here to play Perudo," Paco said. At least, she thought it was Paco. So hard to tell them apart.

"Piero has been looking for you," the other one said.

¡Dudo! she wanted to say. She wedged herself beside Zelda and reached for the plate of leftovers on the table. "He didn't succeed!"

"Ah, but I have," Piero said, coming up behind her.

She nearly jumped out of her soggy wet clothes.

CHAPTER TWENTY-SEVEN

The squall passed, and they returned to their cabins, took turns showering, then changed for dinner. Amy was starving. Breakfast seemed a long time in the past, her lunch got skipped altogether, and the leftover nibbles in the galley were but a few delicious bites. An amuse-bouche that made her want more.

Piero escorted her back to the cabin as if hesitant to leave her side. His behavior didn't make sense. With one hand he drew her in. With the other, he pushed her away. The push-me-pull-you felt confusing. He claimed he searched for her in the storm, and yet, he let her leave the bridge unescorted. He knew the storm was coming. He could have escorted her back to her cabin then, but he didn't. Was he looking for her later because he wanted to protect her, or because he wanted to keep her in his sights for another reason?

Now, peering out the window of the cabin, the sky shifted from storm-dark to night-dark, with no colorful sunset in between, and only a few stars shone from behind the leftover clouds. She heard about storms that brewed quick and nasty in the Pacific, and now she could say she lived through one. It could have been worse. Ancient sailors braved the elements with sextants and common sense, but today's ships were sophisticated with predictive technology that helped avoid the worst of storms. Modern ships had the technology to steer away from hurricanes and gales. And yet, the *Darwinian* seemed unprepared. It seemed as if the captain steered directly into the storm with little regard for his passengers. That didn't make sense. Piero claimed Captain Chavez was a dedicated shipman. If his passengers were still in the raft boats on Bartolomé when the storm swept in, there would have been more than one passenger whose cruise ended badly. Captain Chavez didn't strike her as irresponsible. Was he too distracted by other things going on—like dead bodies and drug deals—to orient his ship away from the storm?

They were informed over the intercom system that dinner would be delayed because of the storm. She suspected Chef Al's pisco sours partly were to blame. Piero invited them to join Captain Chavez for cocktails in the Beagle Lounge while the crew readied the dining room for dinner. She didn't hide her disappointment. More interested in food than booze, there was nothing to do but wait.

The four of them took a table and ordered their drinks. They had avoided the Beagle Lounge since Zelda's birthday bash, and she sensed Zelda's trepidation now. She hoped there were no more screams. No more dead bodies. No more surprises of any kind.

And yet, the mystery had not been solved.

As the room filled with guests, it dawned on her that Simon's killer was among them. Maybe Captain Chavez gathered them here for this reason. Maybe he planned to pull a Spanish version of Hercule Poirot—in the lounge, with the killer, and the gun. The thought made her laugh out loud. Zelda tossed her a questioning look.

The notion that the killer was in this room, acting as casually as the rest, felt as unsettling as any other aspect of this day. As a whole, the day proved treacherous. Her legs were stiff from the climb. Bruises from her fall on the Summit Trail and her somersault into the closet felt sore to the touch. Tenderly rubbing a spot on her leg, she surveyed the room for the killer.

Tobias and Paul looked refreshed from their wet walk on the deck. Their tailored linen suits fit them too well to be off the rack. Were professors in other countries wealthy? Were professors in any country rich? She didn't know. Their relationship was still an unknown to her. They could be a couple—of course, it didn't matter—but she could tell they were close. She saw the ease in how they conversed, the way friends grew and mellowed. She felt the same about Zelda and Rian and Genna. The four of them rode out enough stormy weather to appreciate that they were a sisterhood that stuck, too.

Her one conversation with Paul was about gardening—something she knew nothing about—but his eyes lit up when he talked about his gardens in the foothills of the Alps. Tobias seemed cool toward her, and she hoped he wasn't angry about the scratches on the side of his binoculars. The lenses were not scratched, and he could still use them to spy on the bees in Paul's tulips and poison herbs. Were the two Austrians Simon's killers? Or drug smugglers? She hoped not. She was fond of them. She didn't want to think of them as cold-blooded killers. But if someone died from poisoning . . . She smiled. That seemed more fitting.

Still, what were they doing below deck in the storm? They came up the stairs just after the panga motored away. Was that coincidence? Had they gotten lost as Tobias claimed? If she asked, she'd need a wily way to approach the topic. She turned

to speak to Tobias, but his attention was elsewhere and she let it
go.

The naturalists, in dress khakis with matching blue
monographed polo shirts, milled about the room with ease,
peppering conversations about the grand adventures still ahead.
They downplayed the storm, glossing over the dangers with
funny anecdotes and memories. "And there we were, eye to eye
with the land iguana who would not let us pass . . ." she
overheard then let her attention drift.

Paco and Juan struck up a conversation with Elaine and
Sheila. She'd give anything to be a fly on a glass at that table,
but she couldn't think of a ruse that would give her a reason to
join in. Eavesdropping was Genna's vice, anyway. If Paco and
Juan were looking for American brides, they had a boatful to
choose from. Sheila might be a contender, even if she was older.
So much cougar activity on this boat. The thought made her
laugh out loud again, and Zelda nudged her with an elbow.

"What's with you, Sparks?"

"I'm just silly with hunger."

Paco and Juan would do okay in America. Not top-of-the-
line handsome, and they didn't have a solid handle on the
conversation for the mating male. They did smile a lot. Maybe
their English was less fluent than she realized. Or maybe they
were shy.

Elaine seemed more relaxed than on previous evenings.
Sheila looked radiant. How could it be possible that these two
women came from the same gene pool? She saw nothing in their
looks or manner to give that secret away. Elaine was almost as
tall as Sheila, but willowy thin. Her hair was dishwater blonde,
falling flat against her head in long straight locks. Her features
were nice enough, and she would be pretty if she wanted to be.

Maybe she gave that up when she married Simon.

What was the attraction to Simon? Convenience? Love? Money?

Stop. Marriage was a personal matter. A none-of-your-business matter. Even if Genna did overhear Simon complain about Elaine coming along. She could have jumped to conclusions. Genna and her overarching jealousy.

It made sense that sisters would bunk together while Simon bunked alone. Loads of couples had separate bedrooms at home. She thought of the black bag loading onto the police boat, seen from her perch at the summit of Bartolomé. Without binoculars, she never would have spotted the police boat or the body bag. The captain probably orchestrated the transport when the passengers were away and wouldn't see the police boat approach.

Maybe Elaine made the same wish as Zelda. Maybe she wished her husband gone, too. What woman didn't want her husband dead at some low point in the marriage?

Elaine was a free woman now, too.

Another husband who *was*.

Sheila laughed at Paco. Or Juan. She claimed to resemble her father, and if that was true, it was clear why the mother fell head over heels. He would be tall and suave with a sturdy frame to carry his physique. He would have auburn hair and green eyes. She felt odd sizing Sheila up in this way, as if she were a man in disguise. Victor, Victoria. Sheila, Sheldon. Amy stifled a giggle so Zelda wouldn't complain. Zelda didn't appreciate being left out of a joke, even when she didn't understand the punch line.

Andrew and Bill seemed chummy in club chairs across the room. Secretly, she hoped they would find the common ground they were looking for. Bonds between father and son were different than daughters and their dads. She imagined the relationship between father and son to be a complex one, maybe even competitive. Social pressures often made deep feelings difficult for men who lived in a world of fix and mend, catch and release.

Andrew was an anomaly. A teacher in a religious school with more rules than books. A science teacher. On top of the dogma of his Catholic beliefs, he would be required to teach creation and leave evolution out of it. That would be a hard stretch of faith for a scientist. How did he reconcile his religion with science? She suspected he didn't. Maybe he used gambling as a way to buck a dogma that lost its appeal a long time ago, now nothing more than a habit. So much of religion felt like a habit.

Bill seemed like a trustworthy person, someone you would give your money to and expect the best. Of course, earning trust was the first part of any con man's game. Zelda knew all about that. Until the tiger showed its stripes, you didn't realize the stripes were there. Simon trusted Bill enough to leave him in charge of his company, preparing for an approaching end. Simon could not have grasped how near, but he had to assume it was close. All the more puzzling. What was the point of killing a man when he was dying anyway? But then, why were people motivated to murder at all?

Elaine and Sheila, Bill and Andrew—why would they kill Simon, even if he was a boastful brat of a husband or an overbearing employer? There was tension between Bill and Simon. Even in the brief time at dinner, she saw Simon as someone who made himself bigger by knocking others down. Those kinds of people were everywhere, and she doubted they loved themselves any better than others did. It was a cycle that was hard to break, so most people didn't.

She looked up. Rudy entered the room, and an air of confidence followed him in. Genna stalked his every move, a lustful look in her eyes. He winked at Genna and detoured to the bar.

"Evening, ladies," Rudy said with a grin, drink in hand. He pulled a chair beside Genna and sat down.

Genna gathered all her charm. She was enamored of this Rudy Granger aka unknown. Maybe the unknown was the appeal. Probably the way he wanted it, too, being an undercover kind of guy, although forthcoming about his affairs on the boat. Killers and drug dealers and lots of bling. This business felt out of her comfort zone, even if the four of them did bend the rules a little. Maybe a lot.

Was Simon's murder related to the captain and Piero as Rudy's top-down comment suggested? She tried to keep Rudy's secret, but they were now warned. And the bags in the panga were gone. Maybe they *were* involved. Maybe they *were* covering their tracks. Maybe that's why the security cameras were avoided.

There were so many angles to keep straight. One fact remained. Simon had a gun smuggled on board for protection, and that gun was used to kill him. Plenty of irony there.

From her perch at the top of Bartolomé, she witnessed several things. Now, with what she saw on the video feed at the bridge, pieces were swirling around in her head like an old-time kaleidoscope. The same way snippets tracked through her dreams. Patterns and pictures swirled into shapes, sometimes with sounds. Maybe the pirate in her snippet was Rudy, not because he was Simon's killer, but because he was undercover— because he would help uncover the culprit. She pictured him with a gun pointed at someone, some drug crook he was chasing down. That seemed more likely.

Appearances were deceiving.

While she was certain at first that Andrew ransacked Simon's cabin and briefcase, stole the jewelry, and faced the wrath of Bill in the aftermath, he managed to convince her otherwise. Fury and disappointment fueled the argument witnessed through the binoculars between Bill and Andrew. He had motive and opportunity. He could dispose of the gun and pocket the cabin key. Steal the jewels. Add all that to the evidence on the security video of Andrew at the rail. But then, their cameo on video was equally as damning. She and her best friends didn't shoot Simon. Why think Andrew did?

While Andrew volunteered to help her find her friends, she found him down in the galley playing Perudo. The thought hit her hard. How long had Andrew been at the table with them? She told him to search the top decks, but he went below instead. She recalled his surprise when he opened his cabin door. Had he been expecting someone else? Was he tossing the bags into the panga? Was there time enough to drop the bags in the boat and find her friends in the galley?

Timing was everything.

He could be lying about Elaine and the others as part of his alibi. Or maybe they all were there to help. Could Sheila have passed for a man in the dark? Had she disguised herself in case the cameras caught her with a dead Simon? Sheila, who knew where Simon was. And when.

The comment from the clerk came to mind. She dismissed the interruption at the time, but she found the watch between the cart and the closet. To snap a spring bar from the lugs would take considerable effort. A big tug. A heavy tug. The same effort it took to carry a dead body. And if the diver who dragged the drug bag to Chinese Hat also dragged Simon to the closet and jammed the door, that diver and watch were now reunited. Killer and watch. She nearly inhaled the melting ice cubes in her drink.

Captain Chavez entered the lounge in his starched white uniform looking impressively important. He appeared comfortable, as if being cocktail entertainment suited him. His head was sleek, with every hair in place. Where he seemed severe before, now his face was bright, his smile warm as he made his way through the lounge and its guests.

Piero entered the Beagle Lounge a few minutes later as if it were choreographed to allow the captain's grand entrance. So much pomp and circumstance in this culture. Piero scanned the room, eyes searching for hers, she hoped. The butterflies swooped in. Piero's eyes moved from her to Rudy and back to hers with a question in his look. She nodded.

Rudy turned slightly in his chair toward Genna and turned on the charm. What a sexy scoundrel. "How was your excursion to Bartolomé?" he asked Genna. Amy strained to hear. Nosey parker. All she wanted was to ignore Piero.

"What a romantic place." Genna pressed her hand to his arm. "If I were to describe the surface of the moon, I would describe Bartolomé. Except for the watery dry landing. I have yet to jump from panga to shore without getting wet." Rudy laughed. She intended for him to, sneaky Genna. "Why didn't you go ashore?"

"I had things to take care of on board."

Genna nodded. "Amy climbed to the top, but Zelda and I petered out around step number twenty-nine or so. We enjoyed the sea lions. They are an inquisitively entertaining bunch."

Rudy nodded and drank his beer, casually scanning the room. Today he wore a white linen shirt, with the cuffs rolled up to his elbows. Her eyes fell to the chest of his shirt. Two buttons were missing. Dark hair curled through the gap.

"I'll loan you my sewing kit," she said, motioning to his shirt. "I even have an extra button if you need one."

Rudy laughed. "All these rich foods and wine. I'll wear a bigger size by the time I get home."

"Where is home?" Genna asked.

"Home is wherever I unpack my bags. Not that I have as many as you ladies do. I travel light. My lifestyle doesn't keep me in one place very long."

Genna touched his arm. "That makes me sad. Home is such an essential place. Home is where you keep your friends and your wine cellar, and all the pretty baubles collected over the years. I don't think I would elect to live a gypsy life. I have too many possessions. Do you keep an apartment? Or a house?"

"I have a condo. And a boat where I can live aboard when needed. I used to have a dive boat in the Keys. I sold that for a mortgage two wives ago."

"Oh." Genna's jaw tensed. "Wives."

"Ex-wives, I should say. All very past tense. All very much ancient history I don't plan to repeat."

"I hear that."

Amy startled when Bill touched her shoulder. "May I visit with you briefly? I need some fresh air. Will you join me?"

She nodded and glanced at Piero. He was watching her. Good. Served him right for his attitude on the bridge and for deserting her in the storm.

Bill led her to the rail on the deck overlooking the water. The evening descended on the ocean, with the proverbial calm after the storm. She drew a deep breath of crisp, salty air. The *Darwinian* was back to a gentle rock beneath them.

"I am not sure how to approach this subject without being impolite, so I hope you will bear with me. There is a matter about your friend, Rudy, I feel I must share."

He had her attention. "What is it?"

"It may be nothing, nothing at all, but when we were in Guayaquil at the auction, I saw a man identical to Genna's handsome suitor."

Amy stood a step toward him. "Really?"

"I may be mistaken. But there is something in this man's demeanor that makes me think I am not."

"Why would he be at the auction?"

"For the same reasons we were, I assume. To bid on the narco-assets being auctioned. Usually, the bids are sealed, but this particular auction did not allow for that. This is the reason we made the trip in person. There were several boats we were interested in. That's neither here nor there, but there was a small fleet of fishing boats on the block. This Rudy or his doppelganger bid that fleet. I saw him speak to Simon. My employer. My previous employer. The one murdered a few nights ago."

Amy nodded. How well she knew.

"Their conversation was heatedly animated. They were too far away for me to hear what they were saying, but I witnessed their manner. I am convinced Simon and this Rudy behaved as if they knew each other. Knew each other *before* the auction. And well.

"Simon has been dealing in the boat trade for a long time. He started his business in Florida many decades ago and has since conducted business all over the country. I am certain their paths have crossed, which is not out of the question, and not so much of a concern except . . ." Bill paused briefly. "Except I was struck by his demeanor. I know Simon Monforte very well. He was not only angry. He was afraid. I would say he was terrified. And that is a difficult thing to achieve when it comes to Simon Monforte."

"Terrified? Of what? Of Rudy?"

"I could be wrong," Bill continued. "I may be very wrong. But this man did not wear an eye patch. He wore sunglasses, but I saw no eye patch. Of course, he could . . ."

"Are you saying the patch is a disguise?"

"My question, as well. When I mentioned he seemed familiar, he rebuffed my comment. He would have seen me at the auction. There were not that many of us in attendance. I did not believe him when he said I was mistaken. I believe he knew Simon, and Simon was not happy to see him."

"Wow." Where did that piece fit? Was the undercover cover a pirate patch? How odd. If you wanted to blend in, why choose a disguise that made you stand out?

"There were several things mentioned at dinner that caused me consternation as well."

Amy nodded, urging him on.

"Aside from his comment about my son and my relationship—which he seemed too familiar with—he implied Andrew used my position with the Monforte Company to pay his gambling debts. I assure you, nothing of the sort is true. This comment was carefully worded, but I had the distinct feeling he tried to drive a wedge between me and Andrew. I don't know why, but I couldn't shake the feeling.

"When he mentioned power of attorney, my suspicions grew. That's not an unusual document by any means, but Simon had a copy in his briefcase. Which is now missing. I have a copy, of course, as does Sheila." He paused, and Amy detected affection in his words.

"It didn't sit well with me or with Sheila when he intimated at dinner that she could pass for a man in the dark. She didn't appreciate the implication that she was the person helping Simon to his cabin—as Andrew witnessed—and lying about it."

Amy realized she was holding her breath and blew it out with a noisy sigh. Sheila disguised as a man had crossed her mind, too, and now she felt guilty.

"This is relevant because the captain suspects Simon did not return to his cabin that night. He was put in a towel cart for some reason and then moved to the closet where he was found. As you know. Such a terrible thing. Simon was no saint, not by anyone's imagination, but he deserved better than that."

Amy opened her mouth. If she was going to confess that she and her friends put Simon in the towel bin and why, now would be the moment. She pressed her lips into silence. What good would come of that?

"As I mentioned earlier, Andrew enjoys his poker. Gambling is not a pastime I approve of, but we are working our way through a new relationship, and I do not want to be critical. I have only begun to appreciate the man he has become."

Amy nodded. "Andrew shared the circumstance with me." She placed a warm hand on Bill's arm.

"Yes, circumstance. That's one way to put it."

"Why did you keep that information from Simon? Why didn't you tell him Andrew is your son?"

Bill sighed again. "In hindsight, I was foolish. Cowardly. Certainly not the face of strength to show a son you didn't raise. Simon was not an understanding person. He was a shrewd businessman with a keen eye for opportunity. He never had children of his own, and he would not understand my position. Simon would never appreciate why I remained married to a woman who left with my youngest and cut all ties. He would not sympathize or accept, or give me any peace about it. He was . . . well he had good qualities, but Simon believed he was always right and better than anyone else."

The two grew quiet. The wet chill of the storm clung to the ship, now glistening under the lights. The cabins and common areas were lighted and glowing, and music flowed softly from the intercoms on deck.

"About this man," Bill continued. "This morning, Andrew showed me a piece of jewelry he won in a poker game. I recognized it immediately. The bracelet was one of the narco-assets we purchased on this trip. If I am not mistaken, the assets were in Simon's possession. Probably in his briefcase. When Andrew showed it to me, I became furious with him, certain that he had taken it. But he managed to convince me that he did not. And the reason I believed him is that he claims he won it from this man, this Rudy."

"How does Rudy have a piece of jewelry from Simon's briefcase?"

Bill nodded. "My question as well. Did Simon give it to him for some reason? Was it a payoff of some kind? Did they have a more current arrangement I knew nothing about?"

"Bill, do you think Simon was involved in drugs as well as narco-assets?"

"No! I can't imagine that!"

She moved closer. "You can't tell anyone this. Rudy is an undercover DEA agent. He's been following drug-smuggling activity in the Galápagos, and he's tracked it to the *Darwinian*.

Could Simon have been part of that?"

Bill took a step back and smoothed his hair with his fingers. She recognized Andrew in the DNA and the same mannerism she had seen on the video at the rail. She turned to look over her shoulder.

Piero stood behind her.

CHAPTER TWENTY-EIGHT

She tugged her arm from his grasp. "Piero, you're hurting me."

He loosened his grip. "I don't want to hurt you," he whispered, "but we must hurry." He pulled her up the stairs toward the Moon Deck, all but dragging her.

"Where are we going?"

"*Shh.*"

His eyes were shining in the darkness, but his face stayed in the shadow. Although the deck itself was lighted, they climbed a set of stairs she had not noticed before. Runner lights on the rungs illuminated their feet, but above her, she saw dark sky and stars. This must be the stairway the staff used, how the waiters appeared and disappeared like magic the night she and Piero dined under the stars. Was that only last night? It seemed eons ago.

Was she in danger, or being rescued? There were so many things that seemed to appear and disappear on this deadly sea. Enchanted. Disenchanted. The islands were so aptly named. She let herself be pulled upward, her mind racing. When they reached the last step, he pulled her into the shadows next to a wall.

"What is it?" Her breath felt ragged in her throat.

"Where were you in the storm this afternoon?" His breath, hot on her face, smelled of cinnamon and anise.

"I went out on deck to find my friends, but then I lost my balance and fell into a closet. Something blocked the door, and I couldn't get out. But then it opened and I rolled to the deck rail."

"I thought I saw you."

"You saw me?" Her voice rose. "From where?"

"*Shh*," he warned again. "You saw the panga in the water below?"

Amy nodded.

"Did you see who was commanding the boat?"

"No. It was raining too hard, and the boatman wore a hoodie covering his head. I was above him and he never looked up."

"Did you see anyone else?"

"Paul and Tobias. They were coming up the stairs."

"Did you see what was in the boat?"

Amy hesitated. She waited for him to fill the silence. She wanted more answers. She needed more. She wanted answers now before it was too late. "Piero, are you and the captain involved in smuggling drugs?"

He flashed his teeth. Were they not hushed, he would have thrown back his head and laughed his loud, contagious laugh.

"No," he whispered in her ear. "This is what you thought of me?"

"When I asked about your business on board . . . and you said it was none of my concern . . ."

"Ah, I understand now. You thought my business was smuggling. You thought we were using the beautiful *Darwinian* to smuggle drugs for the kingpins who have no soul."

"Then what *is* your business here?" She knew she was in knee-deep. He would give her what she wanted, or she would go down trying.

He sighed against her. Again she smelled cinnamon and anise. "You were not that far adrift with your thinking. The *Darwinian* is involved in this smuggling operation, but Miguel and I are not. My passage is to uncover the ring. We are certain at least one member of our crew is engaged. This is the third passage I have made to uncover this operation. We have been waiting with keen observation."

"You let the boat leave with the bags?"

"Of course. It didn't travel far. The boat rendezvous was planned for the other side of Santiago, an old cave pirates used when they ruled these seas. The *policía* were waiting. Even if he tried to avoid them, between the storm and the depleted gas tank, he would not go far. We held our position here to allow the storm to serve this purpose."

"You know who these smugglers are?"

"Absolutely."

"Are you going to tell me who?"

"Absolutely not."

It was her turn to smile. "Then what are you doing? Why are we here?"

"Because I wanted to do this . . ." He leaned forward and pressed his lips to hers. His body leaned forward, too, and she felt the lovely weight of his chest.

The moment lingered, but not long enough.

"I have a dangerous job to undertake." His eyes searched hers. "I did not want to let any more time pass between us. I did not want any regrets to follow me home. If I do not see you again, I will rest knowing we have shared this moment."

He leaned in again, lips parting as if to speak, then, reaching for her lips instead, he parted them as well.

CHAPTER TWENTY-NINE

Amy was breathless when she returned to the lounge. Piero slipped up the stairs that led to the bridge, and she went down the same steep stairs he nearly dragged her up. Adrenaline pumped through her veins—from a stolen kiss and a high danger cocktail. Piero told her to return to the Beagle Lounge and remain there. She was to find Paco and Juan and stay as close to them as possible. All of them. Wherever Paco and Juan were, she and her friends needed to stay near. The captain stood inside the door, his arms resting comfortably behind his back. He nodded as he stepped to let her pass. No one would leave the lounge through this door without his permission.

At the other exit directly across the lounge, a man in a white uniform stood his ground there. He was the same crewman who escorted them to the captain's interrogation days before. She looked for Paco and Juan, and one of them nodded, glanced at the captain and then returned his attention to the game in front of him.

Bodyguards. That's who they were. Young, strong, muscular, and probably well-synced mentally, the twins were Piero's traveling bouncers. That made sense now. That's why her friends were escorted to the galley during the storm. There had been more than choppy water and gale winds in the works during that time. A drug sting was in full swing, and Piero intended to keep her friends safe. This was as sound a cover as any—these two guys playing Perudo with Rian and Zelda, who were giggling like schoolgirls well into their cups.

Amy felt the tension in the room. The storm had passed, dinner was delayed, and the lounge felt crowded with anticipation, although empty now of most of the passengers who had gathered there earlier. The music in the background played a decibel or two under the chatter. The Monforte clan, Bill and Andrew included, were in club chairs in the corner, in what seemed to be a deep conversation. Bill caught her eye, a frown of concern on his brow. She smiled, hoping to assuage his fears, and he nodded as if he understood.

Genna swiveled on a barstool at the far end of the bar, the wall sconce light beneath the porthole window illuminating her with a regal yellow glow. Paul and Tobias were at the bar, both looking into the LCD screen at the photos captured over the past few days. They exchanged hellos as she passed them on her way to greet Genna. The room felt electrified with energy and expectation. Maybe it was her expectation that made her shoulders tense.

"Why are you pacing the floor?" she heard Genna ask as she reached the other side of the room. "Have a seat. Let's have another cocktail." Genna patted the stool beside her, eyes focused on Rudy. "Hey, Amy, where have you been?"

He spun around, nearly colliding with her. Rudy's face clouded.

"I'm doing my job," he snapped at Genna's earlier question. "We have an op unfolding. The last thing we need is Uncle Sam's Canoe Club showing up to serve their famous soup sandwich."

He glared at the uniformed man at the door closest to them, but neither made a sign of acknowledgment. Maybe the guard was part of their uncover team, too. Rudy swept the room again, his surveillance quick, an agent on edge. Genna felt it, too, and a frown formed at the corners of her mouth. Rudy's sexy, half-amused grin had thinned into a taut line. Whatever was about to happen, he was ready.

"We need another player at the Perudo table," Amy said brightly, hoping to draw Genna's attention away from the man in front of her. "You are elected. Rudy's busy, anyway. You can catch up with him later. Okay?"

Genna's eyes narrowed and Amy's stomach knotted. They were on opposites sides of the room now, and Genna might give her a hard time if she tried to lure her away. Genna might blast her with the Gregory ire, but Amy needed to get them both closer to the twins as Piero had instructed.

"You should go." His tone was terse. Genna pursed her lips, not used to being slighted. Without another word, she slid off the barstool and glided across the room.

"I hear you need rescuing from my wild and crazy friends." Genna perched onto the chair beside Rian. "Deal me in. Or roll me in. Or whatever it is we do to get this game going."

Amy breathed a sigh of relief. That was easier than she thought.

"Where did you get off to?" Zelda's annoyance showed on her cold-shoulder Michael Kors sleeve. The shirt had buckles and chains as if she were part of the ship's machinery. She had to admit it was a great look on Zelda.

"You left with Bill and disappeared. He said some man whisked you away. What man whisked you away?"

"Piero."

"Mr. Perudo is back in your life? After all the tears you spilled over him?"

Amy reached for a basket of pretzels on the table. "We had a score to settle."

"And?" Zelda pushed.

"We've settled. We had a breakdown in communication the other night. That's all. A misunderstanding."

"Misunderstandings are so easy to have and so hard to get over," Zelda said.

Amy knew all about them. When she had driven off in Zack's Hummer, she never once considered the fuel behind her anger was misconstrued delusion. *Her* delusion. At the time, she was one hundred percent certain a lot of plotting and planning had gone on without her. All behind her back. At least the first part of the journey in the backwoods of Arkansas was spite for being left out, even if it was being left out of murder. Her misunderstanding drove her smack-dab into danger like a blind bat behind the wheel. It turned out okay in the end, but that had been a big, hard hole to fall into, and equally hard to climb back out of.

She turned her attention to the game.

The dice rattled in the cups, which slammed to the table, and the bidding began. They would play Perudo on Genna's deck when they returned home. Nothing would ever take the place of dominoes in this little quartet of fun, but Perudo could carve its own niche. She would glue some dice to the Tiddlywinks Trophy, somewhere alongside the dominoes and the bling.

The Tiddlywinks Trophy started as a bowling trophy she'd picked up in a thrift store for a couple of bucks. A coat of gold spray paint, a few fake jewels, and a line of cheap dominoes hot glued to the base, and she had created a hefty little prize that came with bragging rights for the year. She meant it to be a joke, but the trophy became a coveted reward. The person with the most wins at the close of domino season was regaled the winner, and it had been in her possession for a while.

Zelda took to Perudo as a penguin takes to water. She would love nothing more than for Zelda to score the trophy and bragging rights for their first-ever Liar's Dice Championship. It was possible. Anything was possible when she was with her friends.

The dice rolled, the cups slammed, the laughter got louder. Zelda was in her element, with the disasters of the last few days seeming to fade from her mind.

A commotion at the door caught her attention, and the captain greeted two men at the door. He pointed to the Monfortes, and the men walked purposely toward their table.

"What's going on?" Genna whispered. "Are they being arrested?"

She strained to hear the Monfortes, but the words were a mumble from where she sat. The Monfortes rose and followed in single file between the two men without making further comment. There were no handcuffs involved, and Amy wondered if they were being escorted to dinner. Her stomach grumbled.

Bill nodded at Amy, his brow wrinkled with concern as he passed her table and went out the door. A moment later, Paul and Tobias were led by another pair of uniformed crewmen. The twins followed the two blond gentlemen with their eyes as they exited through the door.

"Are they being arrested?" Amy asked. "The Monfortes and Paul and Tobias, too?"

"We are making the lounge safe for our passengers," one of the twins answered.

"Piero said his plan could be dangerous. Are we the plan? Are you cornering us in the lounge before you arrest us, too?"

The other twin grinned and shook his head. "You American women adore the drama, yes? Please, you are safe with us." His gaze moved over her shoulder, and she caught a nearly indiscernible nod. She fought the urge to run. Was this part of Piero's plan? Were cabins being searched for evidence? Or more dead bodies? Where were the rest of the passengers on the *Darwinian*? In the dining room feasting on steak? And why weren't *they*? Amy felt the heat rise in her cheeks. Her legs were rubber. The captain slipped through the door, and another guard took his place. Rudy smoothed his hair, and his shirt pulled where the buttons were missing. He turned his head and his earring winked in the light. He pulled a watch from his pocket, checked the time, then glanced at the guard at the door.

"I have to take a break," Amy said. "I'm headed for the head."

"I'll join you," Rian said.

She could feel the eyes on her back. Rudy's. The guards' at the door. The twins'. The bartender's, who was probably not even a bartender at all. She thought of Piero's weight against her, and she squared her shoulders for the last few steps to the bathroom door at the back of the lounge.

"Rian, have you ever seen a DEA badge before now?" They were seated in their respective stalls.

"No, can't say I have." Rian's voice sounded hollow from the stall walls.

"Would it be easy to get a fake one?"

"I have no idea."

"You can buy a tin star at the costume shop."

"What are you driving at? I can tell something is percolating in that puzzle-brain of yours."

"Do you remember when Rudy picked us up at the mud farm? When he introduced himself as a DEA agent. How did he know we put Simon in the towel bin?"

"He saw the video, I guess."

"Yeah, I guess. Except he knew Simon Monforte was dead when we put him in the towel bin. Remember?"

"Sort of."

"He knew that before the captain knew. He said as much when he picked us up in the limo. How did he know?"

"Lucky guess."

"And how did he know the gun was a twenty-two?"

"I knew it was a twenty-two."

"But you were there. You saw the bullet hole so you knew. And when I asked why we didn't hear a gunshot, Rudy was ready with an answer."

"Yeah, I remember that. Something about a subsonic bullet. Something about sounding like a deck chair getting knocked over."

"And he knew it was Simon's gun. He asked us how Simon smuggled the gun on board. He didn't ask about the killer's gun; he asked about Simon's gun. Why is that?"

"Because he's the one who smuggled it on board?"

"Nope. That was a crew member. That's what the note was about. The one stashed in your cabin to frame you."

The stalls were silent for a moment.

"And why is it that when Rudy said he was helping with the investigation, he wanted details from the time we found Simon on the chaise. Not before he was shot—after. Remember?"

"Sort of."

"How did he know Simon was on the lounge chair when we found him?"

"The captain told him."

"Except he didn't. Rudy never talked to the captain about us or anything else."

"How do you know?"

"Because neither the captain nor Piero knew who Rudy is. I mean, they know he is a passenger, but he is not part of their investigative team."

"He's undercover. He's not going to tell them who he is."

"And yet he told us. Why would he do that?"

Amy could almost hear Rian's mental wheels turning in the silence of her stall. "So we would trust him," she said finally. "So we would give him the information he needed to mess with the investigation."

"Bingo. Bill Forthright told me Rudy was at the auction in Guayaquil. That he and Simon exchanged words. Heated words. Bill believes Rudy and Simon shared history. They saw each other at the narco-auction and Simon was terrified."

"Bill said that?"

"He also said Rudy wasn't wearing an eye patch. He was wearing sunglasses. No patch."

"Son of a gun," Rian said.

"I think Rudy let Andrew win the poker game so he could give him that piece of jewelry. It was a narco-asset from Simon's briefcase. He wanted Andrew to have it so his father would think he stole it. Rudy wanted Bill to think Andrew killed Simon."

"Did Andrew kill Simon?"

"I thought so at first. But somebody planted those notes in

your cabin trash so we would either get blamed for Simon's murder or for blackmailing who did. Double barrel whammy. You were targeted, Rian. You were targeted because you're smart. Because you were figuring things out."

"Interesting." She could picture Rian steepling her fingers.

"Did you notice Rudy had a button missing on his shirt today? Two buttons."

"No, I didn't catch that, either."

"Well, I found a button. A white shirt button."

"Why is that important?"

"It was on the stair near the closet Simon was stuck in. He put something in his pocket. Rudy, I mean. He was the first one in the closet. He made sure of that. He bent down and picked up something, but I didn't see it, and it didn't trigger anything at the time. But it could have been another button. It could have been a glow-in-the-dark line arrow. It could have been a ring. Or an earring.

"Rudy told Genna he used to have a dive boat in the Florida Keys. That was a diver's watch I found. A spring bar was missing. You can't wear a watch with one spring bar."

"You mentioned it before."

"Did you notice Rudy has a tan line where a watch would be?"

"No, I didn't notice."

"I did. He pulled a watch out of his pocket. Just now. And I saw him do the same thing through the binoculars from Bartolomé, too. It just now clicked. The last piece of the puzzle. I was missing the most obvious clue. I don't think Rudolph Granger, DEA, is who he says he is. I think he's an imposter. He pretended to get close to Genna just so he could get information about what we knew! He's not into Genna. He's into drugs and murder, and God only knows what else!"

"I heard that."

"Genna?"

"Yep."

"Uh-oh."

Cigarette smoke poured over the top of the stall.

"Are you smoking in the bathroom?"

Amy heard Genna exhale. "My best friends have turned rogue and rival," she said between clenched teeth. "I heard you. You're just jealous because he's hot and he's mine!"

Amy opened the stall door to face Genna leaning against the sink, her blue eyes hard, cold fire.

"I can't trust you with a man around! I should have guessed you'd wiggle your way into my romance just because yours fizzled on the vine!" Genna shouted, and the walls echoed her rage.

Amy wanted to throw her hands over her ears, but she forced herself to stand her ground in front of Genna. Her knees turned to jelly, and her gut burned icy-hot.

Rian opened her stall door. "What are you talking about, Genna?"

"Amy's been after Rudy since that stupid little snippet about the pirate and his gun!" Genna shouted. "You and your visions. You wouldn't know a psychic premonition if it walked up and slapped you in the face!"

Genna took a step forward. Amy took a step back.

"You will do anything to make your magic malarkey come true. It was a costume party! There were half a dozen pirates in the room. Including Rian! Why don't you say she's the imposter? Why don't you blame her for ruining your little fiasco of a party? I'll tell you why. Because you were looking for the pirate of your dreams. And he only had eyes for me! Buttons and watches. What a crock! You think you're such a hot tamale detective! Real detectives don't need fatuous dreams. They have facts! They have proof! Not half-brained ideas!"

A trail of smoke swirled from Genna's fingers, which were pointed at Amy, her eyes blazing through the plume.

Tears streamed down Amy's cheeks in huge, hot blobs. They stung her eyes almost as much as Genna's words stung her heart. It was one thing to say such horrible things out loud, even screaming them in a bathroom that made the words echo. But to say them meant she thought them. This was how Genna felt about her. All that sisterhood and friendship loyalty was the real bunk. The true malarkey. The biggest lie in the room. She was Merriweather Hopkins in Genna's eyes. Every woman was a Merriweather out to steal her man.

Genna's lips curled and her eyes narrowed. "You wouldn't be on this cruise if not for Zelda's generosity! You couldn't afford to stow away with the luggage! You're not good enough for him and you're jealous!" she shrieked.

"That's not true, Genna." Rian's voice was as full of reproach as her eyes. "You don't mean any of it. You're just hurt and angry."

"I'm not angry!" she screamed. "I'm disgusted!"

A sob caught in Amy's throat. How could this be happening? She would do anything for her friends. Anything. She put her life in harm's way when they were suspects in Zack's murder. She was the one willing to risk everything to uncover the truth. She was the one who bailed Rian out of trouble with a Mexican border guard, driving four days to bring her home. It was she who kept them calm when a tornado trapped them underground, three damp days that forced them to survive as allies or perish. These were the events where their friendship took root, sprang into this unlikely yet inscrutable devotion, the bloom *and* soil of a sisterhood that seemed almost sacred. They knew her secrets. She knew theirs.

All of that was reduced to this? All of it now falling through the crack of jealous contempt?

No. She would not accept this.

"Please. Listen to me. Rudy is dangerous. He's the one behind the drug operation. He's the one who killed Simon. And I think I know why."

A deep voice answered, "Do you, now?"

"Rudy?" Genna asked. "Is that you?"

"The walls are thin, ladies."

Amy swallowed hard. They could not see Rudy, but it was his voice coming through the wall from the men's bathroom on the other side.

"Guess who I have with me?" The silky-smooth voice that had lured their trust was gone, and in its place was the rugged, jagged baritone of a hungry bear. "Someone you care about. Unless you feel the same way Genna feels about you."

"Zelda?"

"It's me," Zelda moaned. "He grabbed me on the way to the bathroom. He's got a gun."

"A real gun, not a pathetic little twenty-two piece of junk. Stupid old man. But it did the trick. Solid. Right between the eyes." Rudy laughed, and she heard the heartless mirth behind it.

Amy found her courage. "You let her go!"

"That's not going to happen."

"What did Simon ever do to you?"

Rudy laughed again, and it was like listening to a crazed

monster. "We had an old score to settle, me and Simon. He and my old man ran dope down in the Keys back in the eighties. They had fast boats and faster connections. I was just a kid. A kid diving for lobster to sell to the tourists. After all these years, I couldn't believe I found him down here at some two-bit auction, still hustling boats for a buck."

His voice dropped another octave, now vibrating with rage. "He double-crossed my old man, ratted him out, sent him to jail. Left me with a pile of poker debt and a drug cartel thinking I knew something I didn't. An eye for an eye. He owed me that. With interest."

Genna dropped the cigarette on the floor and ground the butt with her shoe. Her eyes were rimmed with tears. Her long arms hung limply at her sides, the bright-painted nails curled into her palms.

"What a great distraction to confuse the captain," Rudy continued. Amy could hear Zelda whimpering. "He was busy trying to find a drunk dead passenger, and I was moving cargo through his high-dollar ship. And you, you ladies were the cherry on top! Dropping a dead body in a towel cart. I thought I was going to lose it. I've never seen anything so funny in my miserable fucking life."

Genna inhaled sharply. Amy reached out to take her hand. Genna tensed, but she let Amy's warm fingers wrap around hers.

"Here's how this is going to happen. We're all going to walk out of the lounge and down the stairs to the panga waiting on the port side. We're going to walk fast and pretend nobody's pointing a gun at your best friend's head. No heroic stuff. You hear me?"

An eerie silence filled the room that now seemed dull and

dark and dank. No one spent enough time in a public restroom to take note of the dirty walls or the mop shreds stuck in the corners, or the streaky haze left behind on the mirror. Genna's back was reflected there, the silver ponytail trailing down a blue cotton shirt dress, with its pressed color and tailored belt at her waist. The wrong dress for the wrong party. She stood stiffly, looking out of place. The best clothes, the best brands, the best of everything. That was Genna's motto. And yet, what she wanted most, she couldn't buy. Amy recognized the longing. She looked at herself in the mirror, too. At the messy curls, the sunburned nose, the tear tracks, and the shame of imperfection that never went away.

"Genna?" Rudy shouted. "Are you still there?"

She nodded but didn't speak.

"It wasn't all a scam." The silk was back. "I liked spending time with you. We could have had a lot of fun."

"You're not a DEA agent!" Amy spat, surprised by the power of her voice. "Or you're a crooked one if you are! You're not tracking down drug smugglers . . . *you are* the smuggler. You're the one I saw in the water. You're the one I saw in my dream! You're the killer pirate!"

She heard the snarl in his voice even through the wall. "If you want off this boat alive, you'll do what I say."

"How are we going to get out of here?" Amy whispered to Rian. "How are we going to get Zelda away from Rudy?"

Amy screamed when the ship horn blew. The two short blasts felt like an electric shock to her already frazzled nerves. The blasts were followed by a gunshot.

Amy screamed again.

CHAPTER THIRTY

It happened so quickly, Amy didn't realize she was standing next to Piero, Paco, and Juan until Piero touched her shoulder.

"Are you okay?" Piero held her at arm's length.

She nodded, her eyes full of tears. The look in Zelda's eyes told her everything. She stood next to Amy, too. Her arm, linked with Amy's, trembled.

Rudy was in handcuffs and being led away.

"What happened? I remember hearing the horn and a gunshot and then . . . I think I blacked out."

Zelda's voice came in raspy breaths. "The ship horn blasted. The police stormed through the door and then the gun went off. I was so scared! I had my eyes shut!"

"Paco and Juan saw him grab your friend and pull her into the bathroom," Piero explained. "We conjectured that if he was going to make a move to escape the boat, he would use a hostage to pave his way. We would not let that happen. When we heard his confession, we had to move in fast."

"You heard him? You heard all that through the wall, too?"

Piero threw back his head and laughed. "As with your eyes of the hawk, yes?"

"What?"

"You saw the ship from Bartolomé with a pair of high-powered binoculars. We heard it through the captain's intercom."

"Intercom!" Rian shouted. "In a bathroom? Video, too?"

"Remind me never to pee in public again," Zelda said.

Piero smiled. "We only use this system when necessity requires. The video feeds stop at the exterior door. We were able to hear la señora Gregory, and we knew you were in crisis."

Genna sat solemnly on a club chair, her long legs crossed at the knee, one Etienne Aigner ballet flat on the floor and the other swinging from her toes. Her face was clouded, and a pang of sadness touched Amy's heart. Genna needed to be left to her private thoughts and demons. And that made her feel even more disconnected. Would the rift be healed? Or was their friendship over?

Amy turned her back to Genna. She didn't want her to hear. "Is Rudy a DEA agent?"

"His status is still being determined, but he will face these capital charges regardless. We knew we were looking for someone privy to cartel and shipping information that the typical tourist doesn't have, but it was your comment about us being at the top of the drug operation that put us on his trail. That's the oldest trick in the book. Point a finger at the person pointing at you. The unfortunate circumstance with the deceased was a snag to our thinking. But when el señor Forthright came to the captain with a complaint that this Rudy had information he could only have obtained from Simon's cabin—papers in a briefcase—we began to study his activities on board more closely. When you mentioned the necklace, and el señor Forthright's understanding of where this asset came from . . . well, they were the icing to the cake."

Amy smiled. Close enough.

"You will be valuable evidence in a court of law. You will give a statement?"

Amy nodded. Maybe she would have to come back to Ecuador to testify. Maybe she would have to pop over to Peru to visit Piero Belaúnde at one of his family attractions.

"I may admit to you," he said with a wry smile, "when you visited the Moon Deck shortly after the body was discovered, and I found you standing outside his cabin door, I wondered did you have the key from his bathrobe. I suspected you and your friends were liable for more than placing el señor Monforte into the towel bin."

Piero *tsk-tsked* with his tongue. "This was not a wise decision. If la señora Monforte chose to press charges, the hands of Captain Chavez would be tied to the anchor that does not float."

Amy laughed. "That's not a safe place—hands tied to an anchor." She thought of Captain Chavez preening as he made his rounds in the Beagle Lounge. She assumed he would be Hercule Poirot with a Spanish accent as he called out the killer, with the gun, in the lounge. Actually, it was the killer, with the gun, on the deck *outside* the lounge. But the killer *had been* in the room. The killer was the pirate. And her snippet had come true. Again.

Piero stood close enough that she felt his heat. She felt the solid, uncompromising weight of his nature. His confidence, like Genna's, was bred into him. Unlike Genna, his nature came from a lifetime of tradition and responsibility, honor, and faith. He was a refined man. An honorable man. And he smelled like starched shirts, windswept dreams, and the musk unique to men. She inhaled him and smiled.

"You suspected him, too," he said, unwittingly spinning her

from her thoughts. "Tell me how you knew."

She wouldn't tell him about the snippet. She wouldn't take the chance. Disapproval. Crazy. Those were not going to be his final thoughts of her. That's not how she wanted him to remember her. The loony American with strange customs and devilish dreams. Would she have suspected Rudy if she hadn't seen the pirate in her dreams? She reached for the charm at her neck and felt the warmth wash over her. Some questions had no answer.

"*¿Qué?*" he asked. She sighed, smiled, and laid her head on his shoulder.

"Was this part of your plan?"

"Yes and no. Nothing ever goes exactly as planned, does it?"

"No, it does not," Amy said. She knew that to be true.

CHAPTER THIRTY-ONE

"Genna didn't mean it," Zelda said. "She was angry, and the green-eyed monster of jealousy took over."

She knew, but she couldn't pull the stingers out. The barbs were in deep.

"I know how you feel about your snippets. I believe in you."

¡Dudo! she wanted to say. Instead, she looped her arm in Zelda's. "I am categorically, undeniably starving. Let's go eat."

"Let's eat and drink and be merry," Zelda agreed. Together they left the Beagle Lounge, and Amy knew it would be for the very last time.

Paul and Tobias were still in the dining room when the two of them entered. There were several tables still in the throes of dinner and conversation, although most of the passengers had eaten their fill and moved on. The Monfortes were not present, and she was glad. She would feel awkward sitting with them. She would feel awkward sitting elsewhere. The little group table had begun to feel like family, a family estranged by their guilty thoughts and wounds. Sitting with Sheila and Elaine, Bill and Andrew would feel like they were at a family reunion where secrets and gossip had been shared, and no one trusted no one, and no one knew what to say. The biggest topic—Simon—

would be taboo. She didn't want to talk about any of it.

Tobias rose from the table and pulled out chairs for her and Zelda. "Welcome. We are delighted to have you join us."

The plate in front of them was empty except for the knife and fork folded neatly in the center, European style. "You've already eaten!"

"We will dine again. The sea bass is exquisite."

"Sea bass. Again," Paul muttered.

"Paul is not a fish person. And there is no mutton on the menu."

"Thank God for small favors," Zelda said.

The waiter brought their first course and a fresh basket of crispy bread, and Amy dug in with fervor. It had been a long, long day. Her spoon soon rang on the bottom of the bowl, and she fought the urge to suck the corn cob slice in her Ecuadorian chowder. She ate another piece of bread instead. Brushing the crumbs from her lap, she turned to Tobias.

"What did you put in your bag that day on Fernandina? Were you smuggling lizard eggs?"

Tobias arched his brow. "Me? Smuggle a wild animal? An endangered species?"

"I saw you. You can't deny it."

Tobias grinned. He reached into his backpack slung on the back of his chair and pulled out a small dark object. He flicked a switch, and hissing, spitting, snorting sounds ensued.

"What is that?"

"The marine iguanas on the rock at Fernandina."

The sound went on for a while, then she heard the grunt of a pig in the mud.

"What is that?"

"The flightless cormorant. This is the only sound the

Galápagos cormorant makes. She is not quite the sound of a *Sus scrofa*, but it is close. Do you agree?"

She nodded, not knowing what a *Sus scrofa* was, but the sounds shifted from grunts to the twitter of birds, to the bark of seals and sea lions. She was thrilled to recognize the animals of the islands from their sounds. Hearing them now, she recalled their journey through the Galápagos. She had learned about the flora and fauna of each island, the history, even how the most seemingly innocent circumstances caused widespread carnage.

"And this," Tobias said, turning the device toward her, a devious smile on his face, "is the sound of two female *Homo sapiens* slipping in the mud."

Zelda laughed. They were squealing and laughing as they slipped and sloshed, trying to get their footing enough to rise out of the mud. They exchanged glances.

"Is this blackmail?" Zelda asked.

"Blackmail did not occur to me," Tobias admitted, his grin still in place. "What a brilliant idea. I could raise money for our cause. Who has more money? You or Zelda."

"Zelda, by a boatload."

"Hmm," Zelda said, wiping the corners of her mouth with the cloth napkin. "How much is it worth? Five ninety-nine?"

"In euros? That's not going to make me rich!"

Tobias flipped the switch, and the adventure in mud subsided. Amy was sorry she thought Tobias was involved in something more sinister. She regretted thinking he might be the smuggler behind the scenes. "What are these recordings for?"

"I am building a database of wildlife in their natural habitat. Both photos and sounds. This is part of my work at university. With the recorder, I can place the machine close enough to capture true sounds without human interference. Humans are noisy."

Amy nodded. She didn't realize how noisy until she experienced the silence of the uninhabited islands and the hum of the sea underwater. She wanted more of all of it, but there was only one day left of their journey. Zelda's big five-oh was joyously celebrated, even if it included an unexpected detour. They crossed the equator, explored islands where no humans lived, dived with penguins—and the hammerheads—and dined under the stars. They caught a killer, too.

Amy raked the last of the rice and raisins onto her fork. Her eyes felt weighted with stones, gritty from tears and trauma. "If I don't get to bed right this minute, I'm going to have to crash here."

"I'm with you," Zelda agreed, and the two of them bid the gentlemen good night.

She linked her arm around Zelda's and thought of Piglet and Pooh. They were braver, stronger, smarter. And loved.

CHAPTER THIRTY-TWO

Amy was still exhausted when the morning light filtered into the cabin. She slept a dreamless sleep, free of strife and struggle. She didn't even hear Zelda snore.

The day's agenda was a brief exploration of Floreana and Española, with a short cruise in between the two islands. She opted to forego both somewhere between nap one and nap three. Even turning over in bed had taken too much energy. She learned, from the daily agenda slipped under the door, that Floreana was a dark basalt island. She would miss the flamingos that hunted in the lagoon. She would miss the famous post office barrel more than two hundred years old, a Galápagos version of the message in the bottle. People still stuffed the barrel with letters for home.

Española was the most southerly island in the Galápagos Archipelago. It was one of the oldest islands, too, and because of its dry climate and lack of vegetation, Española was dying. Tourists were drawn to its sandy bays where albatross and blue-footed boobies and the one and only Galápagos mockingbird called home. Tobias would be in his element, tracking the wildlife with his camera and sound device. She would listen to his recordings and look at his photos, she decided as she slipped back into sleep.

Hours later, gathered on the Moon Deck, the four friends stood at the rail near the bow as the ship cruised steadily toward the setting sun. The sky darkened behind them and glowed red ahead, with the glistening sea spanning out in every direction.

"Behold!" a voice echoed over the intercom as if a deity were speaking. "Behold, the famous Galápagos dolphins!"

Slender gray shapes leaped from the water in graceful arcs off the port side. Hundreds of dolphins leaped and splashed in an oceanic ballet, like a performance on stage. Amy moved closer to the bow. Dolphins vaulted on both sides of the ship, all racing alongside the *Darwinian* on her reach for the last bit of sun. Glistening gray bodies dived again and again from the slate-gray waves, speckled red with the setting sun.

Then, almost as quickly as they appeared, the leaping ceased and the water calmed. The sun sank behind the horizon, throwing out the last rays of gold like a crown.

A hush fell over the deck, even though it was crowded.

"Where else in the world are you surrounded by such wild beauty?" Rian asked. "Where else could we witness such majesty?"

Rian's reverence and wonderment matched her own. She stepped closer to Zelda and wrapped an arm around her shoulder. Zelda smiled. Genna stepped away from the rail and joined them. She pulled Amy to her and hugged her, then pulled Zelda in close, too. Rian joined the group hug.

A thread of angry words and old wounds had pulled free of the tapestry of friendship and sisterhood that wove their stories together. But it was just a snag of thread. Easy to snip. Possible to mend.

"The blood of the covenant is thicker than the water of the

womb," Genna quoted. "We are bound because we choose to be. We are blood because we endure the battles of friendship and our peculiar imperfections. Wherever they lead us."

This was as close to an apology as Genna would ever come, but the words held the weight of honesty and grace—so much so that it meant even more than an apology. Amy swallowed her tears. Everyone had flaws. No one escaped that, and she was not an exception. Genna was proud and sometimes overconfident—forever ambitiously capable. Those were incredible qualities to have. And yet, there was always a yin to the yang. Like the goddesses Selene and Eos, one lifted the great moon into the sky while the other drew the sun with the dawn. In between night and day, life happened. Stuff happened. Some of it good. Some of it not so good. But if you got lucky, you shared life with friends like these, auspicious times like this, and leaping dolphins in the sea.

"I can't believe it's over," Zelda said, breaking away from the hug but staying close. "My life is already half gone. And our trip is done."

"We're not done," Amy said. "We have so many other places to see. So many more bucket list destinations to explore."

"Bucket lists are for people who are old," Genna said. "We will *never* be old."

THE END

ACKNOWLEDGMENTS

Stories are an amalgam of life's events, the people you meet and come to love, and those you overhear in strange places. Without them our stories would be hollow. You never know when an idea will settle in the writer-brain and take root. Sometimes they lay dormant for decades before the spark of an idea sprouts. So, thanks to all those backgammon players down in the Florida Keys who I challenged over beer and fried grouper decades ago. Thanks to my book idol Carl Hiaasen for giving me that nudge of encouragement to write what amuses me. Thanks to Ecoventura for the first-class expedition cruise in the Galápagos, and the dedicated journalists aboard the *Eric* that winter. Jo and Lori, I treasure the friendships we keep. Thanks to Julia and Jill for lending me the best word ever—*wasbund*—a husband that was, and for the adventure we will someday take together. I am grateful for the Writers' Colony at Dairy Hollow in enchanted Eureka Springs, Arkansas, and the chance reading with fellowship author Jeremy Hance that reminded me of my relationship to the wild. Thank you to the members of the Very Important Players Club for letting me kill off your husbands. And finally, thanks to my editor, Cayce Berryman, and cover designer, Bailey McGinn, for helping me build a Cardboard Cottage brand.

ABOUT THE AUTHOR

Jane Elzey is a mischief-maker, storyteller, and bender of the facts. A career journalist, she now writes modern-day, not-so-cozy mysteries without much regard for the truth. Born and raised a wild child on Florida's sandy beaches, Jane now lives in the Ozark Mountains of Arkansas, where there are more trees and rocks than people. An insatiable world traveler, Jane turns her bucket list travels into backdrop settings for her books, sharing destinations with armchair readers on the hunt for whodunnit. Jane Elzey writes about four mature women who play to win . . . while the husbands die trying. The husband always dies. *Dice on a Deadly Sea* is book two in the Cardboard Cottage Mystery series. For more information or to join the Very Important Players Club, visit JaneElzey.com.

CPSIA information can be obtained
at www.ICGtesting.com
Printed in the USA
BVHW040813080822
644057BV00014B/274/J

9 781734 642834